Don't Tell Sybil

An Intimate Memoir of ELT Mesens

Also by George Melly

I Flook
Owning Up
Revolt into Style
Flook by Trog
Rum Bum and Concertina
The Media Mob (with Barry Fantoni)
Tribe of One: Great Naive and Primitive Painters of the British Isles
Great Lovers (with Walter Dorin)
Mellymobile
ed. *Edward James* Swans Reflecting Elephants: My Early Years
Scouse Mouse
It's All Writ Out for You: the Life and Work of Scottie Wilson
Paris and the Surrealists (with Michael Woods)

GEORGE MELLY

Don't Tell Sybil

An Intimate Memoir of ELT Mesens

HEINEMANN : LONDON

First published in Great Britain 1997
by William Heinemann

3 5 7 9 10 8 6 4 2

George Melly has asserted his right under the Copyright, Designs
and Patents Act, 1988 to be identified as the author of this work.

Random House UK Limited
20 Vauxhall Bridge Road, London, SW1V 2SA

Random House Australia (Pty) Limited
20 Alfred Street, Milsons Point, Sydney,
New South Wales 2061, Australia

Random House New Zealand Limited
18 Poland Road, Glenfield,
Auckland 10, New Zealand

Random House South Africa (Pty) Limited
Endulini, 5a Jubilee Road, Parktown 2193, South Africa

Random House UK Limited Reg. No. 954009

A CIP catalogue record for this book
is available from the British Library

Papers used by Random House UK Limited
are natural, recyclable products made from wood grown in
sustainable forests. The manufacturing processes conform to
the environmental regulations of the country of origin.

ISBN 0 434 462500

Typeset by Deltatype Ltd, Birkenhead, Merseyside
Printed and bound in Great Britain
by Mackays of Chatham plc

For Andrée

List of Illustrations

1. First International Surrealist Exhibition (photographer unknown, courtesy of Lee Miller Archives)
2. George Melly and others
3. George Melly with Owen Maddock
4. From *Activities of the London Gallery* (courtesy of the Victoria and Albert Museum)
5. Max Ernst, ELT Mesens, Leonora Carrington (© Lee Miller, courtesy of Lee Miller Archives)
6. Sybil Mesens by Man Ray (© ADAGP, Paris and Dacs, London 1997)
7. ELT Mesens (© Ida Kar, courtesy of Mary Evans Picture Library)
8. ELT and Sybil Mesens (by Carla Dangelo)
9. From *Poemes*: ELT Mesens
10. ELT Mesens (© Michael Cooper, courtesy of Special Photographer gallery)
11. ELT Mesens (© Jacques J. Halber)

It may appear strange that there are no reproductions of works by ELT Mesens. This is because whereas the family of the 'nice cousin', who own half the copyright, were instantly agreeable, the other cousin (who is still alive) didn't acknowledge our numerous requests.

Every effort has been made to contact copyright holders, but in some cases this has not proved possible. Any inadvertent omissions of acknowledgement or permission can be rectified in future editions.

Contents

Acknowledgements

I would like to thank my editor, Kate Goodhart, who came in half way through, saw the point and re-lit the boiler, and Charlotte Mendelson, who saw it through.

Also for encouragement, advice or information from Susanna Clapp, Francis Wyndham, David Sylvester, Sarah Whitfield, my son Tom, Monika Kinley, Tony Penrose, Conroy Maddox and ELT's kinswoman Christiane Geurts-Krauss, author of the invaluable thesis *ELT Mesens – L'Alchimiste Méconnu du Surrealisme*.

Prologue

I was born the twenty-seventh of November
nineteen hundred and three without god, without
master, without king AND WITHOUT RIGHTS.
                                    MESENS

Breathing heavily but rhythmically and sustained by a drip, ELT Mesens – Belgian, poet, collagist, surrealist, art dealer and alcoholic – has less than forty-eight hours to live.

Seated about five feet from the side of the deathbed in a private room at a Brussels nursing-home, and behind one of those tables which can be adjusted in height for bedridden patients able to feed themselves, is a fat man. He is eating, with pleasurable concentration, a large helping of sausage and mash, wheeled in a few minutes earlier and concealed under a large metal dome which I had imagined, until it was removed with a flourish, to conceal a piece of surgical equipment to prolong the life of the dying poet.

The fat man, Mesens's cousin, had offered me a share of the sausages but I had declined, not so much from squeamishness (although the proximity of my moribund friend in this white room smelling of flowers was hardly conducive to appetite) but because I had already offered lunch in a nearby restaurant to a young German woman called Ruth who had been looking after ELT during his last few months.

Was she disinterested? I doubt it. She was the owner of a modest art gallery in Switzerland and Mesens had a large collection of what had become very valuable pictures, yet I believe her to have been genuinely fond of him. Self-interest and real affection are not necessarily incompatible. My sister Andrée and I were both close friends of Edouard Mesens of over twenty years' standing, but that didn't rule out a faint but persistent hope of inheritance despite our suspicion, correct as it turned out, that for all his will-rattling, a vice he was increasingly prone to, he had made no will.

They can't have been easy for Ruth, those last few months. Edouard was drunk almost all of the time and although he could be tender towards her, at certain stages in the ebb and flow of drink, possessed by the spirit of irresistible black humour, he was often abusive and paranoid. Towards the end he was occasionally incontinent, a very upsetting development for so fastidious a man. All this I gathered from Ruth at lunch and, whatever part calculation had played in her devotion, I felt she deserved something.

On the day he had collapsed (he had drunk a bottle of pernod before eleven a.m.), she told me he had shouted from the stretcher before losing consciousness for the last time, 'Everysing for Ruse!' (Despite over thirty-five years in London he had never mastered the English 'th'.) But a cry of intent, however sincere, is of no legal consequence. If he were to die intestate, as predictably turned out to be the case, Ruth was entitled to nothing. Nor of course were Andrée or myself, despite a note discovered later in a diary that we were his intended heirs and which, if initialled, according to Belgian law would have given us a strong claim. Of course he had not initialled it. On his death therefore everything would be divided between his next of kin, two cousins, one of whom at that moment, having finished the sausages, was no doubt attacking a pudding. Still, at least ELT was fond of him; he called him 'the nice cousin'. The other, 'the nasty cousin', he detested. With his last breath they were both to become millionaires.

In the nasty cousin's favour, he had made no effort to court ELT during his last few years. The nice cousin, on the other hand, had made several trips to London to be of practical help. Edouard had dismissed his Italian cleaning lady, and the mansion

2

block flat opposite Lord's cricket ground had become increasingly dusty and squalid while, at the same time, retaining its pathological neatness. Andrée had cleaned it up as often as she could; a frustrating task as Edouard wouldn't allow any of the accumulating piles of unanswered correspondence and what he called 'documentation' to be moved and they soon covered every flat surface including the floor, but the nice cousin washed the paint-work and the windows. On at least one occasion he had even imported his solid Brueghelian wife to make nourishing food for he suspected, quite rightly, that despite an occasional visit to an expensive Soho restaurant, Mesens was eating very little.

I went to lunch at the flat one Saturday. When I arrived the nice cousin was perched on the window-sill looking like Humpty Dumpty, and cleaning what he could reach of the outside panes. His wife was stirring some soup in the dark little kitchen. Edouard, having sent me across the road to the pub off-licence for a bottle of dry martini (his chosen tipple in London, abroad it was always pernod) to replace the bottle he had emptied overnight, was extremely mischievous. He spoke of his cousin as if he wasn't there. 'He eats too much,' he complained. 'For breakfast he has six toasts wiz cheese, salami, ham, liver-sausage, jam and marmalade. Still he is a good old boy.'

When the wife came to serve the soup, and speaking in French because he knew she had no English, Edouard offered me a detailed description of how, when they were boys, he and his cousin had often indulged 'wiz tenderness' in mutual masturbation. The wife, presumably pre-warned that in no way must she appear shocked or angry, whatever he might say, ate stolidly through this deliberate attempt to provoke her. I don't think she returned on her husband's subsequent visits.

Her self-control paid off. Half the masterpieces on the walls of the flat, half the contents of a large storage *camion* in Brussels, were soon to be theirs.

As to why Mesens made no will, despite several warnings that he had little time to live, *his* explanation was always that a gypsy, patronised by the surrealists in Paris during the twenties, had told him he would live to be eighty; he was only sixty-nine when he died. There was of course much more to it than that. As his fanatical need for order confirmed (a vice I inherited) he was certainly anally retentive, but he was also, *vide* the gypsy, very superstitious and felt, I suspect, that a will is a death warrant, a tempting of providence. I had tried several times to change his mind, not solely in the hope that it might be to my advantage, but because he never stopped complaining that if he died suddenly everything would go to the cousins.

'Leave it to a museum,' I said, knowing that some years before, he had teased a curator in Brussels with this notion, asking increasingly stringent conditions until the negotiations had broken down. He would pretend to consider this idea, do a little will-rattling, suggest other possibilities, but finally he'd say that there was no hurry. After all the gypsy in Paris had told him . . .

After lunch I said goodbye to Ruth, returned briefly to the hospital to say goodbye to the now replete nice cousin and to kiss my dying friend on the forehead.

The next day Andrée rang me to tell me that the nice cousin had phoned her to let us know it was all over. We flew over for the funeral but were held up by fog at Heathrow so that we arrived at the cemetery as the mourners were coming out of the gates. There was a tea at the nice cousin's (Ruth was not invited) and we caught the evening flight back to London. For some years the nice cousin sent Andrée very expensive Belgian chocolates for Christmas, then they got cheaper and eventually stopped altogether.

Part One

One

... to find again the only tree
By the unlit road
Of encounter and chance ...
MESENS

Stowe School, Bucks, during the war. The art school, built during the thirties, was a discoloured concrete box in a sub-Bauhaus style, next to the squash courts, tucked away behind the neo-classical chapel. There, under the friendly yet firm guidance of a forty-something Canadian couple, Robin and Dodie Watts, we were introduced to 'modern art': the impressionists, Cézanne, Van Go (sic), Picasso, Matisse and Braque. There was a small library in the Wattses' private room and in it I came across a single number of a magazine called *The London Bulletin*, published in 1938. Leafing through it I was electrified by a full-page reproduction of a painting of a nude woman's body, mounted on a long neck, framed by unruly hair, so that the breasts became eyes, the navel the nose and the sex the mouth. I was both alarmed and exhilarated by this anatomical displacement. I took in the title, *The Rape*, but not, as far as I remember, the artist, René Magritte. I certainly failed to register that the magazine, which also served as a catalogue for the London Gallery in Cork Street was edited by one ELT Mesens.

That summer holiday in Liverpool, in a bookshop called Phillip, Son and Nephews, I bought a remaindered book called *Surrealism*, published to commemorate the great International Surrealist Exhibition held in London in 1936. It had a long introduction by Herbert Read, essays by Breton, Eluard, Hugnet

7

and Hugh Sykes Davies, and was fully illustrated. Everything about this publication excited me, from the Victorian circus lettering on the spine to the assertive if, for me, impenetrable prose, but it was the imagery which hooked me and especially the magic realists: Dali, Tangui, Brauner, and above all Magritte. I spent the rest of that holiday alternating between poring over *Surrealism* and playing my small but growing collection of 78 rpm jazz records (another recent passion) on my wind-up gramophone. Without discrimination, I memorised the name and work of every artist in that book, including a collage of minute horsemen riding amongst vast flowers and an unidentifiable mechanical object. It was by ELT Mesens, who also appeared amongst the poets with an extract from a book of his called *Alphabet for the Deaf and Blind*. I didn't, however, especially revere his contributions, either visual or oral. He was just one amongst the many contributing to this cornucopia of marvels.

In a state of radiant conviction I took the book back to Stowe for the autumn term and showed it to the Wattses. To my dismay they dismissed it as 'old hat' and, with the exception of Picasso, Klee and, to a lesser extent, Miro, rejected Surrealism as 'literary', the dirtiest word in their vocabulary, and on a par with the pre-Raphaelites, another movement we had been taught to despise.

My close circle of friends, however, thought otherwise. We had just reached the age when we experienced the need to revolt against the certainties of Ma and Pa Watts's aesthetic gospel and, following a piece of deliberate provocation – the organisation of a 'surrealist' exhibition in the sculpture room during their day off – we were banished for the rest of that term. We voluntarily extended our absence for another month or so before declaring an uneasy truce. During this hiatus I began to write surrealist poetry which, unlike my earlier sub-Eliot verses, was turned down by the school magazine.

I don't know if my gesture of defiance would have been sustained for so long – the art school was after all a haven of tolerance, a refuge against the hearty rough and tumble of school life outside its rusting metal windows – had it not been for the support of Guy 'Jesus' Neal and Tony Harris Reed, two boys much more intelligent and intransigent than myself. While willing to revolt in the short term, I didn't really enjoy self-banishment for any length of time. Guy and Tony were made of sterner stuff. They were able to decipher the convoluted texts in the book I'd brought to their attention, and explain to me the philosophy there concealed. Permanent revolt, they told me, was amongst the movement's most inflexible principles. With their support I left Stowe to join the navy a convinced, if still rather confused, surrealist apprentice.

Of course, like jazz, Surrealism was only one thread in the skein of life at school. There was homosexuality; there was acting; there were those subjects which appealed to me, especially English and History; there was the debating society, and the avoidance where possible of organised games; there were bullies to be placated, certain masters to be won over, classmates to be amused. Nevertheless jazz, which was eventually to earn me a living, and Surrealism, a movement I still revere, became permanent baggage 'wanted on voyage'.

In failing to describe in more detail this formative period in my life – the style and content of our surrealist exhibition in the sculpture room, the benevolent dictatorship of Ma and Pa Watts – my reason is partially because I have already done so in previous books, but more pertinently because my aim is to indicate my gradual awareness of the existence of Mesens, and to list only those events which propelled me towards him. Even so, I shall be forced when the time comes to reiterate a certain amount I have written about him already, and especially in relation to the early days of our long friendship. I must then rely on the patience of those readers who feel overcome or irritated by a sense of *déjà vu*. In the present context Mesens is not simply a member of a large cast, but the central character. The matter may at times overlap, but the emphasis is entirely different.

At the moment of leaving school and for the first year of my life in the navy, he was, for me, a marginal name on a par with

Leonore Fini or Angel Planells (one reproduction each in my surrealist *vade mecum*). This was soon to change. Objective chance was already shuffling her marked pack of cards.

A rating in the Royal Navy, doing my initial training in a commandeered Butlins holiday camp in Pwllheli, North Wales, I was joined by my school friend, Tony Harris Reed, who was as anarchic and hard-edged as ever. I have always had a tendency to believe that anything which arouses my enthusiasm, New Orleans Jazz for example, is extinct. Therefore, while increasingly obsessed with Surrealism, I had imagined the movement at one with the Archaeopteryx, but Tony discovered a small ad in the *New Statesman* for several pamphlets and books of poetry by ELT Mesens and Paul Eluard, published by the Surrealist Group in England. We wrote off for these and, when they eventually arrived, studied them like holy writs. Finally we were emboldened to send Mesens, the editor of *Message from Nowhere*, a selection of my poems and Tony's rather Ernst-like collages. We heard eventually, not from Mesens himself, but from Simon Watson Taylor, 'Secretary to the Surrealist Group in England', thanking us rather neutrally for our work and suggesting, if we were ever near London, that we contact him. After our training Tony was sent to Portsmouth to await a posting, but I was stationed at Chatham, within striking distance of London and was 'lost' to the navy for over a year on a superannuated aircraft-carrier, a kind of floating thieves' kitchen, in the harbour. Having learnt the corrupt ropes, I duly contacted Simon, who after vetting me, invited me to a surrealist meeting in an upper room of the Barcelona restaurant in Beak Street, Soho. It was there, one wet Monday evening, that I first clapped eyes on Mesens.

What did I know of Mesens as he entered the Barcelona with his wife Sybil? By this time a certain amount. The book of poems – soft cover but beautifully printed on uncut handmade paper, limited to five hundred copies (mine was 439) and signed by the author – was fronted by a short biographical note. I learnt from this that he was Belgian and born in 1903, that he was originally a composer, an early supporter of Magritte and had edited *The London Bulletin*, the magazine in which I had first seen a reproduction of 'Le Viol'. I also gathered that he had taken part in organising the International Surrealist Exhibition in London in 1936 which had engendered Herbert Read's anthology. His poetry, interposed by collages and drawings, struck me as balanced between melancholy and a rather sardonic humour. There were signs too of a love-hate relationship with columns of figures, balance sheets and tax collectors. He also seemed obsessed with bathroom toiletry.

The Mesenses were the last to arrive. (I had been the first.) Simon Watson Taylor and his intense sister Sonja were not long behind me and introduced me to the others as they showed up – a Turkish poet, a Portuguese painter, a woman artist, an extraordinarily charming Frenchman called Jacques Brunius with a prominent nose and a pipe – yet it was evident that ELT was the key figure, the hinge of the evening. When he and Sybil were heard mounting the stairs a kind of static electricity was generated. I watched the door with heightened interest.

How had I visualised the owner of those three insistent initials? Of this man a little younger than my father ('I was born in 1903'), this *SURREALIST*!

His wife entered first. Although later I discovered she came originally from Bishops Auckland, near Newcastle-on-Tyne, I first imagined her to be Spanish, possibly with some gypsy blood. She had an olive skin, a commanding dark eye, a small but somewhat aquiline nose, but especially noticeable was her discreet chic. The other women present were unintimidating in appearance; Edith Rimmington was dressed rather like my mother, Sonja and the other surrealists' girlfriends like students, but Sybil looked like a contemporary photograph from *Vogue*. And the man opening the door for her and following her in, apologising in a pronounced foreign accent for their lateness due to the lack of taxis in distant Hampstead. Well, he didn't look like a poet as I envisaged one, still less like a surrealist (although at that point I had no terms of reference, and was still unaware of their detestation of anything suggestive of the bohemian). ELT was comparatively short, chubby, well turned-out in an entirely conventional way. His tie was discreet, his shoes highly polished, his hair slicked back. He had clearly shaved meticulously and was fastidiously clean. The only mildly exotic touch was that his handkerchief protruded with a certain careful flamboyance from his breast pocket and he smelt deliciously of expensive cologne (in those days scent was very much taboo in England, and confined almost exclusively to homosexuals).

His face was rather like a determined baby. There was something of the music-hall about him too, a touch of the Maurice Chevaliers. The only Belgian I had any visual conception of at that time was Agatha Christie's Hercule Poirot and, despite the lack of spats and a waxed moustache, Mesens had quite a lot in common with my mental image of the detective, including an air of alert intelligence and a colourful if slightly inaccurate grasp of English (which he claimed to have learnt from Lord Beaverbrook, by reading the *Evening Standard*) peppered with unexpected yet appropriate metaphors.

He took his place at the head of the table and, the Spanish proprietor having materialised, we ordered our meagre post-war meal and drank many bottles of cheap red wine before the meeting proper.

In my naïve enthusiasm I didn't realise for some time that the surrealist movement in England was at the point of disintegration, nor that Mesens himself was largely responsible for the hiatus of those British painters and poets who had been published or reproduced in the pre-war *London Bulletin*.

In 1940, very much in the tradition of Breton, he had decreed that the English group swear allegiance to what he considered the basic principles of Surrealism. Amongst those present, Ithell Colquhoun had refused to relinquish her interest in the occult, and resigned rather than break her wand – in retrospect an ironic circumstance given Breton's post-war enthusiasm for the arcane. That strange couple, Dr Grace Pailthorpe and her much younger lover, Reuben Mednikoff, were barred for almost the opposite reason; their insistence on using Surrealism as a tool in their mutual Freudian analysis. Others were unable to accept ELT's papal bull (later revoked when he himself contributed to *Horizon*) that no one should write for any publication which was not surrealist, nor exhibit except under surrealist auspices.

Many not present at that night of long knives (albeit without blades and with their handles missing) later earned their dismissal or quietly took their leave: Paul Nash by becoming an official war artist; Henry Moore for the same reason, compounding the offence later by carving a Madonna and Child for a church in Northampton; David Gascoyne who, together with Roland Penrose, was responsible for bringing Surrealism to Britain in the first place, had been drawn towards Christian-mysticism; Humphrey Jennings accepted an OBE, and others were dispersed by the war. In consequence, by the time I walked up the stairs of the Barcelona in my bell-bottoms, there were very few left from amongst those conscripts and recruits, both genuine and opportunist, who had swelled the surrealist ranks during the feverish call to arms at the time of the great exhibition of 1936.

Yet in all this, according to his lights, Mesens was in good faith. Like Breton, he insisted that Surrealism was never an artistic movement but a commitment to a way of life. You couldn't simply call yourself a surrealist when it suited, only to conform when it paid off. Like Breton, if with less authority, Mesens may be criticised for imposing *his* interpretation, but somebody (especially in Britain) had to interpret the tablets of the law, and ELT's long and faithful service to the movement during the twenties and thirties gave him the authority (and one must add the inclination) to assume that role.

More suspect however, less disinterested, was the del Renzio affair. Tony del Renzio was an enthusiastic volunteer who had published a surrealist manifesto called *Arson* in 1942. It was signed by its editor and the following writers and painters: Conroy Maddox, John and Robert Melville (painter and writer respectively), Edith Rimmington, Emmy Bridgwater and Eileen Agar; all of them still members of the movement at the time I joined, and regular or sometime habitués of the Barcelona evenings.

Michel Remy, that most unlikely creature, a *French* enthusiast for English Surrealism, and to whose research I am indebted, has pointed out that, despite a quote from Mesens on the cover of *Arson* and an admiring reference to him in the preface, he was not, significantly, amongst the signatories, and nor was Brunius. Conroy Maddox tells me that he believes that this was because del Renzio had approached neither of them suspecting, probably correctly, that if he did so ELT would have taken over the whole venture. It is certainly significant that, with the exception of Agar, who always remained discreetly aloof from the in-fighting of the movement, the others who did sign were all based in Birmingham and only able to attend the Barcelona intermittently. Del Renzio went to Birmingham to solicit their signatures; he had telephoned Maddox to try and 'borrow' the fare but, this being refused, had somehow got himself up there anyway and no doubt, for none of the Birmingham chapter would have deliberately opposed Mesens, misled them by the quote on the cover into thinking that the enterprise had ELT's imprimatur. Maddox also believes in retrospect that perhaps del Renzio was indeed making a take-over bid, but if so he failed.

Mesens recognised the challenge, fought it off, and brought his troops back in line. Del Renzio, on what grounds I am unable to establish, was declared heretic, and expelled. He, however, refused to admit defeat and, having first had the audacity to edit a 'surrealist' section in a little magazine, then organised a surrealist poetry reading. The time for action had arrived and the following report of the form it took appeared in Mesens's pamphlet *Message from Nowhere*.

During the latter half of last year the Grey Walls Press published a curious miscellanea entitled New Road 1943. *In this volume appeared a 'surrealist' section edited by the self-alleged Tony del Renzio (son of the late Illus AC Romanov del Renzio, dei Conti dei Rossi da Formia). This, in itself, would not have been significant had the section not consisted of unauthorised translations of work by members of the international surrealist movement, interspersed with a number of strange items such as Mr del Renzio's vulgar little poem 'Morgenroth' (to darling Ithell) which bore no conceivable connection to Surrealism. After reading this nonsense one was forced to the conclusion that the only link between del Renzio and Surrealism was that of a tapeworm in a man's intestines.*

When, therefore, during the early Spring, Mr and Mrs del Renzio were advertised to give a 'surrealist' poetry reading at the International Arts Centre, Bayswater, the meeting was attended by a number of French, Belgian, American and British surrealists who were determined to prevent the further discrediting of the movement by this quaint couple. The Charwoman [sic] of the meeting refused to read the letter of protest from one of our friends.

Mr del Renzio, who has in the past (at different times) claimed to have spent his life riding through the USSR with a white Cossack band, playing 2nd trumpet to Louis Armstrong while studying at Columbia University, deserting from the Italian army to fight with the International Brigade in Spain, and serving in a London drapers, referred, in his opening remarks, to 'his friends' Pierre Mabille and Aimé Césaire! The remainder of his address was inaudible, due to the fact that the brave couple were cowering behind a grand piano, until, after half an hour, three quarters of his audience left the meeting in protest. Mr del Renzio's only vocal supporter was a gentleman of military appearance whose moustaches bristled when he shouted at ELT Mesens 'I know you're no gentleman, Sir!'

As we left the room, Mr del Renzio's white silk tie
flapped symbolically . . .

Ken Hawkes

I have no idea who Ken Hawkes was, but today feel no profound regret at having not been amongst those who disrupted a sparsely attended poetry recital in the middle of a world war. As for the 'unauthorised translations', it is difficult to see how these could have been otherwise, given that the poets were in occupied Europe and hardly in a position to grant their permission anyway. Nevertheless, Mesens had achieved his immediate objective. The del Renzio power bid, if that's what it was, was over.

Later on, at the beginning of the sixties, Mesens and del Renzio met in Milan where the latter was by then resident and became not only reconciled but friends. ELT told me later that Tony had 'a formidable cock', although he didn't say how or why he had established this anatomical distinction. Perhaps it had 'flapped symbolically'.

Yet of all those with whom Edouard quarrelled by far the most painful to him personally and, from the surrealist point of view, the most damaging, was the break with Roland Penrose.

Roland came from a Quaker family and, together with the writer David Gascoyne, had been largely responsible for bringing Surrealism to Britain in the first place. Penrose was both charming and handsome; Breton in his list of what quality particularly personified the Surrealism of his adherents had described him as 'surrealist in friendship'; he was also quite rich. He had acquired two magnificent collections of cubist, Dada and surrealist works; one directly from the poet Paul Eluard, the other, through the intervention of Mesens, from a Belgian, Claude Spaak, brother of the future prime minister. He himself was a painter although without much originality. He was in love with, and officially married to, Lee Miller, an American of strong if wayward character, and a great talent in many fields, especially photography (she had been a mistress of Man Ray in the late twenties). Following the end of the war and the consequent end of her work as a star correspondent for Condé Nast, Lee became bored and restless, and had more or less left Roland in pursuit of adventure.

Roland and, when she was there, Lee had put up ELT and Sybil for much of the war in their house on Downshire Hill, Hampstead. This had of course created certain tensions, but it was not the cause of the split between the two men. That was political, and surrealist-political at that. The main bone of contention was their respective attitudes towards Paul Eluard. Both loved him; Mesens had, he told me, taken part in sexual *partouses* in the thirties with Paul and his waif-like wife Nusch; but shortly before the war Eluard, like Aragon some ten years earlier, had left the surrealists to join the French Communist party and been denounced by Breton who ordered those who remained 'to sabotage by every possible means the poetry of Paul Eluard'. This had not, at the time, involved the English branch especially – the coming conflict, the moral confusion, the French group's adherence to Trotsky, the English alliance with our native anarchists, had masked the imprimatur – but with Breton's return to France and renewed close contact between the British and French contingents, Eluard had again become a test of loyalty and Mesens had accepted Breton's line. Not so Penrose. For him Breton's dictum had become reversed. He was now 'non-surrealist *because of friendship*'. For ELT, in conse-quence, Penrose and Lee were dubbed 'Stalinists', and in Lee's case there was a further bad mark. In her wartime dispatches for *Vogue* she had frequently referred to the Germans as 'Krauts'; an expression contrary and offensive to Mesens's conventional surrealist insistence on internationalism, although in Lee's defence she had been one of the first journalists to enter Dachau. And so as the enmity between Roland and Edouard escalated, only practical considerations prevented an open rift. Their war, throughout the late forties and fifties, was a matter of sniping and booby traps.

In this masked quarrel, I am sure the English prejudice is on Penrose's side. Why banish a lifelong friend over a political difference? Also I'm sure, although Breton had parted from Eluard before the war, it would count in Eluard's favour that he had remained in France during the occupation whereas Breton was safe in New York. It was however exactly this *laissez-faire* pragmatism and sentimentality which made it so difficult to recruit a committed surrealist group in this country. Mesens, however, belonged to the continental tradition and, while he himself fell from grace now and then, he understood why Breton (who I'm sure himself suffered from excommunicating his old companion in arms) had found it necessary to insist that Eluard's place 'is no longer among us'. Had Breton ever compromised, Surrealism would never have retained its authority for forty years. Roland's enthusiasm for surrealist imagery never faltered, but ethically he found no dilemma later in becoming a British Council official in Paris, and eventually accepting a knighthood. Mesens found it almost impossible to excommunicate British surrealists because not only did he lack Breton's majestic aura of infallibility, but most of the British members tended to fade discreetly away rather than wait to be dismissed.

Of this infighting I initially knew nothing but, as a novice, accepted everything ELT told me as our friendship deepened. Far from realising that Surrealism in England was fast disintegrating, I believed myself to be standing on the hub of a great wheel about to turn. Nor of course was I aware that even in Paris the movement was losing its momentum; that Breton's return from the United States heralded not a renaissance, but a decline. Existentialism, pessimistic and absurdist, had usurped its place, forcing Surrealism's retreat into an esoteric position, and its earlier adherents were resigning, individually and in waves.

On the contrary, for me Surrealism was a revelation, the key to a magic kingdom where misery and regression were banished for ever and poetry reigned supreme. The Barcelona restaurant was one of those mountain caves where we brigands of the imagination were preparing to march against the forces of reason and overthrow those obscene myths whose function was to

18

cretinise humanity. In ELT Mesens I recognised the general who would give the signal. Perhaps next Monday evening or the Monday after that the offensive would begin.

Did I really believe this? Most certainly. I always had the conviction (now suppressed, but still part of my nature) that everybody, once exposed, will become as obsessed as myself in anything that obsesses me. Surrealism and anarchism, wine and bread, would solve all human dilemmas. Yet equally I was able to explore, without any sense of betrayal or incongruity, very different, indeed incompatible interests. I was involved for instance with a clique of aristocratic homosexuals, and busy exploring the bohemian and drunken stews of Soho. Nevertheless Surrealism was at the centre of my life in bell-bottoms.

What actually happened at the Barcelona? Not much. If I were to return now, to drag my seventy-one years up the stairs to that upper room, I would feel like that middle-aged and world-weary heroine of *Un Carnet de Bal* who revisits a provincial dance hall, in memory of an extraordinary glamour, only to find a small accordian-led band out of tune, some tatty paper chains and a few stiff and maladroit couples circling the dusty floor.

Yet there is more regret than cynicism in my comparison. In the film the disillusioned heroine finds herself next to a young girl, her eyes sparkling. It is *her* first dance. 'Oh look, Madame,' she murmurs entranced. 'Isn't it beautiful! The lights! The music! The dresses!' So I, at nineteen, would address my older self, 'Isn't it beautiful! The ardour! The poetry! The marvellous!'

I don't mock my naïvety, I only envy it. My faith in the surrealist idea has remained firm. It's my hopes of its realisation which have withered. If Harris Reed had never thought to write to Mesens, if I had lacked the will get in touch with Simon Watson Taylor, it is possible, though improbable, that my enthusiasm might have died away from lack of encouragement. As it was, here were adults to reinforce my convictions. Brunius with his charm and seductive French accent and who I learnt, with some awe, had been assistant director to Luis Bunuel on

19

L'Age d'Or, that legendary banned film which I finally saw ten years later at the National Film Theatre, and of course Mesens himself, friend of Magritte.

After dinner on those Monday evenings we defined the surrealist attitude to current events, planned future publications, most of them unrealised, and played surrealist games like 'Exquisite Corpses', the equivalent of 'Heads, Bodies and Tails' when visual, or 'Consequences' when written. There was not much excitement although Simon Watson Taylor, who was not in awe of ELT, would occasionally oppose an idea, largely I suspect for the hell of it, and there would be a flurry of feathers, but there were no serious rifts.

My contribution was to read any poem I had written aboard the *Argus* during the night watch. These poems were not very good but, in my sailor's uniform and given to histrionics, they pleased the company. One evening I surpassed myself. The poem contained the phrase '. . . in case it is raining knives and forks', and at this point, having secretively harboured about my person a number of these utensils from the knife box, I threw them up into the air so that they came clattering down about me with a most satisfactory din. The surrealists, led by Edouard, applauded; not so the proprietor. Running up the stairs like a furious little Spanish bull, he ordered us all to leave at once. I was a little nervous that this might turn the surrealists against me, but not at all. Provocative behaviour had always been part of their programme. Mesens told me for example that, when they were young, he and several of his friends in Brussels (he didn't tell me if Magritte was amongst them) pissed from the balcony over the audience in the stalls during the première of a patriotic symphony. Admittedly his group was more Dada than surrealist in those days but . . . Hearing this, I felt my cloudburst of knives and forks was, by comparison, a rather feeble manifestation.

In fact ELT, like most Belgians whether Dada, surrealist or good solid bourgeois, was mildly obsessed with bodily functions – it is not for nothing that *Manneken-Pis* should be the symbol of Brussels, and chocolates in the form of chamber pots are on sale at every street *kermesse*. Most evenings we left the Barcelona as a group, full of high spirits and fairly disgusting Spanish wine, and walked together along Beak Street to Regent Street to go our various ways; in my case, unless I was to share the bed of one of the posh homosexuals in Cheyne Walk or Half Moon Street, to the Union Jack Club at Victoria, handy for the seven a.m. train back to Chatham.

On one of the corners in Beak Street was a bombed house. Very little demolition had yet taken place; its rooms, with their unlikely layers of wallpaper, were exposed like those of a shabby dolls' house. At street level was a lavatory and into its bowl, with the rest of us on the look-out for any patrolling 'flic' (as I had learned to call the Law), Edouard would solemnly urinate – a gesture both Dada, surrealist and, especially, Belgian.

After the week of the knives and forks, Simon rang me up to say the proprietor had forgiven us, and we could return as usual. We were after all a source of steady income. Simon also told me he had decided to include one of my poems and a few aphorisms in a surrealist anthology he was editing, this time with ELT's full approval, called *Free Unions*. When it finally came out (it was long delayed by paper shortage and lack of funding) I almost burst with pride. My poem aside, and even that (while totally derivative) was one of my better ones, *Free Unions* was of a remarkably high standard, and is today both rare and valuable.

By the time it was published the movement was further disintegrating. Meetings at the Barcelona petered out from lack of support, and were replaced for a time by less and less well attended rendezvous in a pub in Tottenham Court Road. Although the group answered a Belgian questionnaire as to what one hated most and loved most and, as late as 1947, contributed a declaration to the catalogue of an International Surrealist Exhibition at the Galerie Maeght in Paris, there was little general activity. Mesens himself was more and more involved during 1946 in preparing to reopen the London Gallery in new premises in Brook Street. There, we imagined, under its own roof, surrealist enthusiasm would rekindle. In reality he couldn't have conceived such a venture at a less propitious moment.

Two

An upright piano can be a dangerous possession in the mind of a child, a grand piano even worse on account of the tail.

BBC RADIO INTERVIEW WITH GEORGE MELLY

What were Mesens's origins? We already know his exact date of birth but he himself, in all our years of friendship, hardly ever alluded to his childhood. Even Magritte was more forthcoming.

From other sources I have learnt that his mother came from Lille and that is all I know about her. His father was from Aerschot in Brabant, and owned a drugstore in a working-class area of Brussels. Its stock however was not confined to patent medicines. It also sold a wide range of goods amongst which I have come across a specific mention of chicory.

According to Sybil, whose post-war visits to Brussels on business included making some contact with her husband's surviving relations, there were three aunts. She spoke of them in such a way as to imply they were both comical and formidable. She never met the mother; I presume her to have been dead, but on one occasion at least she did meet 'Papa', by then a very old gentleman. They had a rendezvous at the station and, as she was unaccompanied by Edouard, she asked 'Papa' on the telephone how she would be able to recognise him. He told her he had a beard but also, as he would be wearing a bowler hat, he would raise it at frequent intervals to expose a large wen on the top of his bald head. There were also of course the two cousins, nice and nasty, but they were all I knew of. In concealing his childhood Mesens was very much in the surrealist tradition.

While waxing lyrical at the idea of pre-pubescence, very few of them (Dali and Ernst were marked exceptions) chose to be specific. It may be because most of them came from secure bourgeois or petit bourgeois backgrounds. They were not without snobbery. All I learnt from Mesens was that his first erotic feelings were aroused at the age of six by sitting next to his young piano teacher while practising at the keyboard. Whether this mildly traumatic event was responsible for his aspiring to become a composer I am unable to say, but whatever the reason, and in the face of some opposition from his family, he enrolled at the Conservatoire in Brussels in 1919.

Mesens was considered a somewhat idle but talented student. In 1920 he met the great composer Eric Satie who was visiting Brussels for a series of lectures and concerts and who took a liking to the ardent young man. Mesens once showed me a bundle of postcards Satie had sent him during the early twenties. They were in minuscule handwriting; almost impossible to read without a magnifying glass. Satie strongly advised his protégé to visit Paris, advice soon taken and, on Mesens's second visit in 1922, introduced him to several members of the avant-garde, a step which was to have far-reaching effects on his life and career.

As a composer ELT was quite successful for so young a man. He set several poems to music, including 'Garage' by the French dadaist and surrealist, Philippe Soupault, and a concert of his work was performed featuring a well-known soprano with himself as accompanist. I have never heard a note of his music, although a reproduction of Man Ray's cover to 'Garage' has recently surfaced as a postcard on sale at the Beaubourg. Later in his life he had a grand piano in the living-room of his mansion flat in St John's Wood, but seldom played it, at any rate during my visits, and when he did never conceded to recreate the music of his youth, neither his own, nor Satie's, nor any of *Les Six* for which he had once held some admiration. His repertoire was indeed rather unexpected – the lush melodies of Edwardian musical comedies and in particular Lehár's *The Merry Widow*. During these performances, which I very much enjoyed, he would assume a somewhat roguish expression, but he would never continue for long, breaking off suddenly on the grounds that he was 'wizout practice', nor did he speak much of music, nor attend concerts, although he shared Magritte's liking for Brahms, or so he told me. He would express some pleasure while listening to some, but by no means all, of the output on the Third programme which Sybil usually switched on when she was cooking, but so far as I know would never have tuned in himself, neither did he possess a gramophone or a tape recorder. You would never in fact guess that he had at any time been seriously involved with music, although he always retained his admiration for Satie and would speak of the humility of the middle-aged composer returning to the Paris Conservatoire to sit amongst the young students and improve his knowledge of counterpoint and harmony.

The very last poem published in Mesens's collected poems (*Le Terrain Vague*, 1959) is a homage to the little gentleman with his neat grey beard, pinz-nez, butterfly collar and suit of grey velvet. It's called 'A La Gloire d'Erik Satie', and was especially written for a programme of his music organised by the Société Philarmonique de Bruxelles on 14th February, 1958.

Mesens decided to give up music in 1923. Later on he wrote that this was for moral reasons, but this seemingly mysterious explanation was for the benefit of the Parisian surrealists who dismissed music, with the authority of an essay by de Chirico, as a stupid and meaningless art. Digging a little deeper it probably all boiled down to the fact that Breton was tone deaf. He always displayed this ability to translate his own prejudices and deficiencies into moral imperatives. In 1923, however, Surrealism was not yet born and Mesens had still to meet Breton. His 'moral reasons' were therefore retrospective. I once questioned him on the subject and he was, as he could be, cynically frank. The real reasons he relinquished music he told me were first and foremost that his father refused or was unable to continue paying his fees (perhaps the demand for chicory had slumped), but also because ELT had come to realise that he 'lacked ze mazamatical sense to enrich my work'.

ELT's break with music didn't create a vacuum. He had become increasingly fascinated by the visual arts (for which he was to reveal such a brilliant eye); furthermore, for at least two years before his 'moral' renunciation, he had begun to write poetry. Yet undoubtedly the event which was to have the most profound effect on him was a chance visit to Magritte's first exhibition, shared with a contemporary in a tiny gallery run by two poets. The year was 1920, Magritte was twenty-two, Mesens sixteen or just seventeen.

'We fell in sympathy right away,' Mesens told me some thirty years later and soon, with the encouragement of Pierre Bourgeois, one of the gallery-owning idealists, painter and writer determined to redeem the world through art. It is by no means unusual, even today, for young people in cities to band themselves together for reassurance in the face of uncomprehending hostility and for the fermentation of ideas and, as is usual, this association was short-lived and ended acrimoniously. What was exceptional in this case was that Magritte should turn out to be a genius, and that he and Mesens remained for a long time staunch allies. They were also lucky with their timing. Dada, having delivered its well-aimed kick up the arse of official culture (including academic Modernism), was on its last legs, while Surrealism was stirring in its Parisian womb.

At first the two young men had no clear idea of where they were heading. Magritte's own painting was a mélange of Italian Futurism and the fag-ends of decorative Cubism, although redeemed, as ELT always explained in justification for his enthusiasm, by 'a certain eroticism'. Magritte referred to this period in his work as 'Magritte before Magritte'; an aphorism which David Sylvester believes to have been ELT's invention. Undeniably however, they were, in those heady early days, in complete accord and they complemented each other's nature perfectly.

Mesens was far the more confident and extrovert. It was he, shortly after their first meeting, who suggested writing to the futurists, and they were both thrilled to receive an enthusiastic response from Marinetti. It was Mesens, encouraged by his mentor Satie, who began to visit Paris, to 'breathe a lighter air' as he put it, and was introduced to Brancusi, Picabia and Man Ray through the great composer's generous intervention. He also met Tristan Tzara, the great propagator of Dada, this time off his own bat. Recognising him in the street he boldly and confidently confronted him; a course Magritte would have certainly lacked the *chutzpa* to contemplate.

In 1969, during the major retrospective of Magritte at the Tate Gallery, I interviewed Mesens for the BBC. As he explained, his relationship with Magritte was not always easy. There were 'scenes and rows and even threatenings of killing each other', yet they remained together 'probably because there was something in common between him and me'. One of the things they held in common was a shared opposition to those members of their group who had become drawn towards Dutch Constructivism, not only artistically but in its social ideas. Mesens and Magritte, who had already rejected Futurism once its fascistic tendencies had become apparent, were equally appalled by the human engineering proposed by Mondrian and his followers. During a radio interview with me Mesens said:

> '. . . where a man of enormous talent and
> perhaps genius like Piet Mondrian indulged in
> wrong views like the fact of standardising the
> decoration of the houses built per hundred, the
> workman's houses, where one should have
> imposed in each the same stencilled image
> which we found, Magritte and I, extremely
> sinister.'

They were, in my view, right to do so. De Stijl's ideas were to become manifest in the tower blocks of the sixties, albeit without an identical stencilled image. Nevertheless Mondrian's austere geometry has triumphed in the end although it is doubtful if he would have appreciated the frivolous form it has taken. It may have failed to supplant 'The Wise Old Elephant' or 'The Chinese

Girl' on the walls of council flats, but it erupted all over T-shirts and plastic shopping bags. But if Magritte and Mesens were against standardisation, what exactly were they for? Mesens formulated it as believing that '. . . the poetical was essential, and that a picture could be painted on canvas or on the floor or anywhere it could play its function, as a meaningful thing instead of a decoration'.

One of the things which helped exacerbate the situation was Mesens's habit, following his inhalation of 'a lighter air', of returning to Brussels armed with Dada provocations. 'I brought back to our little capital books of poetry, which I read in the places where we met, mainly cafés or on Saturday afternoons at Magritte's, and which created all the time a fantastic fury on the part of the constructivist element, an animosity leading to real battles and physical fights.' (From our radio interviews.)

This adherence to moribund Dada produced a bonus. Magritte and Mesens both contributed some rather feeble epigrams to the very last number of Picabia's review *391* and Mesens returned the compliment by publishing, in 1925, a magazine called *Œsophage*, beautifully produced as were all ELT's publications, and given over to the works of the beleaguered Dada veterans. Nor were they alone in this venture. Two young poets, Goemans and Lecomte, acted as acolytes at the last rites. Later on Goemans was to become Magritte's dealer and his public relations man in contact with the surrealists during the painter's three years in Paris.

In 1926 Mesens produced another review called *Marie*, but while light-hearted, it was no longer pro-Dada and anti-Breton. In the interim ELT had been taken to meet the Parisian surrealists and, despite some opposition, had been accepted as a 'country member'. Meanwhile in Brussels another figure had emerged, a Marxist, biochemist, poet, and brilliant strategist called Paul Nougé. His ambition was to become Belgium's Breton but, with a far smaller cast to draw on, he realised the need for a less papal stance. Even while *Œsophage* was being put together he had 'borrowed' Goemans and Lecomte to write in rotation with himself a single-page broadsheet called *Correspondence* which came out every ten days. This so impressed the Parisians that Breton, Eluard and Max Morise visited Brussels in 1925 to establish contact, under the pretext of adding their signatures to an anti-colonial pamphlet. (Nougé and Goemans obliged but, in the interim, Lecomte had parted company.)

Nougé already recognised that Magritte had finally discovered the way to make use of the revelation of de Chirico's 'Love Song', which he had been shown as early as 1923, and was emerging as an important surrealist painter, and that Mesens also had a role to play. For the moment however he let them gambol. Meanwhile he recruited two new adherents, Souris and Hooreman, both musicians, for neither he, Magritte, nor any of the Belgian group shared Breton's anti-musical prejudices and, while astute enough not to rock the boat and risk their ejection, Nougé tactfully avoided the danger of becoming no more than Breton's mouthpiece.

Finally Nougé made his move. In 1926 he took leave of *Correspondence* and accepted Mesens's offer to take over the next and final issue of *Marie*. Published in early 1927 it was virtually the surrealist manifesto of the Belgian group or at any rate its *Révolution Surréaliste*. Nougé didn't push himself forward, Mesens was described as 'administrator'. To the public, Nougé appeared to be no more than a contributor. Nor did he immediately take over Magritte. It was Magritte who gradually recognised Nougé's invaluable guidance, and as a result Mesens and he, while remaining friends despite periods of rather childish non-speaking and furious rows, became less and less close. Besides, ELT became a picture dealer and, like most artists, Magritte mistrusted dealers.

Mesens never singled Nougé out as the leader of the Belgian group; he featured simply as one of Magritte's circle. What's more, in radio interviews with him, I proposed that Mesens, Magritte, Nougé and the others had constituted a surrealist group in Brussels. Edouard interrupted with some ferocity. 'Ah! There has never been something called the Surrealist Group in

Belgium nor the Belgium Surrealist Group! It's other people who have called us that.' I countered by asserting that Magritte and the others forged links with the Parisians. ELT again corrected me. 'Ah well, that was after 1927 or '28 . . . Until that date I was the only one who paid regular visits to Paris . . .'

Unable to be the big frog in the little pool of Brussels, Mesens preferred to be a little frog in the big pool dominated by Breton. He thought of himself essentially as a French surrealist, and eventually as the leader of the surrealist group in England. He would never have denied *that* existed, but then in London there was no one of Nougé's authority to challenge his own.

ELT's occasional recollections of his life in Belgium during the twenties and the first half of the thirties were more a series of *vignettes* than a cohesive narrative, and many of his tales related to his early and idyllic friendship with Magritte before Nougé replaced him as the painter's private chaplain. It was a time for him (and possibly also for Magritte) which represented the happiest and most carefree period of his life.

Once, during the sixties, walking with Mesens through the streets of Brussels for the first and only time, he pointed to a building where, he told me, Magritte had painted as a young man, frequently with Mesens present, and how he would suddenly put down his brushes and 'run frantically to the brothel'. (I have decided I shall no longer spell out phonetically Mesens's inability to pronounce 'th' unless the effect is justified by ambiguity.) Here I have no reason to doubt this impetuous lubricity on Magritte's part; certainly his cubist-futurist period delivers a powerful erotic charge despite its formal surface.

Much less reliable, although I accepted it at the time, was Edouard's account of how Magritte re-encountered Georgette Berger, his future wife, after they had lost touch for several years. Magritte, he told me, aged fifteen, had fallen hopelessly in love with a girl of eleven he had seen and spoken with on a roundabout at a fair in Charleroi, where his family were then living. He had neither forgotten her, nor seen her again until one day, when he and Mesens were strolling in the Jardin des Plantes, they were confronted by this Lolita of the carousel, now a beautiful young woman. They recognised each other instantly and it was evident she was much moved. Magritte also, but suppressing all emotion he told her with dismissive indifference that he was unable to linger as he was on the way to visit his mistress. ('A total fabrication by the way,' explained Mesens. 'He possessed no mistress.') It would seem, following this deliberate slight, she had indignantly turned and left, but how she and Magritte found each other again, made it up and got married, formed no part of my friend's narrative. In fact, while immaculately 'surrealist', the story was almost entirely a fabrication.

Georgette and Magritte *did* meet at a fair, but it was not their only encounter. They had bumped into each other shortly afterwards at a bus stop (Charleroi is not an enormous town) and a warm friendship had developed. They had indeed lost touch in 1914 following the confusion and panic of the German invasion. In 1920 Magritte, by now studying painting in Brussels, entered the Coopérative Artistique and discovered Georgette serving on the other side of the counter. This took place in January (the same month incidentally that Mesens first met up with Magritte) and is of course a much more prosaic story.

Is there any truth at all in ELT's account? Certainly Magritte's invention of an imaginary mistress has the authentic flavour of his rare moments of gratuitous bad behaviour. My tentative explanation is that Magritte and Georgette had met each other often before she approached him, whether by design or chance, in the Jardin des Plantes; that they were already committed to each other, and that Magritte, whether to show off his false detachment to his younger friend, or gripped by one of those moments of trapped panic which overcome most men faced by matrimony, reacted as Mesens reported. He could after all apologise later. Furthermore, I got the impression, although it was never made specific, that the happening took place on a spring or summer's day when Magritte and Mesens, far from having just met, were boon companions.

And the reason for Mesens's radical departure from the facts? Georgette, like Nougé, was to come between the two young men. Mesens's story seems to imply that, for a time at any rate, Magritte preferred his company to anyone in the world. It is a bitter tale of lost love.

Less devious was Mesens's original contention that it was he who first showed Magritte the reproduction of de Chirico's 'Love Song', that image which, legend has it, made Magritte burst into uncharacteristic tears and eventually handed him the key to his domain. In the forties and fifties Edouard often told me that he had brought back from Paris a magazine called *Valori Plastici* and there it was. In the sixties, following his own research, he tracked down the reproduction to a later publication, *Les Feuilles Libres*, and brought this to Sylvester's attention. He was prepared to admit that he might have confused the facts – Magritte's tears had flowed after all over thirty years before – but he took care to leave the possibility open. After all whoever had first brought 'Love Song' to Magritte's attention has earned a place in the mythology of modern art and there were several contenders. Even Sylvester is by no means certain. He thinks it was '. . . probably shown to Magritte *and Mesens* by Marcel Lecomte (a member of their circle) probably in the summer or autumn of 1923', so ELT remains a runner.

Besides, although naturally enough he hoped that it was he, his role in Magritte's career far surpassed this solitary act of chance. It is undeniable for example that he was the first to recognise the painter's potential, and he never for a moment wavered in his faith, nor failed to do all he could to impose Magritte's work on an initially hostile or indifferent world. It was not that he was indiscriminate in his admiration either; he knew better than anyone how to tell a good Magritte from an inferior or bad one; he openly detested, much to Magritte's fury, the 'Renoir' period, and never encouraged him to produce inferior pot-boilers or those copies to order which made Magritte a rich man towards the end of his life. Nobody can reduce ELT Mesens's wholly constructive enthusiasm.

Yet, on a personal level, based I've no doubt on Edouard's resentment of Magritte's withdrawal of trust and intimacy, he never failed to denigrate or mock the painter's obstinate provincialism. His stories were very funny and deceptively light in tone, but he spoke of Magritte like a divorced husband who conceals his pain by describing the pretensions and failings of an ex-wife with whom he is forced to remain on good terms for the sake of the children – the pictures. Magritte, for his part, reciprocated by refusing, with some brutality, to acknowledge Mesens's quite modest claims to creativity, either as a poet or collage-maker. Indeed their last serious row – they didn't speak to each other for more than a year – was brought about when someone reported to Edouard that, at a dinner party where one of the guests had announced that he had bought one of ELT's collages (he had begun to have some success towards the end of his life and especially in Belgium), Magritte had reproached the collector for 'spending money on that rubbish'. It was a vicious thing to say about the work of a friend, not to say life-long champion (although it was whoever repeated it that I blame most), and Edouard was both hurt and angry as well he might be.

Sylvester, while praising Mesens as a dealer, exhibition organiser and editor, sides with Magritte in his assessment of Mesens as an artist; I disagree with both of them – not that I would make any exaggerated claims, but I believe my friend to have been a genuine poet with a voice more or less free from any reliance on easy surrealist formulae, and that his collages from 1950 on (Sylvester admits rather grudgingly to some virtue in his work of the thirties) while often repetitive and patently influenced by Klee and Schwitters, revealed at their best a surprisingly tender sensibility, sparkling black humour and, very occasionally, he achieved a minor masterpiece.

But rows on this level between Mesens and Magritte were exceptional. Sniping rather than open war was the norm. In our radio interviews Mesens said: '. . . he [Magritte] still lived in the flat of his father, and therefore had not to earn his living. On the contrary he was, compared with our friends, the best endowed of us and rather practising a certain chic *which I have never known him later* (sic). As a young man he was mysterious in the way he dressed – slightly dandyish. Striped trousers which were then extremely fashionable. He was most comic to look at, because he had this enormous borsalino which gave him the aspect of an old artist and under that an elegant young man.'

Here Edouard has it both ways: to mock Magritte for his early sartorial pretensions, while deprecating his clerk-like off-the-peg appearance in the years which followed. He told me once that when Magritte was in London, he tried to persuade him to buy a superior bowler hat from Lock's in St James's Street, but that Magritte had indignantly refused on the grounds (which the choice of objects in his work makes obvious) that he preferred a mass-produced model. It never occurred to Mesens that Magritte's constant financial difficulties may have also come into it, because he himself, however stretched, always dressed in discreet but expensive clothes, partially no doubt for professional reasons but also from personal preference. He used Magritte's reliance on cheap gents' outfitters (which admittedly later became a trademark) as one of the ways of reducing him to size.

The most elaborate set-piece in ELT's mocking iconoclasm was his description of Magritte's prolonged visit to London in 1936 to execute in situ three large pictures for Edward James. James, whom Edouard described simply as 'a rich pansy', was a Maecenas who was mainly supporting Dali, both as a painter and court jester, but who had admired the Magrittes he had seen in the London exhibition earlier that year, and later met him in Paris. About to redecorate the ballroom of his house in Wimpole Street, he conceived the notion of commissioning three paintings of specified proportions to be placed behind two-way mirrors. Invisible in the normal way, they would materialise as if by magic when concealed lights were switched on behind the glass. (James never thought of Surrealism as a revolutionary movement. He saw it as a way to project his own restless eccentricity.)

33

Mesens had arranged the deal for Magritte: a modest fee, paints and canvases and luxurious bed and board *chez* James. He himself stayed in a hotel to keep an eye on things. Here he was quite justified.

On arrival, James showed Magritte to his room. In it was a large art deco vase filled, not with orchids or lilies as you might expect, but wild flowers gathered on his country estate near Brighton, a typical Jamesian conceit. Asked his opinion of them Magritte said, 'They stink a bit.' Dinner that night was elaborate, the company *haut bohème*. The first course was tiny soles in a delicate pink sauce. Magritte helped himself to eight and refused to eat anything more. He was sat next to Edith Sitwell and spent the whole time talking about his constipation.

A day or two later, visiting Magritte to see how it was going, Mesens found him painting a large expanse of sky in a state of irritation. 'It's so boring,' he kept complaining loudly. 'Be quiet,' said Mesens anxiously. 'You're meant to be a genius.'

Another time he came upon Magritte in a corridor, his eye glued to a keyhole. Edouard was appalled. 'What do you think you're doing?' he hissed. 'Watching Mr James's secretary taking a bath,' explained Magritte. 'But she's very ugly,' said Mesens ungallantly. 'Yes,' said Magritte, 'but very hairy.'

That the painter might have staged these and indeed other events to tease Mesens never occurred to him.

Mesens never let pass an opportunity to put down Magritte, frequently exaggerating to greater effect. He always emphasised, and it was true, that he was accepted by Breton and his circle some years before his friend, but when it came to his description of Magritte's stay in Paris he deliberately misinterpreted his reasons for living in an outer suburb: 'I don't know if you know Le Perreux . . . It's near the Marne where there are fellows going to fish, sadly, the whole day long and there are flats for workers. I don't know the situation now – which dates from fifty years. Very uncomfortable, and he must have paid a very cheap rent, so he must have gone there for two reasons: the cheap rent and being away from Bohemia which he hated . . .' In fact Magritte was desperate to find somewhere more central within his means. The cheap rent came into it certainly; Bohemia was complete invention.

There was one incident in Magritte's life of which ELT must have known, but never discussed with me or even hinted at. On one of the painter's pre-war visits to London under Edouard's aegis, he had a serious affair with a Mrs Sheila Legg, a beautiful surrealist groupie, and this one traumatic lapse in what was otherwise a completely uxorious relationship actually put his marriage at risk for some years. As a rule Mesens (who was on the spot and feverishly interested in everybody's sex life) was far from discreet, but on this occasion, he remained as silent as a confessor. It had certainly nothing to do with any gallantry towards Mrs Legg. He often told me how, during the run of the exhibition of 1936, one of the British surrealists, I forget which, asked him if they could borrow his hotel room for the afternoon. Holding the act of love as sacred, he had instantly agreed, but only on the condition that the surrealist first washed his feet, for he had a low opinion of British hygiene. So why the silence?

It may be that he had encouraged Magritte in this adventure and was nervous that, once it was over, it should get back to Georgette who might well have blamed him for his role as a treacherous enabler. I suspect, however, that to reveal this solitary and uncharacteristic indication of Magritte as a victim of *l'amour fou* would have blurred Edouard's image of him as a model petit bourgeois whose audacity was all of the mind: 'And he lived with his wife a conventional life in which he was charming with her, full of dainty little attentions which middle classes reserve sometimes for their wives. The love of his dog also . . .' (From our radio interviews.)

To have spoken of Magritte's passion for Mrs Legg would have rendered less convincing this patronising, if charming, reduction of Magritte which seemed to have been so essential to Edouard's *amour propre*.

The relationship between Mesens and Magritte remained difficult right up to the end. There were many rows over financial arrangements. (Sylvester prints a complicated proposition from Mesens which reads like Groucho's 'the party of the first part' contract in *A Night at the Opera*.) There were some heated exchanges, not inevitably to Magritte's credit, on aspects of surrealist morality or politics. Yet despite it all they remained linked together with something of the love-hate intensity of Laurel and Hardy. In 1959 *Le Terrain Vague* published ELT's collected poems and Edouard asked Magritte to provide some illustrations. This he did, and they were certainly designed especially; one of them for example illustrated the poem on Erik Satie and depicts a bust of the composer with a bird perched on his head, but the style Magritte adopted was the slap-dash manner of his long-abandoned 'Renoir' period which he knew Mesens detested. He had calculated too, I'm sure, that Edouard couldn't afford to turn down the drawings (Magritte was just beginning to be appreciated on an international level), but that didn't stop ELT complaining to me privately, 'He could eventually have taken more pains.'

And so he could, for, whatever the rights and wrongs of their forty-year needle match, Mesens had always come to Magritte's assistance when he needed it. At the end of Magritte's stay in Paris in 1930, he found himself on his uppers. His gallery, on the eve of his first French exhibition, had failed, leaving him without even means to return home. By purchasing, admittedly at a friendly price, eleven pictures, some of which were masterpieces, Mesens was able to help him out. While certainly amicable, this was also potentially profitable. A year or two later ELT was to do something for Magritte which went far beyond mutual advantage. He stepped in at a time when it appeared inevitable that his friend must face ruin and humiliation, and although eventually it was to make him a multi-millionaire, at the time it was an act of gratuitous faith and love.

By 1932–33, the great slump was at its worst and many art galleries were forced to close down and liquidate their dwindling assets. In October 1932 the entire stock of the Galerie Le Centaure was sent for auction. They had owned one hundred and fifty Magrittes, all of them early and lacking any trace of that 'enormous charm' to tempt the newly impoverished 'good-taste bourgeois'. There was no doubt that if they'd come under the hammer the result would have been a disaster. In the event not one picture was put to the test. ELT Mesens arranged to buy the whole lot in advance. He was twenty-nine years old.

In later life he exaggerated a little. He only put up half the money; the rest came from Claude Spaak, who agreed to take a tenth of the work. What's more, it wasn't Edouard's 'entire savings' as he always told me. He actually borrowed the required amount from his reluctant family. Even so it was an heroic effort.

One hundred and fifty was the number Edouard quoted but, minus Spaak's ten per cent, it would only have been a hundred and thirty-five. Sylvester thinks it possible however that Edouard bought a few more from his ruined mentor PG Van Hecke, so the figure is near enough and a round number is anyway more dramatic – and it is a dramatic story – than an approximate odd number.

'Suddenly,' Mesens would say, 'I found myself with a hundred and fifty Magrittes on my lap, some of great size.' Up until then he had bought only to sell. Now he was a collector and he continued to be one all his life. At his death he owned many fine pictures by de Chirico, Ernst, Picasso, Klee and Miro, amongst others. He had also continued to acquire, with unfailing discrimination, a few later Magrittes. Nevertheless that first courageous, apparently insane, gesture of faith remained unchallenged. Furthermore the pictures were for many years intact. This was not entirely sentimental. Like most collectors at moments of crisis, ELT was forced to sell paintings, including Magrittes, and he was furthermore a professional dealer. The early paintings however remained more or less unsaleable; 'ungrateful' was the word Edouard used to describe difficult paintings of merit. It is after all comparatively recently that the pre-Parisian work, some of it poorly realised, but most of it revealing Magritte's genius at its most poetic, has come into its own.

No wonder that in his last lonely drunken years, Mesens would boast about his early coup to uncomprehending barmaids, waiters, and finally hospital staff – stressing of course the enormous value the pictures had recently acquired; the only element in the story likely to impress them if, which was unlikely, they believed him at all.

Was Magritte grateful to Edouard? Mesens thought not, and when angry with the painter for whatever reason would complain that, 'he has never acknowledged his debt, on the contrary . . .' But then I find this perfectly natural. After I'd got to know him in later life, Edward James told me a pertinent story. A Spanish gentleman was alerted by a friend to the fact that one of his acquaintances was bad-mouthing him all over the village. 'That's strange,' said the gentleman. 'I never did him a favour.'

Even so, Edouard never allowed any of their quarrels to affect, even temporarily, his belief in Magritte as a great artist. He told me that on the night when, unknown to him, Magritte was dying, he had woken up with a start, and seen the word 'genius' glowing against the darkness in letters the colour of flame.

Magritte apart, Edouard seldom discussed his Belgian period. He once, but only once, hinted at a tender love affair with a beautiful young aristocrat which ended, with great sadness, because of what he felt was an unbridgeable social chasm – a strange, rather touching admission. He never mentioned his obligatory army training but, on the evidence of a photograph of himself and a fellow-conscript wearing capes with little tassels and posing with a partially draped double-bass in a field on the edge of a wood, his musical training seemed to have earned him a place in the regimental band. He didn't tell me either that, for a short period, he had run a gallery under his own name, but that was probably because it failed. He did however speak frequently and with great warmth about a couple called Van Hecke.

Paul-Gustave Van Hecke, known as PG (did ELT follow his lead in his insistence on the use of his initials?) was born in 1887. An impresario, he was involved not only with painting, but also journalism, publishing, fashion, poetry, theatre and cinema. Something of a dandy and very much a bon viveur, he was also a convinced libertarian-socialist. Judging by the photographic evidence his shape varied a great deal over the years. He was a tall man but sometimes thin and elegant, sometimes enormously fat and, at the end, frail and much shrunk. He had a remarkable if eclectic taste as a collector; equally enthusiastic about the Belgian expressionists (for which Edouard too retained a rather secretive, possibly chauvinist, liking) and the surrealists, especially Max Ernst and Magritte (to whom Mesens had introduced him), but he had no sympathy at all for Breton's dictatorial exclusivity. Extremely generous and very extravagant, he prospered in good times and went under during recessions. In the 1930s slump, for example, he was forced to sell up, at absurd prices, a fine collection (Sylvester thinks it possible that here again Mesens may have acquired PG's Magrittes to save them from the auction rooms), but he bounced back, and in the post-war years was connected with the casino at Knokke Le Zoute where he organised the film festivals and other glamorous events. Van Hecke was much loved. His nickname was Tartave.

His wife Norine (or Nono) was Brussels's leading fashion designer (Magritte was responsible for some of her publicity). She was thin, tiny and very chic, not a beauty but extremely attractive. Edouard, who was for a time her lover, called her 'a little monkey'. There is a wonderful period photograph of the pair of them in Cannes in 1924 – Nono in a cloche hat, with everything else hanging down in straight lines; ELT in a dark blazer and knife-edged flannels, like the hero of a musical comedy.

PG met ELT when the latter was sixteen, and he immediately took him under his wing. Edouard became in fact a surrogate if Oedipal son of the childless couple; the exact role I was to occupy with the Mesenses some twenty years later. Edouard owed PG a great deal besides his marital complacence. He taught him about picture dealing. He taught him to appreciate food and drink, and how idealism is not necessarily the enemy of hedonism. In fact I never heard ELT criticise his mentor on any grounds other than his extravagance. As an extreme anal-retentive, Mesens tended to despise those who got themselves into practical difficulties although, like PG, he was always extremely generous in restaurants; something which I, in my turn, find it difficult, even if at times necessary, to resist.

When PG died in 1967 a substantial homage was published. Its contributors, both famous and obscure, and the pictures especially dedicated to his memory, give a clear indication of how much love this man inspired during his lifetime. I was eventually to meet him myself, and can confirm his extraordinary ability to make one feel instantly that one had known and admired him all one's life.

Being PG of course there was, on his death, very little in the kitty, and poor Norine found herself in comparatively straitened circumstances. She could hardly blame her husband; she was even more extravagant than he was, but that didn't solve her problem, and ELT felt obliged (he could by then well afford it) to make her an allowance. Being him, he made a big deal of it, attaching strings and criticising the way she chose to spend it. Being her, she gave as good as she got, screaming that it wasn't enough, and throwing what there was of it about like water. Above the mantel-shelf in the fashionable apartment that she insisted on keeping (and why not?), hung a particular bone of contention: that large and terrifying early Magritte, 'Entr'acte', in which creatures consisting simply of a joined arm and leg, draw back a curtain on some slag-heaps, recline against walls, or stroll like lovers. This masterpiece, one of the pictures ELT had rescued during the twenties, had been on long loan to the Van Heckes, who perhaps originally owned it. Now of course Mesens kept threatening to take it back. He didn't succeed, nor did he perhaps intend to, but this kind of bullying was the least attractive side of his nature. The picture was still there when he died anyway, and I hope nobody knew it was his.

Norine, for her part, had visited Edouard when he was in his last coma and started to scream at poor Ruth, imagining perhaps that she had replaced her in Edouard's non-existent will. Hearing this from the nice cousin I was reminded of a line from Ibsen: 'Two shadows fighting over a dead man.' Or come to that, Ensor's satirical etching, 'Two skeletons fighting over a bone'. Death seldom brings out the best in anyone.

An Ensor retrospective was, as it happens, one of the two exhibitions which opened the Palais des Beaux-Arts in Brussels in 1929. This large, partially state-subsidised venture, after a shaky start, became a great show place for modern art, including Magritte. In 1931, Mesens, having failed at private dealing, joined Claude Spaak and his cousin Robert Giron as a member of the exhibition organising committee. This not only ensured Edouard a regular salary, but also allowed him to push Surrealism. (He had no need to push Magritte; Spaak and his cousin were already enthusiasts.)

Of course, being quasi-officials, they had to watch their Ps and Qs a little. At an exhibition celebrating the surrealist painters, Magritte's 'Le Viol' and a Dali which depicted a flaccid but enpurpled penis, were concealed behind a curtain. In general though it was a sympathetic atmosphere, and Mesens always spoke warmly of his years in its employ. He had good cause to feel grateful for another reason. During the war they allowed him to store his entire Belgian collection, including most of his early Magrittes, in the cellars, where they escaped attention.

'Sometimes though,' he told me, 'we had an obligation to hang an official exhibition to ensure the extremely necessary support of the state.' One of these was the work of a nineteenth-century pompier academic, 'of no interest', and it included a huge upright picture of a Polish General, who in some way had been of service to Belgium, mounted on a rearing horse amidst the battle and brandishing his sabre. This work, said ELT, attracted the mischievous attention of one Geert Van Bruaene, one of Edouard's heroes.

Born in 1891, Geert was a tiny, round-faced, pot-bellied, shabby eccentric in granny-glasses who resembled a friendly

41

elemental from Flemish mythology. He had begun as an actor, drifted into art-dealing – Ernst, Klee, Magritte, mixed up with folk-art – and finished up running a small bar, La Fleur en Papier Doré, where he obliged on an antique foot-pedal organ amidst a dark clutter of objects, ancient advertisements and his own aphorisms. He was a natural dadaist and free of all self-importance.

Because of his enthusiasm for modern art, Edouard explained, Van Bruaene was on the permanent mailing-list of the Palais des Beaux-Arts. On this occasion however the public was very different from the usual intellectuals for whom Geert was a familiar and cherished figure. The Belgian establishment in dinner jackets, evening gowns and full-dress uniforms, the foreign ambassadors and their wives, looked with some bewilderment at this small man wearing a disreputable mackintosh, its buttons straining, and carrying an ill-rolled umbrella. Under Edouard's nervous eye, unfazed by the disapproving muttering of those he brushed against, Van Bruaene moved slowly from picture to picture until he stopped in front of the Polish general. He then began to clear a long corridor in front of it reaching as far as the doors the other end of the room. This reassured the ladies and gentlemen. Of course he was a humble employee, although it would have been more appropriate if he had worn a uniform. Clearly, in front of this magnificent picture, an official was about to say a few words; perhaps the Polish ambassador would stress the links between the two countries. They waited in perfumed silence.

Van Bruaene marched some way down the corridor he had cleared. He turned and faced the Polish general. He lifted his absurd umbrella to simulate the raised sword. Then after a long pause he shouted at the top of his voice a 'Polish' battle-cry of his own invention.

SHAPSKA!

Then he turned again and walked calmly out between the shocked and uncomprehending ranks of his natural enemies.

For his whole life Edouard treasured this moment. Faced by

pomposity, stupidity or arrogance, I have seen him raise an imaginary umbrella (or sword) and shout once again that mysterious and unnerving dadaist order to attack.

SHAPSKA!

Three

At the cross-road of sexes
My keenest desire
To anticipate and to place our age
Behind an appearance of refreshed good-heartedness.
LEO MALLET

In the late thirties Edouard began to spend more time in London
until he was, to all extents and purposes, a resident if not a
citizen. In a short while, under Lord Beaverbrook's tuition, he
could both understand and speak English, the latter if not
conventionally at any rate fluently, and the only disadvantage
was that, as an alien, he had to report once a fortnight to a police
station.

His warm friendship with Roland Penrose led to an offer, in
1938, to become director of the London Gallery, at 28 Cork
Street, and this of course confirmed his move across the North
Sea. The gallery, already modern in tendency, had previously
been managed by a Lady 'Peter' Norton whose husband, a
professional diplomat, had been posted abroad, and whom she
had decided to accompany. An exhibition of the paintings and
collages of John Piper was planned for April, the month ELT
took over. At his insistence, it was moved forward to May, and
in its place he arranged a mini-retrospective of Magritte
including such masterpieces as 'Le Viol' and 'L'Évidence Éter-
nelle'. Furthermore, instead of a catalogue, Mesens edited the
first number of *The London Bulletin*, price one shilling, a proper
magazine, surrealist orientated, and containing many reproductions, poems and articles, as well as a list of the exhibits. It was a

brilliant publication and there were to be nineteen further issues, some double, until, in June 1940, the war finally put a stop to it. It was of course the Magritte number which I discovered in the art school library at Stowe some five or six years later, and which sparked off my initial interest in Surrealism.

In a recent interview Tony del Renzio claimed that Mesens had told him that it was Penrose who had prevented him from turning *The London Bulletin* into a totally surrealist publication, but this I doubt. It was after all intended as a glorified catalogue; it contained formidable surreal content; and promulgated very little which, even today, seems irrelevant. Even the John Piper exhibition represented that artist before he became a sugar-coated topographer and, to balance it, ELT mounted on the second floor a small but distinguished collection of drawings and *papiers collés* by Picasso.

By its second issue, the *Bulletin* extended its scope to include two neighbouring galleries: Guggenheim Jeune at 30 Cork Street, who were showing the Dutch expressionist Geer Van Velde (introduced by the then unknown Samuel Beckett), and Miro at the Mayor Gallery at number nineteen. That was in May. In June there was Delvaux at the London Gallery, Léger at the Mayor, and the now forgotten Benno (introduced by Henry Miller) at the Guggenheim. The literary contributors were equally distinguished.

The London Bulletin remains a remarkable achievement – Sylvester maintains that it was as an editor that Mesens showed real genius – and its final number included a moving and unsigned call to arms whose typography and phrasing are clearly his:

> NO dream is worse than the reality in which we live.
> No reality is as good as our dreams.
> The enemies of desire and hope have risen in
> violence. They have grown among us, murdering,
> oppressing and destroying. Now sick with their
> poison we are threatened with extinction.
> FIGHT
> HITLER

AND HIS IDEOLOGY WHEREVER IT
APPEARS
WE MUST
His defeat is the indispensable prelude to the total
liberation of mankind.
Science and vision will persist beyond the squalor of
war and unveil a new world.

Mesens was on good terms with his gallery-owning neighbours. He adored Freddie Mayor, a short, rubicund, cigar-smoking, bowler-hatted bon viveur, whose admirable taste in pictures was equalled by his enthusiasm for the race course (his gallery, when I got to know him after the war, was always closed without question during major race meetings). Peggy Guggenheim, years before she turned into what Edouard called 'an old cathedral' and the unofficial doge of Venice, was for a time his mistress. She was to acknowledge this in her autobiography, *Art of the Century* (1946), although most of the names were altered. She called him 'Mittens', not too opaque a disguise, especially as she went on to describe him as 'a surrealist poet' and 'a gay little Flamand, quite vulgar but really very nice and warm'. Peggy, whom I was to meet in her old age, was witty, difficult, and openly lubricious. Edouard, although only one of a formidable army of lovers, was quite proud of her salute. He kept a copy of her book on a high shelf in his library and got it down to show it me at least twice. 'Don't tell Sybil,' he would tell me conspiratorially as he climbed back on a chair to replace it, although, in so far as I know, the liaison was over before he met her.

There was no doubt that Sybil was the love of his life. During the time I knew him he was occasionally technically unfaithful (and so was she), but he never wavered in his devotion. He would explain away his infidelities by describing them as 'lust', a category of sexual activity which he separated entirely from 'love' and he would illustrate this division visually: for 'lust' he would extend his arms slightly in front of his chest, turn his wrists inwards and place his palms together parallel to the ground. He would then slide them back and forth, apart and together again. For 'love' the action was identical only, by

46

previously curving up his finger-tips, the palms, while still able to rub together, were unable to disengage beyond a certain point.

I must admit that quite often in my life, whilst occupied in an act of lust, or even its contemplation, the near-subliminal mental image of ELT's immaculately manicured hands sliding freely back and forth has flashed across my inner eye. In love however, including the act of love, the locked finger-tip variant has never sought to impose itself.

At some point, as the thirties drew towards their close, while the Spanish Civil War raged on and the Second World War became inevitable, Sybil Stephenson applied for the job as secretary to the London Gallery.

Sybil never told me anything about her background, her school days or her family, but I imagine them to have been provincial middle-class and fairly comfortable. What she made clear was that she was determined to escape Bishops Auckland, near Newcastle-on-Tyne, from adolescence on, and she did so by marrying John Stephenson, a locally born painter of abstract persuasion. They moved to London where he became a member of the Ben Nicholson circle. It was Sybil's intention to earn her living as a frame-maker (she was and remained a firm believer in the protestant work ethic), but for reasons unknown to me she abandoned this idea and joined Edouard in Cork Street.

While the war between the British surrealists and abstractionists was predictably less wholehearted than in Paris, it was none the less ironic that Sybil should have found herself working for a convinced disciple of Breton while still married, although not for much longer, to an out-and-out constructivist. She was always however of fiercely independent character and, while soon appreciating the work of Ernst, Miro and the rest, never renounced her taste for abstraction. She had indeed acquired at some point an enormous Léger, a beautiful purist picture from the early twenties, before the invasion of his tubular-limbed workmen, cyclists and acrobats, and always insisted on it hanging in a place of honour. At first Edouard was mildly

47

irritated by this unsought dowry: 'it belongs with my wife,' he would explain to visitors, but later, and not entirely because it had reached great value, he became proud of it.

Mesens and his new secretary became passionate lovers. 'We were,' ELT often told me, 'fucking everywhere – even behind the desk and in the storeroom.' They soon decided to live together.

They married at the beginning of the war as Edouard knew he would soon be called up and, in the event of his death, wished everything to go to Sybil. Almost immediately he was ordered to report to Brussels but before long, although I've no idea how he managed it, he was back in London, ensconced with Sybil at the Penroses', and working for the Belgian section of the BBC at Bush House, both in the talks department and as an occasional conductor. (His 'moral' objection to music was suspended for the duration.) As Jacques Brunius was employed by the French section, and the two surrealist poets, Sadi Cherkeshi and Feyyaz Fergar, by the Turkish, the movement was pretty well represented on the airwaves beamed towards Europe.

I got the impression that, despite grumbling about it, Edouard was rather happy at Bush House. He had after all a regular salary instead of relying on the vagaries of the art world, and found himself able to write some of his best poetry. Furthermore his life was structured for him; he had to be dressed by a certain time each morning, something which normally he found impossible, and of course he was forced to restrain his drinking. There was, it is true, one incident he much regretted. Since he was a very young man he had been a friend of the great Belgian painter, James Ensor. On hearing of his death he payed him tribute over the air praising, with justice, his early work with its masks and animated skeletons, but speaking rather dismissively of his later and far less original pictures. Unfortunately, not only was Ensor still alive but he was listening, illicitly, to the BBC. He never spoke to Edouard again.

Although he was about to be 'demobbed' from Bush House when I first met him, Mesens was still moved on occasion to celebrate his position there with a short burst of song, part of the signature tune of a popular radio wartime comedy show called *The Happy Drome*. This featured three northern anchor men; a Mr Lovejoy and his two stooges, Enoch and Ramsbottom. I would have expected Edouard to have preferred *The Happy Drome*'s rival, Tommy Handley's *ITMA* (It's That Man Again), especially as it contained genuinely surreal jokes ('Why are you so bent?' 'From shaking hands with cats.'), but he didn't. What he sang, in an emphatically tuneless voice, heavily accented, and with much emphasis on the last word was this:

> We three – the Happy Drome, Working for the BBC.
> Enoch,
> R-r-r-ramsbottom and ME!

In all the years I knew him, Edouard, while very occasionally adding a fragment which had amused him, relied on a mere handful of snatches when he was in the mood to burst into song. Aside from *The Happy Drome*'s signature tune, there was a short Dada round-song about 'The good lady of milk who comes from the good country, the good county of milk', and a French chanson about a crippled *concierge*'s daughter. The point about this last was that its rhythm was intended to evoke her limp and the singer was supposed to simulate her disability. Edouard however refused on humane grounds to resort to this practice, but had invented a compromise. In the street, for it was almost inevitably there that the urge to sing came upon him, and usually late at night, he would walk along with one foot in the gutter and the other on the pavement, thus giving the illusion of the *fille de concierge* as she hobbled briskly along.

Once Edouard had left Enoch and Ramsbottom to their own devices, he began to occupy himself with preparations to re-open the London Gallery. He was to be managing director as before. The other directors were Anton Zwemmer, founder of the famous and still extant art-bookshop in the Charing Cross Road, Peter Watson, a rich homosexual and patron of the arts (he had financially backed Cyril Connolly's *Horizon*), and finally Roland Penrose. It was this of course that created the difficulty. As a surrealist it was ELT's duty to have nothing to do with 'Stalinist' Penrose, but as Edouard was at the same time his employee, this was hardly possible. He was forced to remain polite and, to some extent, co-operative, but with much growling and cursing behind Roland's back. The other two directors presented no such problem: Zwemmer, a Dutchman by birth, was 'a pure business-man' and Watson, a sweet but melancholy man who, Edouard told me, was rumoured to be an illegitimate son of Edward VII. He did somewhat resemble an effeminate and wistful version of the Duke of Windsor.

A lease on a house on Brook Street had already been signed and very slowly, for post-war shortages and proliferating red-tape made any progress extremely difficult, work had begun on it. It was a tall, narrow, Georgian house of which the ground floor, not a large room by any means, had already been converted into a shop before the war, with double windows and a glass door between them.

This was to become a bookshop with low shelves along two walls and space for drawings and small pictures to hang above them. Two steps led down into a much larger gallery at the back. This was a previous extension on the house, and had a cellar for storage beneath it. A door in the bookshop opened onto a side-passage (which also had its own front door), and at the end of it was a rather rickety staircase, with a dangerous little lavatory built out over the yard. Above were four other floors, the first two of which were to become an office, additional exhibition space and a picture restoration studio. The top floors, cut off by a front door, were to form Edouard and Sybil's living quarters: a low but pretty sitting-room facing Brook Street, a bedroom at the back and, above, a tiny dining-room, kitchen and bathroom.

This area was given priority, not only because life *chez* Penrose had become unbearably fraught, but also because it was easier to get round the building regulations when accomodation rather than business premises were involved. It was not long after I first met them that they moved in and, when in London, I often stayed with them, sleeping on a couch in the sitting-room.

The situation was very convenient for Sybil. She had turned her eye for fashion to good use by finding employment at Bourne and Hollingsworth as a sales assistant and then transferring to Dickens and Jones, where she rose rapidly to become chief buyer. Brook Street was within easy walking distance of her work. As a business woman she reverted to her maiden name of Fenton. ELT (who usually called her 'Darlington' on account of that town's proximity to her birthplace in Bishops Auckland) would sometimes tease her by calling her 'Fenton'. While this didn't amuse her, what really irritated her was his frequently referring to her place of business as 'Dickie and Johnny'. Not only did she take her work seriously, but for the next few years it was what Fenton earned at 'Dickie and Johnny' which largely supported them.

She furnished the little flat with small pieces of Regency furniture which looked pretty and occupied the minimum space. I helped ELT hang some of his marvellous pictures, learning a great deal about how to do so in the process. I had become very fond of them both, and they of me, although I was a little in awe of Sybil in her more Fentonish moods. Then, much to my surprise, one Sunday afternoon, there was a dramatic development in our relationship which was to affect my whole life.

I've been prevaricating over dealing with this event, writing slowly, finding any excuse to avoid writing at all, sorting books, accepting other work. This is not because I am in any way ashamed of the incident and what followed from it but because I have written an account of it elsewhere. I have already warned the reader that there would be some repetition of certain aspects of my life with ELT between our first meeting and my full-time entry into the jazz world, but in *Rum, Bum and Concertina* the events of that Sunday afternoon are described in full. Indeed my first impulse was to reprint those pages as they stood, but I have decided against that as they were written fifteen years ago or more and, as one grows older, the emphasis and interpretation of particular incidents shift to some degree. Resisting therefore the temptation to re-read and paraphrase my earlier description here is what happened.

The sitting-room. Edouard and I talking about sex. Sybil reading a Penguin detective novel. Sybil suddenly throws this down, and proposes that, instead of just talking about sex, why don't we go into the bedroom and do it? As Edouard appears unfazed by this suggestion, I accept immediately, although concealing my nervousness – my entire sexual experience up until that moment had been homosexual. In the event all goes well. After a certain amount of mutual foreplay I enter Sybil while Edouard, naked except for his socks, watches in a state of some excitement. At one point he cries, 'You are fucking my wife!' When I've come, he replaces me. His orgasm is quite dramatic. He rolls his eyes and shouts blasphemies (I was to copy this performance for some time). When it's all over Sybil retires to douche. Later we spend a quiet and relaxed evening. On other occasions, although probably not more than six times in all, we repeat the exercise.

My reactions? No sense of guilt, either then or later. A certain pride in having finally fucked a woman. Increased affection for both of them. I speculate also that, whereas I believe that I would eventually (and very slowly) have become heterosexual, this bisexual bridge was probably a help towards this end. A later suspicion: that the event was not as spontaneous as I believed at the time, that ELT and Sybil had probably planned it, and even rehearsed the script. I remember for instance that the conversation, prior to Sybil's proposal, centred on the contrast between Breton's puritanical homophobia and the sub-rosa behaviour of his followers. By such means ELT and Sybil (concealed behind her Agatha Christie) could test my reaction in advance.

Physical reactions? Pleasure rather than ecstasy. Gratitude. Something to swank about aboard ship. A boost to my *amour propre*.

With the *partouses* aside, I once went to bed with her alone when ELT was in Belgium. She said afterwards that it would be better not to tell him as he might be jealous. Later on she began a long-lasting and passionate lesbian affair but, as her lover is still alive and I was not directly involved, I shall leave it at that.

Besides, while remaining a true friend, she began to disapprove of my very promiscuous, rather macho, raving about the jazz world. She much preferred, as she called it, 'Le Petit Marin'. We became much closer again towards the end of her life, but by then there was no question of any renewed sexual activity. Another possible reason for her cooling towards me was that, towards the end of our involvement, she became pregnant and had an abortion. Illegal, of course, in those days, she described it to us in some detail – not the operation itself, but the Hitchcock-like precautions leading up to it. She had to go to a block of luxury flats at a certain hour, ascend in a lift up to the fifth floor, walk down to the third, making sure she was not being followed, and ring a particular bell using a certain code. Edouard always insisted that I was responsible for her pregnancy although, as far as I know, there was no evidence of his infertility. In fact, that same fortune teller whose prediction he would live to be eighty provided him with the excuse not to make a will, had also told him 'Somewhere in the world you have made a baby'. I dare say it was just a way to pass the buck and absolve himself from any guilt he may have felt at Sybil's decision to abort.

I remained sexually involved with Edouard for much longer. On one occasion, during the fifties, he proposed, after a rather drunken dinner *à deux* at the Barcelona, that we pick up and share a whore on our stroll through Mayfair. I was perfectly willing to go along with this. It was many years before the implementation of the Wolfenden Report and the girls were in some cases of great beauty. To my disappointment, but he after all was paying, he chose a stout, middle-aged woman in a fur coat. By chance (unless he had patronised her before), she turned out to be Belgian. She led us up the stairs to her room off Hanover Square where we both undressed while she remained fully clothed except for her fur-coat.

It was soon evident that she had mistaken our intentions, imagining we were gay and had paid her for use of the room. Edouard disabused her of this idea and she reluctantly removed several outer-garments, keeping on a formidable corset. She then conceived the notion that what Edouard was paying for was to see me beaten. To this end she threw open a large Victorian wardrobe which contained a wide selection of canes and whips. ELT again corrected her. Our requirements were perfectly straightforward. Incredulously she complied and, with Edouard seated naked in a chair, again wearing his socks and far too drunk to accomplish anything when his turn came, I climbed on top of her (for in those days nothing, however grotesque, could put me off) and eventually came. It must have looked like a Weimar Republic painting by Grosz or Dix and was, although it hadn't occurred to me until this moment, a hideous caricature of the affectionate threesomes with Sybil a few years earlier. Edouard was rather disgusted with himself afterwards, and with me also for going along with it. The event joined Peggy Guggenheim's memoirs as something to be concealed from Sybil, but then Sybil had her own secrets: our solitary love-making and a confession that once, on a business trip, she had spent the night with a businessman who had picked her up in an hotel bar. I never used any of this ammunition although at times, under fire form one or the other or both of them, I experienced a certain temptation to do so.

When the London Gallery closed in the early fifties, and the Mesenses moved to a mansion block off Baker Street, I would visit ELT regularly, and usually in the afternoon when Sybil was still at work, for I saw no reason to submit voluntarily to her criticism of my way of life and scruffy appearance. My pleasure in these visits was in Edouard's company, in his wonderful stories of the past, and the bonus of examining again his beautiful collection, which he would sometimes ask me in part to re-hang. First however he would expect us to engage in mutual masturbation or fellatio and, while I can't pretend I enjoyed this very much, it didn't especially worry me. I was always fascinated to see how, before we started, he would squeeze the end of my dick while watching closely. I presume his object was to make sure there was no discharge, a trick I imagine he had learnt from the Flemish whores of his youth.

Sometimes he would be in a more experimental mood. We once tried sodomy but, as I could have told him in my case at any rate, found it too painful. Not painful but certainly odd was his request one afternoon that we should both masturbate onto a plate and then, on our hands and knees, lap it up like pussy cats. I went through with this but found, and still find, it a rather melancholy and depressing moment in my erotic life probably because it was, of necessity, post-orgasmic. Not so ELT and in later years, long after we had abandoned any sexual contact, he would mention it to me with a kind of retrospective glee. Long after he was dead I told this story to a girlfriend of mine. It was something I regretted. She had a low boredom threshold and liked to 'liven things up'. To this end if, at a dinner party, the conversation turned towards Surrealism in general or Mesens in particular (both usually my doing) she would intervene with a cry of 'The plate! Tell them about the plate!'

And that is about all I have to say about my sexual experiences *chez* Mesens. It may appear inexplicable to some as to why I continued to indulge him, plate and all, long after my initial enthusiasm had evaporated. My answer in general is, that while still young, I was well aware that wrinkles and a pot-belly lay ahead and that the time would come when I too would one day rely on sexual generosity. Furthermore, in this particular case I loved him and knew it gave him pleasure. There was, however, one element which I did find difficult to handle. I promised earlier not to continue to reproduce his pronunciation phonetically but I must just once. His difficulty with the 'th' sound meant that he pronounced 'mouth' as 'mouse' and I found it very hard to control or suppress my laughter when, during our bouts in the flat off Baker Street, he demanded passionately that I kissed him on 'the mouse'.

Four

Pictures and works of art might be called safe
depositables; the spirit is inside and becomes
increasingly inspired as the auction prices mount.

PICABIA

I was in the navy for three and a half years – the unusual length
of my service is accounted for by the fact that, post-Hiroshima,
there were all those who had been called up or recruited since
1939 to be demobbed first. I didn't resent this at all; it was quite
comfortable in the iron-clad womb. However broke I might be
there was always a deck over my head and food, however
disgusting, on the table. Furthermore my 'lost' year in Chatham
dock yard had introduced me to London and the surrealists. I
was not complaining, although I knew it couldn't last.

When they finally winkled me out of Chatham and transferred
me to a sea-going ship I began to worry. Not at going to sea; on
the contrary, the war was over and we were sent on 'goodwill
visits' to Scandinavia and the Med. I'd never been abroad as a
child and found it all extraordinary and dream-like. Furthermore, after each expedition, we returned to Chatham for a
variable amount of time, and I was able to pick up the threads of
my London life where I had dropped them, the Mesenses et al.
No, my apprehension was fixed on the future. Now the
Admiralty had rediscovered me, there must be only a finite
period before they demobbed me, and I must face life in Civvy
Street. I was realist enough also to recognise that, once out of my
glamorous bell-bottoms, I would be of much less interest to rich
homosexuals. I was, all in all, in a bit of a quandary, and even

contemplated signing on, although not very seriously and usually when drunk.

There was however the writing: I had already contributed several articles on Klee, the Picasso-Matisse exhibition at the V & A, and my feelings on Merseyside to a small monthly journal called *The Liverpolitan* and had shown them to ELT who read them with close attention and praised them moderately and with certain reservations. I had also been taken on by the *Liverpool Daily Post* to cover, as and when it were possible, important London exhibitions at two or three guineas a time. These I neglected to bring to Edouard's attention as some of the exhibitions were in no way surrealist. I remembered also his insistence that no member of the group write for other than surrealist publications and, while this had certainly been modified, saw no reason to twist the tiger's tail.

I didn't feel too bad about it though as I had used the *Liverpool Daily Post* pieces of silver to buy, in pound instalments, a beautiful little frottage of a bird in a cage by Max Ernst. I'd found it in Roland, Browse and Delbanco, an old-established gallery in Cork Street, but when I showed it to ELT he was far from encouraging. He said that at twelve guineas it was much too expensive and also 'of weak tendency'. Later I realised that what really irritated him was that I hadn't bought from him; indeed it was rather thoughtless given that he was about to open a gallery. This was soon corrected. To demonstrate the 'weakness' of my little bird (an opinion he was quite prepared to moderate when it suited him) he showed me a beautiful small oil; one of Ernst's 'Lop Lop' series. 'For you Doctor,' he told me, 'forty pounds. A very friendly price.' I mentioned this offer when I was next home on leave and, rather to my surprise, for he was not generally prodigal, my father offered to give it me. I had begun a collection.

In my naïvety it never occurred to me that my father's generosity led to Edouard's next move.

He must have discussed it with Sybil because one lunchtime, with the same apparently casual air which preceded my bisexual

57

initiation, one of them asked me the question I had been avoiding thinking about. What did I intend to do after the navy had no further use for me?

'Well,' I said, unable to think of anything else, 'perhaps I might get a job on a Liverpool paper . . .' This tentative answer produced as violent a reaction as if I had proposed training for the priesthood or becoming a Stalinist spy. Journalists were hyenas, scorpions, vultures, swine first-class, yelled ELT in that harsh high voice he usually reserved for surrealist rows, and although Sybil was less hysterical she backed him up completely. If I wished to retain their friendship, to remain within their circle, I must forget that I had ever contemplated such a course. Pretty overwhelmed by this ultimatum I asked them what, given my lack of any qualifications, I could do?

'You could come,' Edouard said, 'and train as an art dealer.'

Well, it had never occurred to me but, like so much else in my life, immediately appeared inevitable. ELT painted a convincing enough picture; the days spent in persuading the rich to invest in art, the nights in organising subversive surrealist manifestations. The building struggling to life on the floors below us was only a beginning – we would later open branches in Paris, Brussels and New York. I would be able to accumulate a magnificent private collection of my own. I think we all went to bed together to celebrate, and later to a restaurant for dinner where we drank champagne. Edouard suggested at some point that perhaps he and Sybil should come to Liverpool to discuss it with my father. He hadn't met him at that time although he had already met my mother on one of her post-war trips to London – probably for the re-opening of Covent Garden – and she 'didn't care' for him. 'Lays down the law' and 'Holds the floor' were her principal objections. She'd liked Sybil though and marvelled at her patience, but it was my father who mattered in this instance. Although I was unaware of it at the time, Edouard had decided that, if I was to learn the trade, a certain amount of money must first be invested in the business. Nine hundred pounds was the amount he had fixed on – in 1946 a not inconsiderable sum.

My father was, on the surface, a much less complex person than my mother. A not particularly successful or enthusiastic businessman; lazy but charming and with few needs – draft Bass, golf, shooting and fishing – he nevertheless exhibited certain sympathetic aspects: a deep hatred of pomposity for one. He was good-looking but, while there were rumours of one liaison, gave the impression that extra-marital affairs would have used up too much energy. He voted Conservative from self-interest rather than conviction, but was unfazed, even amused, by my enthusiastic belief in anarchism and, unlike my mother, immediately got the point of Surrealism. Having been bitten once or twice he was suspicious of any form of speculation (he had lost heavily in the twenties by investing in a roller-skating rink just before the craze collapsed) and was generally careful with money. How he would react to ELT's proposal was an open question. They got on immediately. Edouard made Tom laugh for one thing – always a strong factor in how he judged people – and they shared a mutual veneration for the pub, a ritual guaranteed to alienate my mother. Edouard's judgement of my father was that he found him 'a good old boy', a form of commendation he applied to very few. They enjoyed themselves that weekend, but that didn't guarantee that Tom would agree to my apprenticeship. While gratified that the two men I most loved seemed to be getting on so well, I was in a detached state about the whole thing and totally fatalistic as to its outcome.

From their arrival at Lime Street Station on, I couldn't really believe that Edouard and Sybil were in Liverpool; it gave me that uneasy sensation of displacement I experience when meeting someone entirely out of context or whom I believe to be dead. The Mesenses were London, Surrealism, triolism. What were they doing in Liverpool? Liverpool was home, my family, my childhood.

My mother meanwhile was coming to the boil over Edouard's morning routine. He would come down to breakfast on time in his dressing-gown, but then disappear into the bathroom for two hours. 'The obligers can't get in to do it,' she'd complain angrily under her breath. 'They always do upstairs first.' ('The obligers' were what my mother called the cleaners; my parents could no longer afford a full-time domestic staff.) What Edouard actually did in the bathrom, a complicated ritual, will be touched on later. Even if she had known it would in no way have placated my mother.

My sister, who was about sixteen, enchanted the Mesenses, and she would also become their life-long friend. She had already decided, pushed by our mother, Maud, to become an actress and, as it was around Christmas, she was appearing as a member of the small chorus in a seasonable 'review' put on in the evenings at the Liverpool Playhouse. We all went to see it and Edouard was very tickled by the final chorus. On the surface it was banality itself: the whole cast prancing about with fixed smiles, and singing in that curious theatrical-posh accent they taught at drama schools in those days the following words:

'This we're afraid is the end, of the laughter and singing and dancing . . .'

Afterwards we all had dinner in a small restaurant close to the theatre, a pretentious place with an absurdly obsequious owner which was nevertheless the best that post-war Liverpool could offer. My father had expressed some opposition to this – he resented spending any money on eating out – but I had stressed how often the Mesenses had taken me to the Ivy, and Maudie didn't want to feel obligated. Edouard was in a very good mood, partially because he had been so seduced by the finale, and he made Andrée repeat it several times until he had committed it to memory. The reason of course lay in its dadaist absurdity; the intimation of mortality reduced to an inane jingle.

Edouard added it to the limping daughter of the *concierge*, the good lady of milk and Messrs Enoch, Ramsbottom and Me, as part of his late-night repertoire of catches.

'This – we're afraid – is the END!'

On the last evening of their stay my father and Edouard took me to the pub and Tom explained that he had decided to pay the

London Gallery nine hundred pounds so that I could be trained as an art dealer. The nine hundred wouldn't just vanish, however. I would use it to choose pictures at trade prices which would then be mine, but available as part of the gallery stock. If I sold one, the gallery would take its commission and I must reinvest the money in another work or works. I was delighted by this news, and later asked my father why he had agreed to it. His answer was typical: indicative of the disappointment and even anger which lay behind his easy-going manner.

'My family,' he began, 'paid for me to become a partner in a wool-brokers, a job I've always detested.' (He once told me he'd have liked best to manage a sporting estate.) 'I didn't see therefore,' he added, 'why I shouldn't give you some money to do something you were actually keen on.'

But this explanation came when we were alone. In the pub all he gave me was his intention to support me. When he'd finished, Edouard said his piece. It was much less agreeable and revealed for the first time a side of him I had never suspected – the businessman.

'Naturally,' he began, 'you will at first receive a very small salary – three pounds a week would be suitable in my view.' Three pounds was of course worth a great deal more in 1946, but it was still pretty basic. 'This would be increased proportionally to match with your progress. Your love of art is proven, but to succeed you must acquire shorthand and typing. Perhaps after your demob you should return to Liverpool for a few months to attend a college. French also – your French is a disgrace for an educated boy. Once you are in London there are excellent night-schools . . .'

While continuing to pretend to listen I had by now more or less cut off. Words like 'double entry book-keeping' and 'annual stock-taking' went in one inattentive ear and out the other. The thing was I didn't really believe (but I was wrong) that ELT meant what he said. I thought it was for my father's benefit – to reassure him that dealing in modern art, unlike investing in roller-skating, was a serious business. Edouard was after all a surrealist! What had Surrealism to do with double entry book-keeping?

Eventually he finished and I expressed my intention to do everything he suggested to the best of my ability. Rather to my father's embarrassment we all shook hands. ('Still at least we didn't have to embrace,' said Tom later.) Then the jokes began again and he had two more halves of draft Bass. With the first they toasted my future, and later we went home for supper in rather too ebullient a mood to please my mother (*en route* 'This we're afraid is the END!' was given its first Edouardian public outing).

And so I went back to Chatham to complete my service, another six months as it transpired, and during that period in limbo saw something of my future employer, and not all of it entirely reassuring.

The gallery was at last taking shape: the rebuilding was complete, the walls were all white, the built-in bookcases installed, the coconut matting laid. Facing the entrance, flanked by display windows, was a high-relief mural by FE McWilliam of displaced and enormous human features: eyes, nose, ear, mouth. In front of it was a large desk. Behind this, it was explained at every visit, I would sit addressing invitation envelopes when not answering the telephone switchboard, typing letters and invoices, or attending clients. Only the last had much appeal; I began to wonder if, despite ELT's opposition, I wouldn't have been better off as a 'swine first-class' on the *Liverpool Daily Post*.

During this period all attempts to divert Edouard's attention by discussing Surrealism were briefly dismissed. The group had largely disintegrated anyway, but even apart from that it was obvious that the poet Mesens had been temporarily banished. ELT was for the moment entirely possessed by the demon of commerce. I was quite shocked when he took me with him to negotiate the purchase of two beautiful Paul Klees from someone (possibly a German-Jewish refugee) who was clearly in need of ready cash. Thirty-five pounds was the modest asking price, but, not only did Edouard expend an inordinate amount of time beating it down to thirty, he then took me to a public house to boast for almost an hour on his cunning and perseverance.

This incident however was merely unattractive. What really disgusted me, and alarmed me about my future, was the discovery that he had written to my parents behind my back to remind them to insist I enrolled immediately after my demob at a college of shorthand and typing. Was this the act of a surrealist? Not in my book. Nor was any of his behaviour when it came to running a business, and at the time I was both saddened and puzzled at this revelation. Listening again however to a BBC interview I had with him in the sixties (it's strange to hear one's own much lighter, younger voice interrogating the dead) I picked up several clues.

'My father,' said Edouard, 'absolutely refused to give me money. He didn't pay for me even on the platform of a tram. I had to pay from my own pocket . . .'

It was also of course his father who had cut short ELT's ambitions as a composer, and so at some point he had decided to show the old man that he too could earn a living.

'. . . otherwise what would I have been? One of those poor devils hanging on a café table writing on little pieces of paper – no, no!' It was then that he became a very well paid picture dealer attached to the Palais des Beaux-Arts. He dressed meticulously, collected pictures, ate in good restaurants, and yet those he most hoped to impress, his parents, remained unconvinced.

'. . . living with parents who were not understanding me at all. They took me more and more – the more I progressed the more they took me for a wild man . . .' Yet Edouard still believed, and was to continue to believe his whole life, in Surrealism, poetry and revolution.

'I always succeeded in making a poem now and then, in organising manifestations . . .' (and in pushing the work of those artists he believed in) 'whenever I got the opportunity to shove them in . . .'

But as a result of this dual role, especially in that his 'merchandise' was at the same time part of his ideological baggage, he created a pull-baker pull-devil situation which made him terrible unhappy and which he never resolved. For the whole of his life this caricature of a businessman fought it out with the wild man; Mesens *père* in one corner, André Breton in the other. It was for his father's sake that Edouard haggled over the Klees, or scrutinised a restaurant bill for a quarter of an hour, checking and re-checking it before confirming '*C'est juste*', and leaving a tip exact to the last franc or penny.

I believe, also in retrospect, that his attempt to turn me into an efficient employee sprang from the same source. He had frequently declared himself my 'father' and he knew very well that, while I was as committed to Surrealism as he was, I detested discipline. He sought to bring me into line, to break my spirit, to make me as unhappy as he was, but my obstinacy and ineptitude saved me. I was helped too by the way that, even at the gallery, the other Mesens would occasionally break through, especially after his drunken return from the pub.

For six months in Liverpool, the last consecutive period I was to spend under my parents' roof, I attended, as per Edouard's instructions, a college of shorthand and typing, officially restricted to women. I believe that my mother was in some way responsible for this bending of the rules.

To begin with I turned up every day, but neither concentrated whilst in class, nor did any homework. As I was very fast with two fingers I saw no reason to learn touch-typing, and as for shorthand, I ignored it completely. London and ELT seemed far into the future. So I flirted with the embryonic secretaries, and sometimes with the children of my parents' generation and with one of whom, the beautiful and spirited daughter of a gynaecologist, I began an affair which lasted intermittently for some years. Meanwhile, I established a parallel homosexual life centred on a fat and intelligent middle-aged queen prepared to spend on me what little he had left of a considerable fortune, and, less profitably, a circle of university students, the majority of whom were reading architecture.

In my ex-nursery hung my two Ernsts, the drawing and the painting, and on a shelf below them sat my small library of surrealist literature. On the ping-pong table stood my wind-up gramophone and a growing stack of jazz records. After a time I more or less stopped going into the college and sloped off to the pictures almost every afternoon.

I was not however out of touch with ELT during this idle hiatus. Fudging, when questioned, my lack of application in the acquisition of secretarial skills, I went up to London several times and especially to attend the private view of the gallery's wonderful exhibition, 'The Cubist Spirit in its Time'.

This was held soon after the gallery opened its doors and, in the light of what was to come, assumes in distant retrospect an almost tragic significance. The fifty-seven exhibits, while dominated certainly by the masterpieces of Picasso in the Penrose collection, were more than an assemblage of beautiful artefacts. Mesens and his assistant Robert Melville saw their aim as a re-evaluation of Cubism from a poetic and surreal viewpoint.

The thin but well-illustrated catalogue included contributions from Apollinaire and (predictably) André Breton, but it is ELT and Robert who separate the inventive sheep from the systematic goats; those who had simply turned Cézanne into a rigid system from those who had created what Melville called 'magical presences of . . . persuasiveness and grandeur'.

To create this exhibition today could cost so much in insurance as to be beyond the means of any private gallery. It was a revelation to me, but I was surprised as to how few people attended the *vernissage*. In this I was naïve. There were at best a handful of serious collectors of modern art and most of those preferred to buy British. The late and lukewarm reaction of a few intellectuals between the wars had evaporated. The sparse public who turned up that chilly spring evening were an indication the London Gallery was doomed from the start.

I wasn't due to become a Londoner until June but, out of the blue came a letter from ELT saying I was needed two months earlier. It must have been at Easter that this rather unwelcome news arrived as Edouard referred to the unreliability of the post during the religious festival. 'The Holy Post,' he wrote, 'suffers its Royal Relapse.' He suggested in consequence that I replied in the affirmative by return.

I was not pleased by this turn of events. Admittedly it gave me an excuse for my failure to acquire shorthand and for remaining a two-fingered typist, but on the other hand I would be unable to occupy my room in Chelsea for several weeks as its landlord, a bohemian civil servant and ghost-writer who had once accommodated Simon Watson Taylor, would not be rid of its present occupant until the week I was originally due. I couldn't very well refuse however, so on a freezing April day, carrying only the minimum necessities (for there was no point in lugging down all my possessions until I had somewhere to put them) I caught a train from Limestreet and booked into a shabby hotel in Shaftesbury Avenue and the next day, for I had travelled at Edouard's suggestion on a Sunday, reported for work at the London Gallery, Brook Street, W1 at 9.55 a.m.

I remember almost nothing of my first fortnight at the gallery. Waiting anxiously to move into my room in Chelsea, to become a 'real Londoner', I felt myself floating in limbo. Both the name and the decor of the small private hotel in Bloomsbury where I had put up have vanished entirely, and my sole recollection is of a genteel yet quite spiky disagreement at breakfast between two middle-aged ladies seated at 'separate tables' as to whether *Oklahoma* or *Annie (Get Your Gun)* offered superior entertainment. At the gallery itself (how did I get there? Tube, bus or on foot? I've no idea) my shortcomings were at first concealed during the inevitable but none the less welcome 'honeymoon period'.

Upstairs in a studio a beautiful German picture restorer dabbed away at a saint's eyeball rolling heavenward or the elbow of a Rubensian nymph, while kindly Robert Melville helped to distract ELT's attention from my sloppy innumeracy.

Robert, who was later to become art critic at the then prestigious *New Statesman*, had published a pre-war book *Picasso – Master of the Phantom*, and more recently several essays which, following Edouard's papal edict, had been confined to surrealist publications. I had read these and was tremendously impressed, but also naïvely surprised at the contrast between the extreme eroticism of Robert's imagery: the suggestion at one point that de Chirico's biscuits were baked from sperm: and his modest and respectable physical appearance. small frame, large head, neat beard, spectacles and decidedly projecting teeth. ELT had a schoolboy's taste for slightly malicious nicknames and took to referring to Robert, although naturally not to his face, as 'Doctor Toothpaste'. He didn't deny however that he was a conscientious employee.

Edouard was also something of a sexual fantasist. He claimed for example that one morning, descending the stairs from his flat to the gallery, he had surprised Doctor Toothpaste and Mrs Johnson, the cleaning-lady, emerging red-faced and 'with giggles' from the staff lavatory on the half-landing. What made this story grotesque was that, while Robert was slight, Mrs Johnson was enormous and the lavatory extremely small, but what raised the incident to a level above that of a Donald McGill seaside postcard was that the lavatory was not only minuscule but precarious. Built out over the back and, given the age of the building, unlikely to be cantilevered, its occupation suggested a suicidal urgency on the part of Dr Toothpaste and Mrs Johnson. Sex is after all a rhythmic business, at any rate in part. Soldiers are ordered to break step while crossing a bridge. If the worst had happened and the ill-matched couple, especially (as ELT predictably suggested) if in the throes of mutual orgasm, had plunged to their doom in a cascade of bricks and Victorian plumbing, they would surely have earned their place in sacred surrealist annals of *l'amour fou*.

Even at the time I didn't entirely accept this story, and, while naturally keeping an eye open, could detect no spark of sexuality or regret pass between Robert and Mrs Johnson when their paths crossed. I had no doubt that Edouard had come upon them behaving oddly on the stairs, but felt it was more likely that Robert had wanted to use the lavatory only to find Mrs Johnson cleaning it. The transition with its difficulties (Mrs Johnson in relation to the size of the lavatory suggested in retrospect Magritte's image of a huge apple occupying an entire room) was enough to explain the nervous giggling.

Finally I was able to move to Chelsea and went back to Liverpool to fetch my trunk and the rest of my possessions, including my jazz records, wind-up gramophone and my two Ernsts. My mother, given to dramatic gestures, told me that she hadn't really believed I was leaving Liverpool before the pictures went.

The following weekend I went to lunch with the Mesenses and afterwards, in the large gallery beyond the bookshop, I brought up from the cellar those items of stock, some of them in fact belonging to Edouard or Penrose but available for sale, and made my selection. It was one of the most exciting and intoxicating afternoons of my life. Certainly Edouard, who with no attempt bar one to influence my choice, could find no fault. In this, of course, he was in a tiny minority. The artists I admired were in the main completely out of fashion. There were some exceptions: the young Lucian Freud (who was at least taken seriously by the *Horizon* crowd clustered around Cyril Connolly) and of course Picasso and Klee were acceptable, but Magritte, Ernst and Miro, especially the former, were beyond the pale. Had my father known anything about 'modern art' in the late forties, he would surely have despaired at the way I was wasting his money. Luckily he had at that time no opinions, although he was always to favour Magritte for his 'neatness' and realism.

I shall not list here my whole choice – there was a lot, including some lesser but interesting artists, Scottie Wilson for instance, and the entirely forgotten Peter Rose-Pulham. Nothing as far as I can remember cost more than a hundred pounds, most of it less. Outstanding was a Magritte masterpiece, 'The Black

Flag', showing fantastic aeroplanes (one had wings constructed from a window sash with little draped curtains) floating in a night sky. It is now in the Scottish Museum of Modern Art. There was also a huge Miro of two parrot-coloured savage women against a menacing blue background, the surface built up in places with lumps of plaster. Painted in the thirties when Miro was reacting strongly against the coming of the Spanish Civil War, it was the reverse of those charming and playful pictures of his début. Edouard applauded my courage in choosing this awkward work, but warned me it was 'ungrateful'. Amongst the rest there was a fine cubist Picasso drawing of a harlequin which had once belonged to André Breton; two further Ernsts, a frottage drawing from 1926 and a beautiful dark little forest under an orange sky with a pale green polo-mint moon. The Freud was a big pastel of his then wife Kitty (née Epstein) staring out from under some fig leaves, and there was also an early (1914) Klee watercolour of North Africa.

Today most of my choices would seem to be acceptable, even perspicacious, but not so Klee. Once a great star of modernism, chamber music to Picasso's full orchestra, he has become almost invisible. What the avant-garde found 'poetic' is today generally dismissed as whimsical, that gravest of contemporary sins. I've no convincing explanation. Does size come into it? Perhaps. Intimacy is not a quality much rated any more, perhaps wrongly.

When I'd finished choosing, and there were prints and etchings involved too, Edouard made his calculations, a slow, much re-checked process which I was used to from our visits to restaurants. He told me that there was still ten pounds in hand but, while I was moving forward to select the final item, said that *he* in this one case would decide what it should be. I wasn't best pleased by his choice – it was a near-abstract 'butterfly' by a forgotten Belgian painter called Guiette, sloppily realised on coarse flapping canvas, and hideously framed. Amused by my obvious displeasure, Mesens was insistent. 'You have otherwise been well served,' he told me, and I was aware it was true. The Guiette, which I soon 'lost', was some kind of moral joke. I couldn't exactly analyse the lesson it was meant to teach me, but in a strange way I took it on board.

I was soon allowed to take most of my collection back to Chelsea where I hung as much as possible on the walls of my top floor bed-sit and stored the rest on the landing over the stairs. I had to agree of course to bring in whatever pictures were needed either for special exhibitions or because a known collector of a certain artist was due.

Indeed, the beautiful Freud went within the month. Alfred H Barr, director of the Museum of Modern Art, New York was over on his first buying trip since the war and snapped it up. I wasn't there at the time but ELT told me later that there had been no hesitation. Barr, as soon as he saw it, pointed at it and said 'Wang, Wang, Wang!'. He didn't really say 'Wang, Wang, Wang!'. That was the way Edouard always imitated an American.

As agreed I re-invested the money, less the gallery's commission, but this time not from stock. I had spotted a large and magical Max Ernst in the nearby St George's Gallery, a tiny rare bookshop with a small stock of pictures, run by a diminutive and elderly Jewish lady, a pre-war refugee whom Edouard called 'Mother Jarra'.

On a brown-orange floor stood a creature constructed from flat, semi-transparent squares and rectangles; the customary format for Ernst's 'Lop-Lop' series. In this case it seemed to be screaming in bird-like rage and holding in front of it a pale canvas as if it were a shield, across which sinister creatures writhed in metamorphosis. It illustrated convincingly Breton's description of Ernst as 'the most magnificently haunted mind in Europe'.

ELT didn't mind me buying this Ernst elsewhere because it added a fine picture to the stock without the gallery paying for it. Although the turnover was very slow, my little 'forest' by Ernst sold only a month later. The buyer was Lady Hulton, a glamorous-looking lady married to the proprietor of *Picture*

Post, and she was advised in this by the art critic Robin Ironside (one of the first writers to set about restoring the reputation of the pre-Raphaelites after their long banishment to the museum cellars by Fry and Grant).

This sale somehow provoked Edouard to insist on me offering Ironside my first purchase, the tiny frottage of the bird, as a kind of commission. He had of course been put out when I'd bought it without his say so, and perhaps that came into it, for it was not the gallery's usual practice. Perhaps he thought it might tempt the critic to return with Lady Hulton but I've never really worked it out. Anyway I wrote to Ironside to tell him it was his, but before he could collect it he unexpectedly died. I didn't get it back though, or at least not then. For ten years Edouard kept it leaning on his mantelpiece, turning apparently stone-deaf when I mentioned it was mine. As he had initially dismissed it as of no account, this was a very odd example of his anally retentive tendencies. It was indeed Sybil who finally ordered him to return it to me. His argument against doing so was that the little bird no longer belonged to me, but to the late Robin Ironside.

One weekend, not long after I had begun to work at the gallery, both Edouard and Sybil were away and, as there was an exhibition to hang, asked me to stay in their flat during their absence. The week before, some more of ELT's pictures had arrived from Belgium and amongst them, to my awe and delight, was Magritte's 'Le Viol' which I had first seen five years before at Stowe in *The London Bulletin*, and of which I had stuck a reproduction on the back of my locker-door in the navy.

That Saturday, the exhibition hung, I thought I would plan a nice surprise for Edouard and Sybil on their return, and hung 'Le Viol' over the fireplace in their bedroom. In doing so I revealed my total naïvety. Even then, thirty years before the feminist movement, it was not an image to reassure women, and especially a woman as independent and intelligent as Sybil. She demanded its immediate removal, and I went back to Chelsea rather hurt. When I got in the following morning ELT told me that, not only had she banged on about my insensitivity and

71

stupidity, but had insisted that he dispose of it altogether. What would I feel, he asked, about exchanging it for my little Klee watercolour of North Africa? I didn't hesitate for a moment and that is how 'Le Viol' entered my collection. Many years later, when he suspected he hadn't long to live, Edouard gave me back the little Klee. Even when it came to retention he was, as indeed in general, remarkably and even touchingly inconsistent.

Five

Your occulist, accustomed to mirages, will tell you
nevertheless that it is preferable by far to choose
glasses which are black on the outside and looking
glass inside.

MESENS

My early social life in London was at first rather constricted as I
was only earning three pounds a week. I had become great
friends with my landlord's family, and spent many evenings with
them. I occasionally visited the Chelsea Palace to see Max Miller
or Wilson, Keppel and Betty, and was for a short time, and
rather to the Mesenses' disapproval, taken up by the painter
John Craxton, who was one of the mostly gay circle around
Gian-Carlo Menotti, the composer of operas. On two evenings a
week, at ELT's insistence, I caught a bus which took me across
the river into the unknown bad-lands of South London. There I
got off in Clapham outside Arding and Hobbs (a name which
always made me suspect a missing aspirant) and walked up a
steep hill to a huge and gloomy state school where I attended a
French night-class. As usual I did no homework, paid little
attention to the elderly lady who taught there, and gradually
stopped going at all. If Edouard was aware of this he said
nothing. He seemed to accept it, as he had my two-fingered
typing.

He and Sybil still took me out a lot, mostly to the Ivy where I
sometimes resented what he spent on me – it was almost double
what I had to live on for the rest of the week. At the same time he
would often reproach me for eating my lunches in the working

73

men's cafés tucked away in the mews and alleys of Mayfair where a three-course 'dinner' cost only half a crown.

'Why,' he used to reproach me, 'do you eat at rat cafés?' The answer, as he knew very well, was that it was all I could afford, although I actually rather liked the food and still do. Sybil also took me to the cinema and, with Edouard, the Café de Paris to see Marlene, and to the Palladium when Harpo and Chico, but not alas Groucho, were appearing there.

This was all pleasant enough, but it didn't stop them nagging at me during the day: Sybil for my shabby appearance, Edouard for what he called my 'impressionism'. Both were absolutely justified. My suits were hand-me-downs from my uncle Alan, a much larger man than I and, furthermore, well splashed with gravy and custard at the rat cafés, nor could I afford to have them cleaned very often. As to 'impressionism', a typical example was the lack of concentration that I brought to my most boring task. This was to copy out three or four hundred names and addresses every month onto envelopes containing invitation cards to the next exhibition. Whenever Edouard in passing picked one up at random there was always a mistake, a wrong postal code perhaps or an incorrect spelling. It was this kind of sloppiness which led him to class me with Renoir or Monet. The other thing which drove him mad was my inability to learn which light switch turned on which light, which key fitted which lock and so on. He invented a word to describe this failing. He said I was 'unconscient'.

There was one aspect of my behaviour however of which Sybil very much disapproved but Edouard vigorously supported. There were, screwed to the bookshelves in the front shop, several small metal ashtrays. Visitors would often stub out their cigarettes on entry, sometimes after only one puff. When they had left or passed through into the big gallery, I would jump on their discarded fag ends, smoke them if they were long or unravel them if short. I would then store the resultant tobacco into a tin on the lid of which I had engraved the words 'Poet's Mixture', and, when there was a sufficient quantity, re-roll it. This rather squalid practice was yet again economic in its origin. Because of the duty-free tobacco available to naval ratings, I had become a heavily addicted smoker and could no longer support my habit. The 'Poet's Mixture' ploy helped me solve this dilemma.

Inevitably after a short time, Edouard caught me at it but, far from being angry, was both amused and supportive. It fitted with his own inability to throw anything away (to Sybil's rage, he kept drawers full of flattened Gold Flake packets). On learning what I was up to, Sybil thoroughly disapproved on both professional and hygienic grounds, but Edouard would not be moved and would often help me harvest the ashtrays after we closed. He did however accuse me of 'impressionism' even here. He reproached me for rejecting very short dog-ends. He was later to make a collage, 'The Profits of the Smoker', which he told me was based on our scavenging in the late forties.

My faults were emerging: scruffiness, innumeracy and, increasingly, a tendency to arrive slightly late. The arrangement was that I should ring the bell at 9.55 whereupon Edouard would come downstairs in his pyjamas and silk dressing-gown and let me in. It was usually between two and eight minutes past ten when this took place and Edouard, looking pointedly at his watch, would react always with some irritation, but with variable intensity according to the strength of his hangover, the contents of his mail, or the stupidity of the world as presented in the pages of the long-extinct *News Chronicle* – a newspaper he in general approved of despite its weekly religious column. On good days his reproach would be addressed to me as 'Doctor', 'General' or 'Professor', but it was rare to be awarded one of these honorary titles, and it became rarer. In Edouard's book there was only one valid excuse for arriving late and that was 'making love'. I did use it occasionally if especially tardy, but not too often. Had I done so I suspect that ELT would have moved the goal posts or, in this case, bed posts. As to whether I lied or not, in this context it really depended more on the time and Edouard's body language. My wigging over, I would take the keys (he retreated grumbling upstairs to complete his long and ritualistic toilet), open the glass front door of the gallery, switch on the spotlights, and transfer the telephone from the flat to the little cubbyhole in the corner behind my desk, another task threatened by the emergence of the 'unconscient'.

Why was I so often late? It was a mixture of indolence and optimism. If the 19 or 22 bus drew up within five minutes of my arrival at the stop, some fifty yards from my room in Chelsea, if the traffic wasn't too bad up Sloane Street and along Piccadilly, and if the 25 bus arrived simultaneously with my change at Green Park, I would be ringing the bell in Brook Street half an hour after closing the front door in Margaretta Terrace. It was however very seldom that all these conditions were fulfilled, and depressingly often the 19 and 22 bus would be so late that I would be forced to hail a taxi. Admittedly this cost only three shillings, but two or so a week had a serious effect on my tiny salary. The absurd thing of course was that if I could have left my lodgings quarter of an hour earlier I would have avoided all this stress and anxiety. It has however done me a considerable favour in the end. Just as Edouard's obsessive love of order transformed me from a slut into a maniac of geometric tidiness so, and more usefully, my daily bollockings have made me a near model of punctuality.

And my defensive reaction to Edouard's reproaches for this or that failing over the course of a day? I can hardly credit it now, but it was to burst into tears. Did it at least work? Not at all. Lucian Freud told me that Mesens had told him of the ease with which he could make me cry. 'Why do you let him do that?' Freud asked me quizzically. 'He obviously enjoys it.'

My parents were kept posted, or at least my mother was, as to my flaws and inadequacies. On one of her visits to London she came to the gallery at an unfortunate moment. Not only had I arrived especially late, allowed the unconscient principle to take over entirely in the addressing of the invitations, forgotten to re-route the telephone, and been obliged to type a letter, transcribed from Edouard's immaculate handwritten French, three times over for serious inaccuracies, but also ELT had two witnesses to impress: the surrealist painter and future suicide, Oscar Dominguez, and his companion, a woman of alarming fetishistic appearance, whose name, like my mother's, happened to be Maud.

Edouard made great play on this coincidence, suggesting that he and Dominguez, a bear-like figure with a rolling bloodshot eye and important moustache (my mother had always detested facial hair) should take the two Mauds upstairs for de Sadeian frolics, or that at least he and my mother should ascend to 'make a baby'. 'Oh I think I'm too old for that,' said my mother, irritated but not especially alarmed by these clearly frivolous proposals, and recognising that at least she could 'dine out on it' on her return to Liverpool. Suddenly Edouard changed tack and began to blame her, with evidence, for my professional failings. It was she, he claimed, who had spoilt me, indulged me, fed my conceit and so on. She let him finish and then said something which I found extremely impressive.

'You forgot he has a father.'

What Maud said was true.

When my father, always under duress, came up to London there was no mention of my shortcomings. All that happened was that ELT might try to sell him a picture. 'Too messy,' was Tom's reason for refusing to buy a large and wonderful Picasso ink-and-wash drawing of a woman. Edouard offered to reduce the price a little – it was a hundred and fifty pounds for the public – but my father wouldn't budge. This created no ill-feeling; realistically Mesens knew there was no more money forthcoming, and they went off laughing and joking to the pub. My father however, developed quite a liking for modern painting as time went by and when, during the fifties, Edouard had begun to make collages again, Tom followed his example, signing his by no means untalented works 'Le Père Melly'.

It did irritate Tom, however, that both Andrée and I felt him obliged, despite his dislike of spending money in restaurants, to return the hospitality that Edouard and Sybil had extended to us. We suggested the Ivy and rather grumpily he accepted, although certainly to his partial relief I wasn't able to be present. Afterwards he complained to me bitterly, not only about the bill, but about the way Andrée and Sybil discussed at such length and in such detail what they would eat. He despised fuss about food. The next time it was his turn to be host, he asked me to find somewhere cheaper and I came up with an establishment on the Chelsea Embankment called, as far as I can remember, the Purple Parrot, offering a set three-course dinner at one pound a head. Not only was the price acceptable to my father, but he enjoyed the food more. The Mesenses, although too polite to say so, were of another opinion. We had however told them about my father's mistrust of restaurants, and Sybil especially was much amused at Tom's open satisfaction at the small bill.

Was there nowhere I could have suggested between the Ivy and the Purple Parrot? A restaurant where the food would have passed muster for Edouard and Sybil, and yet the bill, while a little more certainly, prove modest enough not to cause Tom pain? Well probably, but on my salary I hadn't really had the chance to shop around and nor, as a young actress waiting for her break, had Andrée. Yet even if we had, decent restaurants were still thin on the ground in the shabby, bomb-scarred, rationed austerity of immediate post-war London. Apart from the rat cafés, and they of course were out of the question, or the Lyons' Corner Houses – good value but a little too petit bourgeois, rather too standardised, to placate ELT – there was very little between the established continental restaurants of Soho and Covent Garden, and the 'dainty', usually rather amateur ventures like the Parrot, with their gate-leg oak tables and heavy 'folk' crockery. There were a handful of Chinese restaurants, but given Tom's deeply conservative approach to food we knew better than to risk them. It was not until well into the fifties that 'amusing' little restaurants began to open. But even if they had existed these places would have been too expensive to have pleased Tom, while Edouard always preferred 'serious' restaurants where the waiters 'knew their *métier*'.

So did I learn anything useful at the London Gallery during those three years? Yes – for one thing I absorbed a great deal about pictures, and not only those painted by official surrealists. Indeed Edouard, although only when we were alone, could be quite dismissive about those painters that Breton was pushing after the war, and he admired many artists who in no way subscribed to the movement's ideology.

But the principal thing I learnt from Edouard was how to hang an exhibition. First he taught me 'the classic rules'. Leaving aside eccentrically shaped pictures – triangles, fan-shaped, diamonds, ovals and circles – there are only two kinds to take into account: a 'landscape', that is to say broader than tall, and a 'portrait', taller than broad. A portrait should always be flanked by two landscapes and vice versa. If possible the larger or strongest picture should be the central one. If the central picture is dark in tone the two others should be lighter, or the reverse. If the flanking pictures were indeed portraits, or their general composition was anything but face-on, they should gaze or point inwards. The centre point of interest in a work should, where possible, be hung at eye level. If for whatever reason two pictures had to be hung one above the other, the smaller should be uppermost. The perpendicular spaces between a group of pictures should be even; those parallel to the ground also but twice as big. Oils in general should not be hung in association with other media. There are more refinements, but these are the general rules I absorbed from ELT Mesens on Saturday afternoons as we hung a new exhibition under the glass roof.

When I had taken all this aboard, Edouard went on to tell me how these rules can be broken. It could sometimes be effective, he explained, to hang a picture on a wall by itself and, in contrast, crowd an adjacent wall with smaller pictures in mixed media to give a kind of stamp album effect. In my concluding lesson he told me that when hanging a private collection in a house or flat the classic rules, while certainly to be borne in mind, should of necessity be more or less ignored. Furniture insists on different levels, and, unlike a gallery, we often sit down near to a wall. There is also the function of a room: no violent eroticism in the nursery certainly, and no excrement, real or represented, or the activities of maggots in the dining-room (perfectly possible nowadays) nor (*pace* Sybil and 'Le Viol') pictures inimical to either partner in the bedroom.

Throughout my initiation we laid out the pictures to be hung in front of the appropriate wall. This makes it possible to adjust and correct before knocking in a single disfiguring nail or x-hook.

When it came to framing his work Mesens took immense pains. At the London Gallery he had been forced to frame everything as cheaply as possible. Now that money was no object he could afford to consider each work on its merit, but he knew better than to over-frame. There were no velvet mounts or heavy gilding just for the sake of it. He had certain fixed concepts that he passed on to me and for which I am still extremely grateful.

A mount or frame should never extend a picture but confine it. A picture whose colours are predominantly 'hot' should have a cool frame. A drawing should always have a mount in slight contrast to the paper on which it was drawn. A mount should be twice the width of its top and sides along the bottom edge. Never cut an engraving to fit a frame.

I'm well aware that this didactic excursion may have glazed many an eyeball. I'm going to let it stand though and for two reasons; on a practical level it may help anyone who for whatever reason – marriage, divorce, a pictorial legacy, a new acquisition, a move to smaller or larger premises – is about to hang or rehang some pictures, but for my own sake to demonstrate that I acquired and have retained at least one skill during my three years at the gallery and, in contrast to what I had learnt in the navy (how to pipe an Admiral aboard, how to wank in a hammock without waking up the whole mess-deck), it has proved useful in later life.

At the time too it helped in part to placate Edouard. It meant that at least he could leave me to arrange and hang the gallery shows, and there would be an occasional word of praise

80

although qualified instantly by a reiteration of my failings in every other direction.

Yet my pleasure and pride in the creative stage of a hanging was seriously reduced by the unnecessary and prolonged labour of getting the pictures up on the walls, and this was entirely due to ELT's obsessional penny-pinching in his managerial role. He was a prototype recylcer certainly, a cause for admiration these days, but he carried it to the very edge of madness.

At the heart of my misery were the eye-screws, and especially the smaller ones, most of them bent through use and all of them blunt. What's more, as most often the frames they were expected to support were utility-thin and of the cheapest wood, it was extremely difficult to gain a purchase. When this had been effected, the crooked eye-screws, few of which were even an exact pair, either splintered the wood or went through the outer edge. Big, heavily-framed pictures were less of a problem although here, if it was hard wood, it could be difficult to get the eye-screw started. This, and indeed every problem, would have been made far easier if the London Gallery, Mayfair, w1 had invested in an awl. Edouard, although I asked him often, refused to authorise its purchase, still less new eye-screws and certainly not string. No piece of string, however small, was to be thrown away. Every knot, however fast, was to be untied. All the string was kept in a large biscuit tin (Peak and Freen as I remember), and returned to it after use.

Actually, as far as the exhibition went, the string problem was as nothing compared to the eye-screws. The string came into its own in the bookshop in the execution of parcels, especially as most of it was coated with powdery whitewash – a legacy of its exhibitionist function where my last task before opening the doors was to apply this whitewash with a decrepid watercolour brush to make the supporting strings invisible against the white walls. And then of course there was the question of wrapping paper . . .

The bookshop had a glass-fronted shelf for large and precious books, many of them surrealist. Sometimes, not very often it's true, someone would buy one – a set of pre-war *Minotaure* perhaps, or a post-war *Verve* – and express a not unreasonable request to have it wrapped. Then it was panic stations. First I had to run down to the basement and find a suitable piece of paper and sometimes, if there wasn't one, stick two ill-matching pieces together. Then came the string, trailing clouds of whitewash and never quite long enough, and now under the eye of an impatient customer (a fashionable woman late for her crimper; a sleek middle-aged man, shoes by Lobb, whose younger lunch-date must by now be glancing at her watch). The resulting parcel, enclosing as it did a luxurious and expensive volume, was lamentable. While less puzzling to the customer (wartime shortages had familiarised people with the improvised and the shoddy), my smaller parcels were even more of a dog's dinner. The horror of wrapping parcels was at least in part alleviated by ELT, knowing that as Gallery Manager he could be held responsible, making himself scarce.

During our evenings together, I attempted and indeed succeeded in recruiting Sybil to my side. 'Would you,' I asked her, 'in your role as "Miss Fenton", allow your staff to wrap up your customers' purchases in odd bits of brown paper tied with whitewashed string?'

She could only say no. When it came to professional standards, by her own admission she was something of a martinet. She told me herself that she lined up her girls every morning to sniff their armpits and advise the less-than-fragrant to purchase deodorant and look to their laundry. On one occasion she gave me a terrible pasting when, entering the gallery, she caught me cutting my nails, so I was on completely safe grounds in presenting my case and soliciting her for support.

Edouard just turned grumpy and pleaded the gallery's poverty. Sybil was not placated. We were in a good trading address. People expected high standards of service and so on. It made no difference whatsoever. Helping himself to a large whisky under her disapproving eye, he hid behind a word compared with which a straight refusal might have been construed as hopeful.

'Eventually,' he said.

Yet for all that, the bookshop, of which for some time I was in sole command, did proportionally rather better than the gallery.

It contained – limited and rare books aside – poetry, smaller art books, anarchist literature, avant-garde magazines and even some fiction. It wasn't hard to decide what to buy: the traveller from Zwemmer's called to show what art books they were importing; the anarchist literature was always on sale or return; for the rest I relied on my Chelsea landlord's *Times Literary Supplement*.

Edouard took no interest in the book department. He claimed to have 'read everything' when he was young.

The reason the bookshop did better than the gallery was that young people who visited us (many of them provincial, working-class, autodidactic art students who had become unfashionably fascinated by Surrealism and its off-shoots) could *sometimes* afford a book but never a picture.

I did pull off one financial coup in the bookshop. At the opening of an exhibition of Freud and Craxton – amongst several other little dramas taking place of which more later, and incidentally our only crammed and fashionable *vernissage* – I overheard Cyril Connolly telling Peter Watson (our director, Connolly's backer) that Evelyn Waugh had, for whatever reason and for free, offered *Horizon* his new novella *The Loved One* for publication prior to the hardback edition. Still a total secret of course . . .

But not to me! Armed with this insider knowledge I ordered fifty copies instead of our usual half-dozen. They sold out in a morning. Rather pleased with myself I told Edouard who, after a desultory glance around the empty gallery, was on his way to the pub. I thought not only might it cheer him up, but also win me much-needed extra brownie points. Neither. He reacted exactly as he did when, in his later desolate years, Andrée and I would feed him anecdotes we believed might interest him.

'And then?' he said.

My routine at the gallery hardly varied: the slightly late arrival and subsequent bollocking; the opening of the front door and replenishing of the till; the mounting treadmill of the invitation card envelopes; the occasional attendance, if required, on visitors.

At eleven fifteen the managing director made his second appearance, bearing two or three business letters usually in French and handwritten during the small hours which I was to type later. This was followed by his departure at five to twelve, and his return, elevated and jovial, at five past three (in those days public houses in the West End of London opened at twelve and closed at three).

After half an hour or so of jokes and pranks he would retire upstairs only to descend again in a filthy temper at about five fifteen. His subsequent scrutiny of my work led inevitably to re-addressing many of the envelopes, re-typing at least one of the letters, and the prolonged struggle with the till until the balance between petty cash and takings made some kind of sense.

Dr Toothpaste, abandoning his clerkly work upstairs, would relieve me for my lunch hour in the rat café round the corner. Miss Fenton, as her responsibilities at 'Dickie and Johnny' increased, returned less and less to feed her husband, thereby allowing him to spend more and more time in the pub. He used two pubs actually, and occasionally, if I had done better than usual or he was less hungover, he would invite me for a drink after work. One was a 'lounge' just across the road beneath a smart tobacconist – all leather and oak panelling. He called this the Aristoc. The other was a more cheerful and proletarian establishment off the other side of Bond Street, and where he was clearly considered something of a wag. This he called the Democ. It made no difference which he'd been to during his lunchtime sessions (perhaps both of them). Both led to euphoria and, later on, depressive rage.

I welcomed the euphoric interludes. For the half hour or so they lasted the old Mesens, the Dada-sympathiser, the surrealist-anarchist, was reborn. There was one day when he led me to the window and, peering over the oatmeal coloured curtain which in part concealed the gallery from the street, drew my attention to a rather pompous-looking man on the opposite pavement. A shop there was about to open – a shop with nothing for sale, but where rich foreigners – Americans staying at Claridge's most likely – could order replicas of the expensive and luxurious luggage on display to be delivered duty-free on their return home.

The man, whose officiousness was almost visible, was engaged in a kind of ballet, the object of which was to direct the young woman in the window as to how the gold and pig-skin suitcases of various sizes were to be displayed to their best advantage. The girl seemed not very adept at carrying out his mimed instructions and he was clearly becoming irritated. Edouard suggested that I should cross the road and touch the man on the shoulder and, when he turned around, deliver the following formal speech.

'The managing director of the London Gallery opposite has asked me on his behalf to wish you Good Luck, Sir.'

'He will thank you no doubt in a perfunctory way,' said Edouard. 'But then, after a few moments, repeat the formula, Good luck, Sir, and continue to shout it louder and louder – GOOD LUCK, SIR! GOOD LUCK, SIR! GOOD LUCK, SIR! – until he becomes mad with rage.'

So while Edouard watched from behind the Picabia in the window, I carried out his suggestions to the letter. It worked like a dream. Puzzled irritation ('Yes, yes, yes') was soon replaced by total hysteria. 'I shall call the police!' the man yelled, shaking his fist at me as I darted back and forth across Brook Street still wishing him good luck. It was perhaps a shame he didn't fulfil his threat.

'And what is the charge, sir?'

'He wished me good luck.'

'Sir?'

'Several times.'

Edouard was so delighted at the success of his joke that he came down in a comparatively amiable mood after his usually disastrous siesta, and as a result invited me out for a drink, although whether at the Democ or the Aristoc I can't remember. He did suggest though that we didn't tell Sybil as he suspected, I'm sure correctly, that it would have offended Miss Fenton's code of business practice. As a result 'Good luck, Sir!' joined 'Mittens' and the elderly Belgian whore on the shelf of the proscribed index.

With the absurd egocentricity of youth I seriously believed, and felt occasionally mildly guilty, that Edouard's growing depression and obsessive drinking were due to my failure to become an immaculate French-speaking, shorthand-taking, touch-typist. In retrospect, while acknowledging that my failure to become these things offered him a useful target for his anger, they were extremely marginal. Approaching fifty, Edouard was responsible for a gallery whose closure was in no doubt. Its doors would remain open only for as long as its backers chose to cover its losses. Its stock-in-trade, Surrealism, which before the war had excited everyone and had indeed attracted Mesens to these shores, was now considered hopelessly *passé* and spoken of, if at all, in the past tense. English Surrealism had entirely disintegrated; in France too it was a shadow of itself. Edouard had returned from his first post-war visit to Brussels complaining about its provincialism and on bad terms with Magritte after refusing to accept his Renoir-like period. Significantly, too, his own poetry, never a torrent, had dried up completely.

There was of course his marvellous collection, but even its most established painters – Picasso, Gris, de Chirico, Klee – were still modestly priced. The next generation, led by Ernst, Miro and Tangui, were worth very little, while his enormous stock of early Magritte would have raised little more than when he had saved them from the auction room in the early thirties. To have sold to live would have been an act of complete folly. Luckily Sybil knew this too and, as she was earning an excellent salary, was able to keep them both.

Meanwhile, to keep things going a little longer in the hope of a turn around, Edouard would often take his salary in the form of a picture at trade price and sometimes, if things looked especially grim, Sybil would buy a picture (the large Tangui refused by the Tate for instance). They were not to regret these measures, on the contrary . . .

What I didn't understand, and still can't, is how Edouard could afford not only his formidable daily intake of drink at the Democ or the Aristoc, but also the frequent visits to the Ivy. Of course they'd no rent to pay; the flat went with the job, but even so – unless Sybil chipped in there too.

Certainly between 1948–50 things became increasingly tense between them. One Sunday, when I was staying with them to hang an exhibition, there was an enormous shouting match and Sybil threw a cup of coffee across the dining-room table. She was either a very good shot or a very bad one because the coffee just missed a quite large and very beautiful 'empty' Miro of 1924: untreated canvas, a red circle, a blue splodge, a few lines and arabesques. Had she connected I don't think the stain could have been removed. Perhaps, like the cracked glass in Duchamp's 'Bride Stripped Naked by her Bachelors', it would have become accepted as an element in the work. Whenever I see this picture – now in a public collection; it has played its part in many great exhibitions of the last few decades – I always smile to remember the drama and near disaster of that Sunday lunchtime in the tiny dining-room all those years ago.

One dark wet winter's morning I arrived a little late as usual only to find the gallery already open and the lights on. More surprisingly Edouard was dressed, Sybil hadn't left for work, and I was unreproached.

Sybil told me that the previous evening Edouard had been arrested in a public lavatory for smiling at the man in the next stall. The man it transpired was a young and handsome policeman, an *agent provocateur*. There was to be a case.

I waxed furious on ELT's behalf. They must fight it of course. It was monstrous. And so it was, but it never occurred to me that

Edouard, almost certainly rather drunk, had smiled at the policeman's no doubt provocatively displayed penis. In this I showed myself naïve. The days of 'the plate' still lay far ahead, but the fact that Edouard had taken part in our *partouses* should surely have alerted me to the possibility of his bisexuality.

Sybil was touched by my blind disbelief, and gently told me that their lawyer had advised them to plead guilty. Leaving me in indignant charge, they set off for court. Their lawyer turned out to be right. As no physical contact had taken place, and as Sybil spoke for him, Edouard was fined a small amount and cautioned.

I was pleased and relieved when he returned with this news – Sybil had gone straight to Dickie and Johnny – but a few minutes later when he went out to the Aristoc he said to me, although in not too reproachful a manner, 'You were late again, Doctor.'

As a post-war gallery director committed at heart to Surrealism, Edouard's principal dilemma was what to show. With a monthly change-over, and one large and three smaller rooms to fill, this was a real problem and it was not enough to simply revolve the stock. Of contemporary painters on the gallery's lists, only Lucian Freud and John Craxton proved to be money spinners. Craxton was certainly a big seller and his landscapes, influenced by the Greek painter Ghika, offered vines, olive trees, goats and languorous neo-romantic, mildly cubified fisherboys and shepherds. While certainly popular, they were not at all to ELT's taste, and had been imposed on the gallery probably by Peter Watson.

This left only Craxton's friend Freud, but not only did he produce very slowly, but it was obvious that, with his passion for gambling, he was sure to leave as soon as there was a better offer. To put off this day, Edouard tried unsuccessfully to recruit him to Surrealism, but Freud was far too wily to swallow this not especially tempting bait. Edouard's 'evidence' were two pictures of zebras poking their heads through apertures into the artist's studio, but Lucian dismissed this argument by claiming objectivity. He possessed a stuffed zebra's head and had painted it. There was nothing surrealist about it. In fact this denial was suspect. Freud may not have *been* a surrealist, but he had certainly learnt from Surrealism. His animal skulls and tiny glowing fruit littered Dalinian plains; his dead birds, hares and monkeys; the intensity of the early portraits, all displayed, whether he liked it or not, a surreal sensibility. In all events it was this surrealist flavour which made him the only contemporary painter that ELT felt able to defend.

Edouard was, of course, too conscientous a managing director to dismiss Craxton out of hand, but instead rather feebly defended it by claiming that he himself was 'a grocer' and that Craxton's work was 'butter, but honest butter'. He resorted to it when at the only glamorous *vernissage* in the post-war London Gallery's history, a joint show of Freud and Craxton, I told him that I had just overheard Douglas Cooper advising a couple on the point of buying a Craxton that it was rubbish.

Writing this memoir I find myself in constant danger of turning into the equivalent of those people at a dinner party who discuss at length mutual acquaintances entirely unknown to the rest of the company. Cooper was up until his death such a famous monster of art-land that it is difficult for those of us who either feared or loathed him to imagine he isn't well known. I doubt it though, and feel obliged to interrupt this narrative to offer a short profile of this brilliant and odious creature who I suspect still haunts the nightmares of ageing curators, art historians and German airmen.

As to this last category, surprising perhaps in this context, ELT told me later that during the war Cooper, who had perfect German, was responsible for interrogating captive members of the Luftwaffe, but did so with such sadistic enthusiasm as to be removed from his post. I cannot swear to the truth of this anecdote, but it is perfectly in character.

Cooper was of Australian origin and immensely rich. It was said, although he rigorously denied it, that his fortune came from sheep-dip. Nothing wrong with that, but then Cooper was very snobbish. He had however a remarkable eye for modern art and particularly Cubism, and during his later years sold many masterpieces by Miro, Klee and others which he had accumulated outside the cubist cannon to reinvest exclusively in Picasso, Braque, Gris and Léger – in his view the only authentic cubists.

Although Edouard would have extended this list to include Marcounis, Delaunay and a few others as worthy of attention, he was, as in so much else, in broad agreement with Cooper, but this carried no weight. Malice alone fuelled Cooper's engine. He would turn on friends with as much enthusiasm as enemies – in the seventies, despite a long friendship, he attacked Picasso's current work as no more than the 'terrified gibbering of an old man in death's ante-chamber'. Nearer home, he had only recently accused Edouard of selling a fake Klee.

Cooper was fat and yet seemed to float. He dressed in bright colours and bold patterns, in clothes a little too tight so that every button was forced to do its work (and I'm aware that I seem to be describing myself here). His face was round, and his mean, small eyes glinted behind thick spectacles. Although obviously overweight he didn't seem flabby so much as taut, like a balloon. I had the feeling that, if pricked by a fork, he would have spurted like chicken Kiev, but bile instead of butter. Edouard, seeing him come in, had warned me to keep an eye on him, but I was actually standing by the couple who were hesitating over the Craxton when Cooper struck.

'It's rubbish!' he hissed and, already worried that it might be 'too modern', they withdrew.

As the last visitor left and ELT and I walked round the gallery uncharacteristically bristling with red spots, almost the only picture still unsold was the fisherboy in conté crayon heightened with white on blue sugar paper that had been jinxed by Douglas Cooper. 'Defend him to enter the gallery again!' Edouard told me. He used 'defend' always to mean 'forbid', a literal translation from the French 'défendre'.

What did we show apart from Craxton, Freud and the great surrealist masters? There were the British surrealists: the exquisite, almost pre-Raphaelite fantasies of Edith Rimmington, the rather splodgy satirical gouaches of John Banting (drinking had coarsened his previously refined technique). There was Scottie Wilson, about whom Edouard had written enthusiastically in *Horizon*, but whose compulsive cross-hatched world of fish, birds, flowers and monsters sold very little, especially as he would often exchange them for the price of a drink elsewhere. There were artists who came in with work whose sincerity touched ELT but whose talent alas was flimsy. There were two cheerful young Australians, Klippel and Gleeson – the former a sculptor who made abstracts out of bent canes stuck together and painted in jolly colours (I bought one but the glue soon melted and it sprang apart), while the latter painted Wagnerian Dalinian fantasies, mostly rather large. Years later, singing in Australia, I found both of them represented in every state museum – although Klippel had sensibly rejected the rebellious canes in favour of more solid materials. There was a jovial bearded pipe-smoking Pole, Alexander Zyw, who was close to expressionism and did quite well, and there was Peter Rose-Pulham, an ex-*Vogue* photographer and a friend of the still-obscure Bacon. I have always felt that Rose-Pulham, despite the early influence of de Chirico and Magritte, might have become an important painter if drink hadn't carried him off. His eggs and lemons on the mantel-shelves of cheap Parisian hotels, his grey humanoids copulating precariously on athlete's bars, were in advance of Bacon's screaming popes, and equally intense. Of course they were also unsaleable.

Now and again we had the pleasure of attracting an artist whose work reflected a genuine and original eccentricity. Such a one was Austin Cooper, a white-bearded Canadian dressed in good if threadbare tweed, who before the war had designed for the London Underground in the restrained cubist style of McKnight Kauffer. A nervous breakdown had totally reorientated his work. Mostly rather small, his collages were very dark and mysterious, sometimes built-up, at other times torn or incised. He told Edouard that, apart from glue, he used his own bodily fluids including sperm. The pictures were named after

Canadian-Indian Chiefs whose spirits he claimed to guide him. He wanted Edouard to paint above the picture-rail a quotation from William Blake: 'The Lust of the Goat is the Gift of God.' Sales, of course, nil, except for one piece each to Edouard, Robert Melville and me. I have mine still. It's very beautiful and, although I never expected to hear of Austin Cooper again, recently a gentleman from Canada got in touch. There is to be an exhibition and a monograph.

Peter Watson, the only gallery director who came to all our shows, walked around his exhibition muttering 'The man is sick' over and over again, but at least it was an improvement on his usual tune: 'No tension, no tension.' He was a sweet man, but an utter depressive, certainly in the post-war years leading up to his death.

Occasionally, very occasionally, someone famous in arts or letters would visit the gallery. Osbert Sitwell, all of whose sympathetic if over-ornate volumes of autobiography I had bought as they were published, came comparatively often and would invariably engage me in conversation. This, in stark contrast to most people's rudeness or indifference, helped prop up my increasingly fragile ego.

Wyndham Lewis, his fiery Vorticist days when he edited *Blast* long behind him, was another near-regular, but his visits were not voluntary. 'The Enemy', as he had once called himself, was employed as art critic of the *Listener*, an appointment I suspect to have been more or less charitable as he was almost blind and I had to guide him down the three steps into the main gallery. This didn't stop him from dismissing a wonderful exhibition of Max Ernst as 'undistinguished'. How had he arrived at this conclusion?

It seems surprising to me now that I actually came across figures – Connolly, TS Eliot, Wyndham Lewis, Ernst himself – who have become part of history, but it's a common enough sensation, as Browning recognised in 'Memorabilia':

> 'Oh did you once see Shelley plain?
> And did he stop and talk with you?'

The most memorable event in the three years I spent at the gallery was the afternoon Kurt Schwitters recited the 'Ursonate'.

Mesens had often spoken, and always with great admiration and affection, of Schwitters, the maverick dadaist from Hanover who had fled Germany and Norway just ahead of the Nazis, arriving eventually in England. As an enemy alien he was immediately interned in the Isle of Man. On his release, after a short period in London, he had somehow landed up in the Lake District where he earned a meagre living painting realistic, rather muddy portraits – a compromise which allowed him to continue with his 'real work', the construction of poetic collages created from the world's detritus: tickets, torn paper, fragments of wood, press headlines, advertisements, words selected and truncated at random. He called his particular Dada tendency *Merz*. There is no such word; it is part of the word *commerz*, which he had incorporated into an early collage. In Hanover, *Merz* took over his entire house. In what he called *Merzbild*, he constructed a huge architectural collage which writhed through every room, sometimes going out of one window and coming in another. He also called his poetry *Merz*; some of it a kind of caricature of sentimental German romantic poetry, some absurd-ist like the recitation of a sneezing fit, but much of it involving entirely made-up sounds and culminating in his great 'Ursonate' ('Primitive Sonata'), forty minutes of divine gibberish carefully orchestrated.

He had already recited this at the gallery one afternoon in public while I was still in Liverpool pretending to learn shorthand and typing. Few had attended and a BBC Third programme producer, whom ELT had invited hoping that he might record it for the archives, had left half way through. This new visit however was in the hope of selling Edouard some of his recent collages, for few people in the Lake District wanted their portraits painted and in consequence Schwitters and his charm-ing young companion Wantee Thomas were very poor.

Wantee, without whom Schwitters might have found himself unable to cope, was so called because she would so often poke her head round the door when he was working to ask him, 'Do you *want tea?*'

It was a cold wet Saturday morning when Schwitters with his cheap attaché case and Wantee in her thin coat arrived in Brook Street. Although it was Saturday the gallery was open as it was during a short period when Mesens decided to truncate my weekend 'for the benefit of students'. Eventually, as no students chose to take advantage of this offer, he withdrew it, allowing me to stay in bed in fuggy Chelsea, but on this occasion, knowing that Schwitters was coming, I would have showed up anyway; Edouard's tales had made me very curious to meet him.

One anecdote above all delighted me. One day, in the streets of Hanover during the 1920s, Schwitters was accosted by a man, clearly from elsewhere and burdened with a bad stammer: 'C-C-C-C-Could you t-t-t, t-t-t-tell m-m-me, where I c-c-c, where I can b-b-b-b-b-buy some c-c-c, some c-c-c-copper n-n-n-n-n-n-n-nails?' Schwitters gave him a long and complicated route which would lead the man eventually to a large hardware shop.

As soon as he was out of sight, Schwitters ducked down a short alley which led directly to the ironmongers in question. He entered and asked the proprietor if he had in stock any 'c-c-c-c, any c-c, any c-c-copper nails'. Answered in the affirmative, he demanded to see one, but declared it too small for his purpose. He was shown another – still too small – and another – not big enough, and eventually, somewhat irritated, the man brought out a huge nail, used perhaps in ship-building, and told Schwitters that it was the largest manufactured. Schwitters then told him to shove it up his arse, and ran out of the shop.

Ten minutes later the genuine stutterer, following Schwitters's directions, found the shop and entered. Schwitters, concealed across the street, observed with satisfaction the man, terrified and totally bemused, running out of the ironmongers and legging it down the street pursued by the enraged shopkeeper brandishing a mallet.

Now in the gallery, Schwitters opened his suitcase and displayed his exquisite little *Merz*-collages. Edouard bought them all at five pounds each. Later they were put on sale at twelve pounds framed; a minimal profit, but again no one bought except for me and on this occasion my sister. It had been an act of pure altruism on Edouard's part.

At midday I locked up the gallery and joined Kurt, Wantee and Edouard in the Democ (Sybil worked on Saturdays). We returned, all of us rather drunk, at three and Schwitters proposed quite spontaneously that he recite the 'Ursonate'. He stood in a corner of the main gallery – I cannot remember the pictures on the walls – and begun to intone:

> 'Fumms bö wö taä zaä Uu,
>   pögiff
>   Kwii Eee
>   Oooooooooooooooooooooooooooooooooooooo,'

He finished forty minutes later:

> 'Rinnzekete bee bee. Rinnzekete bee be.'

His white hair stuck out wildly. His eyes were bright blue and staring beyond us. His mackintosh was open. He was over six foot tall anyway but seemed to have grown taller.

What did we feel?'

According to Hans Richter,[1] Schwitters first read 'Ursonate' in about 1924 to an audience of retired generals and rich ladies, until that time unexposed to modernism. After a few minutes hysterical laughter broke out, but he continued unfazed at a louder volume until silence reigned once more. There were no more interventions and then, when it was over '. . . the same generals, the same rich ladies who had previously laughed until they cried now came to Schwitters again with tears in their eyes, almost stuttering with admiration and gratitude. Something had been opened up within them, something they had never expected; a great joy.'

While neither retired general nor rich lady, the recital I heard

[1] *Dada: Art and Anti-Art*, Thames and Hudson, 1965

had a similar effect on me. Later on, Schwitters's son, a Norwegian businessman, recorded the 'Ursonate' and, having heard it frequently as a child, offered an accurate if dry and academic reconstruction. There is certainly no 'great joy'.

Recently I was invited to Manchester University where there was a big celebration of Dada including, among other pleasures, a reconstruction of an evening at the Cabaret Voltaire. Elsewhere a plump, bearded German, not young but certainly too young to have heard Schwitters, gave a reading of the 'Ursonate'. He caught the spirit brilliantly and shutting my eyes I could imagine myself back in the London Gallery forty years earlier.

Incidentally, it was in Manchester that in the middle fifties, although already seven years in his grave, Schwitters saved if not my life at any rate my face, the features of which a band of yobs were threatening to rearrange with broken bottles in a dark cul-de-sac. This was to pay out Mick Mulligan, my band leader, who had restrained and ejected one of their number after finding him systematically kicking another young man on the floor of the gents.

At the end of the session I had gone out of the pub where we had been playing to take a little air, and they'd been waiting. They had not yet broken the bottles, but had begun to beat them rhythmically against the brick walls which enclosed us.

Suddenly I thought of Schwitters.

'Rakete Rinnzekete,' I shouted. 'Rakete Rinnzekete. Rakete Rinnzekete. Kwii Eee. Fumms bö wö taä zaä Uu. Ziiuu rinnzkrrmüü . . .'

They turned and fled.

In Ambleside Schwitters struggled on. A kind farmer offered him a barn in which to create a new *Merzbild* to replace the one that had taken over his house in Hanover until destroyed by Allied bombing. Schwitters had only managed to work on one wall when he died in 1948. In 1965, the Fine Arts department of Newcastle University acquired the wall, and transplanted it with great difficulty to the university art gallery. This was largely through the efforts of Richard Hamilton, 'the father of pop art', who was teaching there.

Within eighteen months of its opening it became evident that the post-war London Gallery would sooner or later fail. There was however at least one occasion when ELT's obstinate commitment to Surrealism worked in our favour.

In 1945 a Hollywood film company had sponsored a competition to paint the most convincing version of 'The Temptation of St Anthony'. The winner would be featured in Albert Lewin's film *The Private Life of Bel Ami*. In 1947 these pictures were sent off on a world tour, both as a boost for the film and to display the company's enlightened patronage. As most of the eleven artists invited to participate were either surrealist or quasi-surreal, when the exhibition came to London we were the obvious venue and were able to pocket a substantial fee in dollars.

None of the pictures were much good and the worst was the winner's, Max Ernst at his most tricky and elaborate, a swampy collaboration between Disney and Bosch. Edouard was disgusted by it although not altogether surprised; his enthusiasm for Ernst's work in the twenties and the first half of the thirties remained inviolate, but from what he described as 'the spinach period' and on from there, he expressed growing reservations. Indeed on this occasion he felt forced to admit that the renegade Dali (St Anthony on one knee in the desert holding up a cross to ward off a rearing demonic horse and five elephants supported on spiders' legs and bearing on their backs an obelisk and several nude women some of them encased in baroque architecture) should have been awarded the prize.

Neither picture has disappeared. The Ernst, by some lapse of judgement, was included in the Tate retrospective of 1991, and the catalogue acknowledges that it appeared in the film. The Dali, while it formed part of the huge exhibition at the Pompidou and the scaled-down version at the Tate (1979 and 1980), failed to acknowledge the connection, presumably because it didn't win. In neither case is there any reference to them being in competition.

It was just acceptable for ELT to play host to distinguished or erstwhile distinguished painters (albeit involved in a dubious commercial venture) from the surrealist point of view, but when things got really tough he was forced to adopt a much more painful strategy to pay the bills. In the final spasms of the gallery's short post-war life we were obliged to let off rooms to anyone prepared to pay a fixed sum; the pictorial equivalent of vanity publishing. The rate varied according to the size and position of the room, but the deal included not only wall space, but the hanging, an opening, a catalogue (minimal) and invitation cards to all our usual list. What I didn't understand though was why Edouard felt it necessary to print 'ELT Mesens presents . . .' above the name and checklist of these intruders. It meant nothing to them and caused him considerable pain. Once the deal was made however, he had as little to do with the show as possible. It was I who had to hang the oils of silver beeches on Hampstead Heath, the twee gouaches of aspects of Brighton. He made it slightly better for himself by exhibiting in those rooms which were un-let small exhibitions of Miro or Tangui, or even of unknown artists who had touched him, but it was a bitter time.

By far the most uncomfortable yet memorable of these lettings was to the loving mother of a schizophrenic girl, a sculptor. For her daughter's benefit she hired the bookshop and the large gallery behind it for a month on condition that we conceal that it was she who was paying for it, and that ELT pretended that he had recognised the poor creature's talent. There was however what Mesens called 'a further toad to swallow'. When the list of works arrived for printing in the catalogue, it became clear that all the subject matter was religious.

One morning the sculptures were delivered. They were all of plaster (even the mother hadn't gone so far as to have them cast in bronze) and they were enormous. Plinths were provided and I decided where these should be placed first. The two very strong van men had some difficulty lifting the sculpures so I didn't think it fair to dither or change my mind.

Edouard came down from his ever-more prolonged ablutions

particularly late that day. He dreaded having to face 'The Last Supper', 'The Crucifixion' and so on, but was nevertheless curious about them. After all, the work of schizophrenics is often extremely interesting and the surrealists had always admired the compulsive art of the insane. In the event he was as surprised as I had been. The vast accumulations of plaster looked like collapsed wedding cakes and nothing more. Even Benjamin Peret, the surrealist poet who found it difficult to pass a priest in the street without insulting him, would have had no suspicion that they were intended to be religious iconography. He might on the other hand have been puzzled as to why ELT had chosen to exhibit them.

We became rather hysterical about them, but were both depressed later. The saddest thing was the uselessness of the mother's gesture. In so far as I can remember at the opening that night, Edouard of necessity present, the girl didn't react at all and completely ignored the embarrassed congratulations of her relations and a few friends of the family, the only people, despite our many, if ill-addressed invitation cards, to have turned up. This event was surely the nadir in the decline of the gallery. Afterwards Edouard and I went round to the Democ and got very drunk.

Six

A soldier had lost both arms in a battle. His colonel
offered him a five dollar bill. The soldier responded
'No doubt you think sir, that I have lost only a pair
of gloves'.

MAX ERNST

You might imagine that I, whose meagre livelihood and future
prospects were tied to the gallery's prosperity, must have felt
considerable anxiety as everything slid towards the abyss. The
reason I didn't was that a few months after arriving in London, I
discovered something I'd never suspected to exist, the revivalist
jazz world. Shortly after that I began to impose myself as a
singer. My next step was to join Mick Mulligan's Magnolia Jazz
Band, and slowly we began to acquire a reputation.

Within a year, as the jazz movement expanded, Mick and I
had become quite famous, appearing not only in the London
suburbs, the potting sheds of jazz, but eventually in the West
End, and at weekends in the provinces. We didn't earn very
much then or ever, but it was enough to double my income, but
it was never the money that counted. My popularity was based, I
feel obliged to admit, more on my extrovert exhibitionism than
on my musical ability but it helped to restore my belief in myself,
a belief much diminished by ELT's constant depreciation. It was
true that the till remained unbalanced, my typing full of errors,
my French rudimentary, but several evenings a week, when
Mick, the band and I travelled out to appear in Acton or
Edmonton in front of appreciative and at times hysterical
audiences, my deflated ego re-inflated, my *amour propre* restored

itself. Let Edouard rant and roar as he chose, I would cry no more.

My growing involvement with the jazz world is irrelevant here except in so far as it infringed on my work at the gallery, but infringe it certainly did. Mick Mulligan, with my eager collaboration I feel obliged to add, was largely responsible here. He had at that time quite a lot of money and a large if rather dented car. Each day, suffering badly from a hangover and completely exhausted, I would promise myself an early night in Chelsea, but then at about five, and always at the exact time ELT came down into the gallery at his most difficult, Mick would ring ('Mulligan!' growled ELT) to tell me where we were going to listen to jazz that evening. Worse, more often than not we would finish up at his place in Ealing drinking and playing early Louis Armstrong and his peers until dawn.

Inevitably what little concentration I had to begin with soon evaporated entirely. Acting on a tip from a friend, I managed to keep awake by ingesting the inside of a crushed benzedrine inhaler, but while this certainly made me lively, it also turned me manic. Faced with this gabbling fuckwit Edouard asked me if I was taking drugs. I denied it indignantly.

Yet Edouard, however much he might deplore Mick's effect on me, was at times seduced by his anarchic sexual free-wheeling and willingness at any time to repair to the pub. Sybil on the other hand was completely resistant to his louche charm, especially as she saw drink as an enemy and Mick as an enabler. What's more, she suspected, and correctly, that I had told Mick about the threesomes when I was in the navy. For her, Mick was simply bad news and I, increasingly, a lost cause.

Then, to confuse the issue thoroughly, Mick spontaneously proposed to invest a thousand pounds in pictures. I have never really understood why. He was not very interested in art, but he did admire Surrealism on two counts: its eroticism and its anti-clericism. The first accounts, on his very first visit to the gallery, for his purchase of a rare, limited, beautifully produced book called 1926. It contained hard-core pornographic photographs by Man Ray with suitable poems by Paul Eluard, but as Mick was very careless with his possessions it soon vanished. Mick suspected that his mother, a kindly but easily shocked woman, had come across it and destroyed it, a likely explanation, but why did he leave it lying about? As to the second, as part of his investment, he bought a fine civil war drawing by Masson, in which two priests and a general, with faces resembling pigs or donkeys, greedily consumed the guts of eviscerated dead peasants. Yet this doesn't explain his decision to lay out a thousand pounds, a considerable sum in the late forties, and I suspect it may have been competitive. If I could have a collection in my single room in Chelsea, well so could he in Ealing!

In the event he chose well. Apart from the Masson drawing and a small brilliantly coloured oil by the same artist depicting two witches eating a grasshopper, Mick homed in on a large and beautiful Magritte, at that time the most despised painter in the world. It was called 'The Flying Statue' and was originally painted in 1927 although, Edouard told us, it was radically reworked around 1933. It shows a statue, possibly based on the Venus de Milo, with cupboard doors for wings and surrounded by other Magrittian props, including a large piece of fretworked wood penetrated by metal pipes, a *bilboquet* in front of a low wall, and beyond it the void. As well as draping the legs of the statue in the final version, Magritte had decided to make it all much more sombre. It was framed in a curved art deco style, painted matt silver. As pendants to this central work, there was a fine Ernst frontage, a Feininger drawing and several lesser things but all in all it was a good instinctive choice and, as in my case, Edouard declared Mulligan 'well-served'.

And so he was, but unfortunately at the beginning of the sixties Mick hit a financial crisis, and while happily this turned out to be temporary, it seemed very serious at the time. He was forced to put his collection on the market, but as it was several years before Surrealism began to move, everything went under the hammer for about the same as he'd paid for it; a misfortune of which, in his sarcastic cups, he never failed to remind me. Had he only been able to hang on for another ten years, or better still twenty, his investment would have been sensationally successful, but then I am in no position to gloat. Personal difficulties never seem to coincide with soaring values.

Mick's purchase was my only substantial coup as a trainee dealer; I did occasionally shift the odd picture but always at a modest price. One day a young schoolmaster visited that same Ernst exhibition which the almost blind Wyndham Lewis had dismissed in the *Listener*. The schoolmaster didn't share the old Vortecist's opinion, in fact he fell in love with a delicious picture in the '100,000 dove' series, and regretted his inability to buy it. It was I think about twenty pounds, a formidable amount for a schoolmaster, but when I proposed that he should pay five pounds down and the rest in instalments he eventually decided, although with much heart-searching, to agree to these terms.

At the private view of Ernst's retrospective at the Tate (that same exhibition reduced by the inclusion of 'St Anthony') I was approached by quite an elderly bearded figure. It was of course the schoolmaster forty-five years on. He told me that he still had the picture, although from time to time he had been offered increasingly large sums of money for it. I was quite moved by this revelation. At the time of the sale though it was no big deal. Five pounds down and a pound a month for fifteen months buttered no surrealist parsnips. There was, however, one more occasion when ELT, displayed in his worst light, was very disappointed in me. The potential situation involved a member of the Moores family (the Littlewoods tycoons) and I was accused of bungling it.

My uncle Fred, my mother's brother, had married a sister of John Moores, the founder of the business (ironically later he would sponsor the Liverpool Biennial). In the forties, according to Uncle Fred, he still had reproductions on his walls of pictures like '. . . and when did you last see your father?'. Anyway 'Mr John', as his staff called him, was not involved here. It was his younger brother Cecil.

Cecil was holding a lunchtime family cocktail party in one of the great hotels in Park Lane. It was only ten minutes' walk from the gallery and Uncle Fred had got me invited. When I asked ELT he was originally reluctant to allow me extra time off, but he soon changed his tune when he heard who was to be my host. I went along then with his blessing and Fred, very helpfully I must say, introduced me to his brother-in-law and told him what I did for a living.

Cecil, unlike his shy older sibling, was something of an extrovert. He called for silence. He asked for his young daughter Pat to step forward. He put one arm round her, the other round me. 'Ladies and Gentlemen,' he boomed in a rich Lancastrian brogue, 'this young man is Freddy Isaac's nephew. He's just started working in an art gallery round t'corner. My daughter Pat is very fond of art,' I could see her almost fainting with embarassment 'and I want young Melly here to take her to his gallery where she can choose a picture of up to ONE 'UNDRED POUNDS!'

There was scattered applause and off we went. Pat turned out to be a sensitive if rather shy girl. Edouard couldn't believe it when we walked in and I explained our mission. He had a vision of all those huge Edwardian houses backing onto the Lancashire golf links hung with the great modern masters.

Pat eventually hesitated between two pictures: a beautiful line drawing of a 1924 nude by Picasso or a lightweight if charming small oil of a sailor by Craxton. I tried to push her towards the Picasso (one of my failings as a gallery assistant was that I always tried to persuade clients to buy what I liked) but she couldn't make up her mind, so we took them both back to the hotel for her father to have the casting vote.

It was clear he didn't like either much, but predictably went for the Craxton. 'There's more work in that,' he argued, 'and besides it's in't colour.'

'Marry her!' commanded ELT when I returned with the Picasso. 'She would be sweet with you and you could form a magnificent collection!'

I was angry with him. I could forgive him everything except that greedy cynicism; the legacy I dare say of generations of Belgian petit bourgeois, which I had first recognised when he beat down the price of the two Klees when I was still in the navy. Much as I liked her I was not attracted by Pat nor she by me, but even if I had decided to court her like a Dickensian fortune-hunter and gained her trust and love, the Moores, well-used to spotting conmen and financial opportunists, would hardly have welcomed me, Freddy Isaac or no Freddy Isaac, with open arms and cheque books. 'Besides,' I thought looking at Edouard almost salivating at the idea of all that money, 'what about *l'amour fou*, the cornerstone of surrealist faith?'

What I didn't realise of course was that Edouard was salivating from spiritual hunger. He knew the gallery was doomed. He saw liaison with the Moores as a solution to all his woes.

Despite some mention of the secretary, Robert Melville, alias Dr Toothpaste, and the picture restorer Gigi Richter, I have tended up until now to describe my life at the gallery as if only ELT and myself were involved, whereas in fact this was true for only the few months prior to our closing down. Up until then there had always been someone else, some kind of buffer.

That terminal and solitary period was the worst. It's true that my salary was doubled, from three to six pounds, but Edouard, while ensuring that I realised this was only because I was alone and nothing to do with my value as an employee, made my life less bearable in other ways. I don't think I would have stuck it out but for one thing. Even I could see we were heading for the rocks and that I was in consequence in purgatory rather than hell while, at the same time, Mick Mulligan and I were offered more and more gigs, far more indeed than I, with my gallery commitments, was able to fulfil. This led us to discuss when, rather than if, the gallery closed the possibility of turning pro. Once the date was established, the possibility became a certainty. Goodbye Kahnweiler! Hello Jelly-roll Morton! And that is what happened. All my life I have relied on the certainty of chance. I have never planned anything, and while a modicum of strategy might well have made me richer, and less passivity helped me avoid a few desperate or even dangerous situations, I have no regrets. If you don't believe in luck, She won't believe in you.

Our picture restorer left soon after I arrived, but that had nothing to do with ELT. Indeed, her picture restoration was the only profitable side of the gallery and might have kept us afloat. It was in fact Lee Miller, Roland Penrose's formidable consort, who sent her packing.

The stormy relationship of Lee and Roland is of concern here only as far as it affected Edouard, and for those interested in Lee, and she has a remarkable story, I can warmly recommend Tony Penrose's fine biography of his formidable mother; a book swinging between subjectivity and objectivity like the photograph of an eye (Lee's eye as it happens) that Man Ray attached to the clicking pendulum of a metronome.

Lee never minded Roland having casual affairs, on the contrary, but as a much acclaimed war photographer for *Vogue* she was reluctant to return to fashion and Downshire Hill. To avoid this fate she remained in Europe, ignoring Penrose's evermore desperate letters, but an either-or ultimatum brought her belting back from the Balkans where she pulled off the oldest trick in the book and became pregnant. Then, to make assurance double sure, she persuaded her amiable Egyptian husband to divorce her, divorce her, divorce her, married the future knight and thereby legitimised her future biographer.

A reluctant wife and bad mother she left the registry office with the demon of boredom already yawning in her ear. Roland however was ecstatic and painted a series of pictures inspired by Lee's return and the conception of an heir. He asked Edouard to exhibit them, and naturally he was in no position to refuse.

In general Penrose was a much better artist than he is given credit for. The blue-faced portait of his first wife Valentin, with birds for hair and butterflies and moths replacing her eyes and mouth is an iconic image, and if much of his work is over-influenced by others, especially Ernst, his use of identical postcards fanned out in collage is his alone. But his exhibition of 1947 was a real bummer. Its centrepiece was a picture of Lee, her stomach transparent, revealing a lizard-like Tony floating in the womb. This, and indeed all the works, were painted in acid colours, the visual equivalent of a fingernail scraping down a blackboard. The idiom is based on the sentimental sub-Cubism of the Parisian communist painters Pignon and Fougeron. The opening was pretty grim. Lee, as far as I can recall, didn't show.

The picture restorer's departure depressed Edouard, if at all, on a purely commercial basis, but the next defection enraged and upset him on an emotional level. Dr Toothpaste handed in his resignation and, even worse, did so to join a new and rival venture. On the surface, ELT claimed to be concerned on a business level. He pretended to believe that Robert would take with him as a dowry a list of all those who had ever bought anything from the gallery and that, as a back-up, he may well have copied out the file of invitees. But as our 'serious clients' would hardly have made up a rugger team and I had become convinced that most of our invitation cards, drawn in the main from the pre-war London Gallery visitors' book, were addressed to people now either dead or gaga, I felt that either Edouard's castigation of Robert's supposed sharp practice was his way of concealing a sense of personal betrayal. Robert was a long-term surrealist. At a moment when, even in France, the movement was losing its momentum, his defection was a body blow to ELT's *amour propre*. He might deny it, but he *was* after all Pope Breton's papal nuncio in London. Was he unable to rely on the allegiance of even one of his rapidly diminishing flock? So it would seem.

On a practical level, too, Robert would be missed. He alone had both the drive and expertise to carry through the increasingly lethargic Mesens's ideas. ELT knew that, without Robert, there was no chance at all of any future surrealist activity. On the other hand, keeping the books presented no problem; there was after all very little to enter and Philip Sansome, a red-bearded anarchist not long released from prison for disaffection of the troops, took over Robert's book-keeping with no difficulty at all on a twice weekly basis.

ELT's 'court' became more and more Lear-like and I was his fool, the only role I was qualified to play. He could rely on Jacques Brunius, *his* surrealist purity was never in doubt, but Jacques used this as a stick to beat ELT for his lassitude and pessimism. There were a few artists too, but most of them he suspected, probably with some justification, of hanging on in the increasingly wan hope of an exhibition.

So he sat there, ELT Mesens, ranting and roaring in his cups, taking refuge in the bathroom, surrounded by an Aladdin's cave of wonderful pictures, most of them rejected as valueless and irrelevant by the 'aesthetes', critics and the art establishment. His own creative spring had long run dry – he had written no poetry since the end of the war – and it was ony Sybil's tough love which held him back from what he pronounced 'Swiss-side' or at any rate from drinking himself to death.

I supported Edouard without reservation over the Dr Tooth-paste affair. At a party given by Simon Watson Taylor, secretary of the fast-failing surrealist group, at his basement flat in Tregunter Road, I started a fight with Robert's very nice daughter Roberta, who flew at me tooth and nail, and with every justification, for insulting Daddy. In perspective I don't blame 'Daddy' at all. Robert was a very nice and honest man and recognised from his book-keeping that it was only a matter of time before the gallery went under, leaving him without a job. He would have been a fool not to take his chance.

Erika Brausen, Robert's seductress, was an intelligent and sympathetic lesbian with a good eye and admirable audacity. Her master-stroke was to realise that contemporary art was about to become fashionable on an international scale, and must be presented as a way of advertising not only the taste of the collector, but also that he or she had the money to pay for it. The Hanover Gallery with its thick carpets, Regency desk, and luxurious framing was the antithesis of the London Gallery's

Hampstead-like austerity. There was no question of recycled string or paper.

Amongst the older galleries, while it must be pointed out that many of them still exist, only the Lefevre in Bruton Street had the panache of Erika's new venture, but then the Lefevre (which served champagne instead of filthy wine at its openings) had its cellars full of great masterpieces from the Impressionists on, and any picture dealers whose co-founder, Alex Reid, had been painted by Van Gogh could afford to assume a bantering hauteur towards its clients. Erika of course had no such back-up. She had to rely on flair, and that she held in trumps. It was she who had the nous to grab Francis Bacon when most people recoiled from him in horror, even though it transpired eventually that she was only fattening him up for the Marlborough Gallery to gobble up later.

Aware that he stood on the threshold of this new big business international art world, Edouard felt completely out of it. He was without a role to play, selling a few of his pictures to keep going but relying otherwise on Sybil's rapid professional ascent at Dickie and Johnny.

He had initially placed some hopes in the Institute of Contemporary Arts, seeing it as a potential way to promote the modern spirit in general, and Surrealism in particular. The founding committee, while admittedly lumbered with the hold-all presidency of the didactic Herbert Read, also contained such allies as Jacques Brunius, Robert Melville and indeed Roland himself (their quarrel was still to come). There were two important and initial exhibitions: '40 Years of Modern Art' (held in the basement of the Academy Cinema) and '40 Thousand Years of Modern Art'. Premises were acquired: a bar and club-room and a gallery-cum-performance space in Dover Street. Eventually, however, the inevitable split happened, and Edouard and his supporters resigned *en masse*, joined, rather to ELT's surprise, by Geoffrey Grigson, an admittedly irascible poet and critic but in no way a surrealist sympathiser.

The next day Edouard delivered a blackly humorous if perhaps over-subjective view of the fracas but recently I found some of his notes which present, in my view, a complete justification for his disillusion. In his slightly 'slipped' English (an adjective he invented to describe the flavour of strawberries out of season) here are his objections:

> '. . . I again formulated the idea of an experimental centre that we called the Institute of Contemporary Arts. All this will have taken soon 3 years! And *did we realise the slightest part* of our original intentions? My answer: No we have made only concessions and to whom? for what? I am getting terribly exasperated when I see that day after day we have been bending more and more towards an activity imitating British Council, Arts Council, the Film Clubs and *even* the Anglo-French Art Centre. Moreover, as Penrose seems to satisfy himself with what he calls authoritative opinions of Museum officials and artists who are on their way to the tomb, there seems nothing fresh or young to be expected!'

This was, in retrospect, an almost prophetic insight as to Roland's intentions. Penrose was indeed to become more and more conformist. His acceptance of the position as head of the British Council in Paris led eventually to a knighthood. Later on, in the seventies, he resigned as President of the ICA as a protest against a punkish clique who were behaving, it seemed to me, entirely in the spirit of Dada (Roland accused them of lacking talent, never a priority in that seminal movement and of disobeying the council!). Later all was forgiven. On his eightieth birthday he was given a party at the ICA's vast premises in the Mall (to many people's regret it had long moved there from its cosy origins in Dover Street). It was a sentimental occasion and why not? He was offered and accepted to become Honorary President for life.

As for the ICA, during its twenty-five years in Dover Street and later in the Mall it did put on some good exhibitions, films, concerts, and so on. Furthermore, Edouard's 'nothing fresh' proved to be quite unfounded. During the fifties a number of young artists, sculptors, architects, critics and thinkers invented pop art there. There was some confusion to start with. Was pop art an appreciation of juke boxes, finned limos, leather jackets and comics, or was it the creation of ironic if enthusiastic homage to these icons? At all events, ELT remained indifferent to pop, although in fact it represented the 'fresh or young' in full revolt against the establishment and good taste, but then ELT deplored most art created since the war. He stopped with Gorki. He felt, quite correctly, that his idols had dried up: Ernst turned whimsical; Magritte increasingly slick, repetitive; Dali a monster of commercial opportunism although never (as Edouard had admitted to me) unintelligent; Miro, weak and decorative; and even Picasso, although Edouard didn't live to see his wonderful angry/terrified finale, he considered finished. The only post-war artist he really admired was Baj, an Italian with a truly inventive spirit, if limited vision. Otherwise there was nobody.

I suspect that many people suddenly lose their gift to recognise talent. Early in the sixties I bought a painting by Kossoff, admittedly an ungrateful picture, in paint of a formidable thickness, but to me a very moving demonstration of the heroic struggle to trap the human image. Edouard, visiting me, looked at it in genuine perplexity.

'Why,' he asked, 'do you buy this sad marmalade?'

With Robert gone I faced a worsening situation. Edouard was naturally the main threat, but Sybil was no help at all. While in private life she and even Edouard, if less consistently, remained my best friends, in public her recent elevation to Chief Buyer at Dickie and Johnny led to her treating me, increasingly, as if I were one of her own staff. Admittedly she didn't go so far as to sniff my armpits on a daily basis, but she gave me hell when she caught me clipping my nails at my desk (the gallery was otherwise empty) and she also banned me from wearing an admittedly seedy, but I thought rather dashing moleskin waist-coat I had rescued from the acting box in Liverpool. I felt got at from all sides, with only my growing fame in the jazz world and the anarchic friendship of Mick Mulligan to sustain me.

On a social level Sybil had developed a new vice. Her recent apotheosis and its consequential contact with male executives meant that she was exposed to the latest rounds of dirty jokes. These she enjoyed, not only in themselves, but because she believed them to be proof that she had been accepted as 'one of the chaps'. Unfortunately, however, she felt it necessary to pass them on to Edouard and myself only, like most women (and many would claim it in their favour) she was hopeless at telling them. Even I, well-trained in this area, found it difficult to follow her, but usually managed to recognise the punch line just in time to simulate appreciative laughter. Edouard on the other hand was completely at a loss. Sybil's 'jokes' were simply an addition to her other two flaws: her exclusive reading of detective stories and her vigorous singing of Anglican hymns whilst about her household tasks. He would hear her out in bewildered silence but, far from reacting when she had finished, or following my lead when I was present, would simply enquire 'and then?', his customary if undeliberate put-down in any anecdotal situation. Yet Sybil, jokes and all, remained, while strict, admirably fair, and prepared to spring to my defence when she considered that Edouard was behaving like a monster. She was an original and remarkable person. ELT was lucky to have won and kept her love and loyalty.

Just now and again during this unhappy period I was able to achieve something which so delighted ELT that for a time, but only a time, he could overlook my failings. One such moment was my physical ejection of Douglas Cooper.

Cooper, barred as you may recall, for actively dissuading a couple from buying a Craxton drawing, swept in one cold brisk autumn morning while I was talking to the amiable young book rep from Zwemmer's. I was initially surprised that Cooper had chosen to visit this particular exhibition – it had been paid for by a fairly dapper young man to expose his bland if competent fantasies on the theme of Brighton. I concluded therefore, that he knew the artist, who was admittedly rather good-looking, in some social context. I also knew that here was my very own *High Noon*! It must have been about that in real time too; Edouard had only recently gone out and was by now knocking them back in either the Aristoc or the Democ.

Nervously, I approached the plump yet burly figure and told him that Mr Mesens had said that he was no longer welcome. He paid no attention, but moved on to peer at the next picture with apparently the same concentration he would have given to a Braque *papier collé*. More loudly, if in an escalating squeak of panic, I repeated myself. He could no longer pretend he hadn't heard me and swung round, his eyes glinting dangerously behind his thick spectacles.

'I don't know you and I don't want to,' he hissed, 'you whipper-snapper!'

I've no idea what I'd have done next if he hadn't emphasised the word 'whipper-snapper' by striking me quite hard in the face with one of his leather gloves and catching me by chance across the lip with its metal popper. It was this (it not only stung but drew blood) which propelled me into uncharacteristic physical response. I grabbed him by the back of his collar and the seat of his expensive bespoke overcoat, frog-marched him to the door, and pushed him out into Brook Street. He turned and shouted, 'I've been waiting for this moment. I shall sue, and I have a witness!' 'Oh no you haven't,' said the young man from Zwemmer's, 'not the way you treat our sales staff.' As for myself, flooded with adrenalin, I empathised for the only time in my life with the pub-brawler and the football yob.

Cooper never forgave me this humiliation. On the rare occasions I bumped into him afterwards he would do his best to equal the score. At a smart party where I was wearing a white dinner jacket he affected to believe I was a waiter, and casually held out his glass for a fill-up. 'Get your own fucking whisky, Cooper,' I snarled. Once, rather more effectively I must admit, he grabbed hold of a woman's arm, a great friend of mine with whom I was visiting a large Magritte exhibition at the Marlborough Gallery, and looking pointedly at me, whom he knew to be a great admirer of Magritte (often we know more about our enemies than our friends), propelled her away with the loud promise of convincing her that the Belgian master was the worst painter who had ever lived. His final coup was, however, so outrageous that it made me laugh. Finding out that my second volume of autobiography, *Rum, Bum and Concertina*, had just been published, he took it away to review for *Books and Bookmen* and tore it to shreds. He wrote of it in tandem with a memoir by Annigoni, guessing correctly that I would despise the inept Italian academician. He asserted that I had obviously no knowledge of literature or art and finally, that I had worked for 'a vulgar and drunken Belgian picture-dealer now dead'. I know Cooper *could* wound his victims. I once saw Roland Penrose reduced to tears by Douglas's verbal assault on his perfectly respectable book on Miro, but I certainly didn't cry. I simply reflected with glee how much that ejection in Brook Street all those years ago must have humiliated him.

Douglas Cooper was one of the very few people in my whole life (my prep school headmaster was another) whose death caused me a moment of savage exultation.

One morning, instead of vanishing upstairs in his paisley dressing-gown to begin his complicated ablutions, ELT followed me into the gallery. Roland, he told me, had imposed another employee – a young man with a year off between leaving school and military service. He had got to know Roland by sending him poems and collages (exactly as Harris Reed and I had contacted ELT a few years earlier). 'As a director,' said Edouard, 'Penrose can insist his young poet who is certainly a spy first class.' I must be wary. The young man's name was Roy Edwards and he came from Brentwood, Essex, where he lived with his mother. He would be arriving at noon to learn his duties and would remain until we closed. 'He is also perhaps a pansy.' Edouard had talked to him on the phone and, while given to allotting almost everybody a deviant sexual role, was very often right.

The morning was, as usual, uneventful. At eleven fifty, his

114

current norm, Edouard came down, as immaculate as an old-fashioned couturier. At midday precisely ('You see, my friend, it is possible to be on time,' ELT muttered in my ear) Roy Edwards, just seventeen but looking younger, came in.

Dressed in a black polo-neck like a French student of the period, grey flannels and a sports jacket, obviously purchased for the occasion, and with his shoes well polished (I could see Edouard comparing his appearance to mine and not to my advantage) neither over-confident nor timid, he came towards us without hesitation and held out his hand, first to Edouard and then to me. 'Hello,' he said, 'I'm Roy.'

A banal enough greeting I grant, but it was the voice which made it so extraordinary. The Essex whine is rather ugly in my view but Roy had thrown across it an extreme 1890ish drawl, a languorous elegance of diction, all the more enigmatic because it was impossible to make out if he had deliberately decided to retain the hint of Estuary man.

Physically he was solid but not burly. His face, with its thick black eyebrows and long upper lip, was a shade simian but attractively so, but his eyes were entirely remarkable, very dark and conveying prodigious intelligence, sardonic humour and an emotional depth. Here then, I thought, was Roland's Spy and I have to say that as Edouard, after a short appraising conversation put him in my care and left the gallery 'on business', the thought of Roy sharing my burden for the next twelve months was extremely comforting. I'd taken to him immediately and although I was almost eight years older, he too felt we were to be friends.

My only reservation was his hair. It was black and spiky (a crew cut would have been one solution) but he chose to wear it just acceptably long and then plaster it down with hair-cream. It looked greasy and his skin also, but I never, right up to the end of his life, dared speak of it. Roy wouldn't have dreamed of making a personal remark to anyone else, and it was inconceivable that anyone should assume the right to breach his personal presentation. Even Miss Fenton, who came home early that evening to examine the new member of staff, never dared. Edouard was allowed just enough gel to keep his hair in place, and she was equally severe about how much *eau de cologne* he could splash on but although she kept saying that something must be done about Roy's hair, not a word she said to him.

It was Sybil alone who resisted Roy. (Edouard was soon as much in thrall as I.) She didn't like what she felt was his detached sardonic appraisal. There was one instance however when she had to laugh. She reported it as follows:

> ROY: (*on her return from D&J*): Good evening, Sybil.
> SYBIL: Good evening, Roy. Oh, by the way, did you ask if you could call me Sybil?
> ROY: No. (*long pause*) May I call you Sybil?

She had no alternative except to say yes.

In the daily grind, as I had predicted, Roy made my life far easier. He was numerate for a start, so when it came to balancing up petty cash and adding up the till, it took him five minutes to come up with the right answer instead of the half hour it took me to get it wrong. His share of the invitation cards were clearly written and correct (a mixed blessing in that it gave Edouard a point of comparison, but at least they took us half the time). His typing was slower than mine but more accurate and he could read (although I never heard him speak) French. I could hang an exhibition better and was, whenever a rare opportunity presented itself, a better salesman. I'd hoped he might mask my daily lateness, but ELT had foreseen that. Because Roy had a long way to travel every morning he was allowed to arrive half an hour later. Of course he always arrived on time, on very bad days, the same time as I.

I did have another advantage. Roy's insistence on leaving on the dot sometimes irritated Edouard, and once even caused him to lose his temper, something that rarely happened as far as Roy was concerned. Later on however, not only did Mesens see the funny side of it, but it gave him Roy's nickname; something which had been eluding him. One Friday Edouard told us that the following day he expected us both to come in for a stock

ELT and others (ELT front row third left, Dali in diving helmet) at the International Surrealist Exhibition in London, 1936

Le Petit Marin (second from left)

Overleaf: When Mesens was right. Two inner pages from a paper catalogue, when the gallery was on its last legs.

THE LONDON GALLERY LTD. was founded in October, 1936, by Mrs. Clifford Norton a Cunningham Strettell. The premises were then at No. 28 Cork Street, London, W.1.

Under Lady Norton's management, the Gallery presented one-man exhibitions by: th Norwegian painter Edvard Munch, by L. Moholy-Nagy, Herbert Bayer, Fernand Léger (13 year the Tate Gallery Exhibition), Oskar Schlemmer, Naum Gabo, the cartoons of David Low, collective exhibitions:— "Children's Drawings", "Young Belgian Artists", "Surrealist Objects",

E. L. T. Mesens, former secretary of the Palais des Beaux-Arts, Brussels, took over the man in April, 1938.

Under his direction the Gallery presented first London one-man exhibitions of work by:
    René MAGRITTE (April, 1938) 46 exhibits.
    Paul DELVAUX (June, 1948) 17 exhibits.
    Humphrey Jennings (October, 1938) 26 exhibits.
    THE EARLY CHIRICO (October, 1938) 18 exhibits.
    Man RAY (February, 1939) 95 exhibits.
    F. E. McWilliam (March, 1939) 47 exhibits.
    Louis MARCOUSSIS (April, 1939) 20 exhibits.

In the same years we also exhibited in our galleries:
    John Piper, paintings and collages (May, 1938) 31 exhibits.
    Drawings by Pablo PICASSO (May, 1938) 14 exhibits.
    THE IMPACT OF MACHINES (July, 1938) 87 exhibits.
    MAX ERNST Retrospective (December, 1938) 51 exhibits.
    LIVING ART IN ENGLAND (January, 1939) 49 exhibits:
        36 exhibitors including Piet Mondrian, Naum Gabo, and Frances Hodgkins
    Paul KLEE (March, 1939) 12 exhibits (6 years before the National Gallery Exhib
    Joán MIRO (April, 1939) 19 exhibits.
    PICASSO IN ENGLISH COLLECTIONS (May, 1939) 51 exhibits.
        (6 years before the Victoria and Albert Museum Exhibition).

The London Gallery Ltd. has also collaborated with other galleries and societies:
    Roland Penrose Exhibition (at the Mayor Gallery—June, 1939) 51 exhibits.
    Ithell Colquhoun Exhibition (at the Mayor Gallery—June, 1939) 16 exhibits.
    Max ERNST (Cambridge University Arts Club—1939).
    SURREALIST PAINTINGS (Oxford University Arts Club—1940).
    FROM FAUVISM TO SURREALISM. (Three exhibitions at Dartington Hall—Totne
    SURREALIST PAINTINGS (Isokon Flats—Hampstead, 1940).

E. L. T. Mesens was Belgian representative at the INTERNATIONAL SURREALIST EXHI (New Burlington Galleries, 1936) and responsible for the hanging of it.

He was the organiser of the Belgian section of the ARTISTS INTERNATIONAL ASSOCI Exhibition (1937), and Honorary Organiser of the showing of PICASSO'S "GUERNICA" (New Bu Galleries, October, 1938).

He arranged also at the Zwemmer Gallery:
    MIRO EXHIBITION (May, 1937).
    CHIRICO – PICASSO (June, 1937).
    SURREALISM TO-DAY (June, 1940).

The premises at 28 Cork Street were closed at the end of July, 1939, and the London Gall did not re-open during the war.

About one hundred paintings belonging to the directors of the gallery, and a whole docu library were destroyed in one of the first heavy air-raids over London.

★

945, E. L. T. Mesens organised at The Arcade Gallery, the exhibition:
SURREALIST DIVERSITY FROM 1915 TO 1945. (4th October)
ame Gallery presented in conjunction with The London Gallery Ltd.,
30 WORKS BY "SCOTTIE" WILSON (18th October).

e meantime new premises for The London Gallery Ltd. were found and—one remembers the
of both the administration and the building trade—slowly reconditioned.

all section of the gallery opened on the 5th November, 1946, at the present address of No. 23
reet, London, W.1.

first exhibition was also the first appearance in London of the name of:—

The outstanding Cuban painter, WIFREDO LAM. 20 drawings.

w mixed shows followed while the repair work was being completed on the premises, leading to
tion of exceptional quality and importance:

THE CUBIST SPIRIT IN ITS TIME (March, 1947). 57 exhibits.

e same year also:

THE TEMPTATION OF ST. ANTHONY by 11 contemporary painters. (September, 1947.)
JOHN CRAXTON AND LUCIAN FREUD (October, 1947). 42 exhibits.
THREE TYPES OF AUTOMATISM (February, 1948) including work by the Roumanian
Paul Paún.

exhibitions in England of :

Oskar Dalvit (April, 1948), Stefan Knapp (May, 1948), Aleksander Zyw (October, 1948), the
s James Gleeson and Robert Klippel (November, 1948), the Colombian Pedro Restrepo, Samuel
nuary, 1949), Gordon Bird, Kali, sculpture and drawings by Inge Winter (March, 1949), Magda
h (April, 1949), Vivien Roth (June, 1949), Henry Bartlett (December, 1949), Sonja Sekula
950).

The revelation of Austin COOPER (October, 1948).
The Wroclaw Congress seen by Feliks TOPOLSKI (January, 1949).
Paintings and Drawings by André MASSON (January, 1949).
SERIOUS NUDES (March, 1949).
Portraits of famous contemporary painters and writers by the photographer ROGI-ANDRE
(April, 1949).
THE EARLY CHIRICO (April, 1949) 13 exhibits.
Twenty drawings by PICASSO (May, 1949).
John CRAXTON (June, 1949) 56 exhibits.
Estéban FRANCES (October, 1949) 10 exhibits.
Baron BRAUN, a true Sunday painter (November, 1949).

one-man exhibitions by :

mington (June, 1948), John Pemberton (November, 1948), Phyllis Bray (January 1949), Sven
(May, 1949), Allan Milner, Stephen Gilbert (October, 1949), Ann Lewis (November, 1949),
Morris, Cyril Hamersma (February, 1950), sculpture by Sean Crampton (March, 1950).

man exhibitions by :

keham (May, 1948), John Banting (June, 1948), Peter Rose Pulham (June, 1948 and November,
cian Freud (November, 1948), Roland Penrose (May, 1949), new work by Austin Cooper
1949).

recently :

Joán MIRO (February, 1950) 14 exhibits.
Max ERNST (March, 1950) 16 exhibits.

o the date of proof reading of the above text, The London Gallery Ltd. has not sold a
nting or sculpture to a Public Art Gallery in Great Britain. All our internationally known
 represented in Museums and the most authoritative collections in Europe and the U.S.A.

Mesens said that he would double my salary if I would relinquish 'the jazz'.

'Max,' ELT told me several times, 'received me with tenderness.'

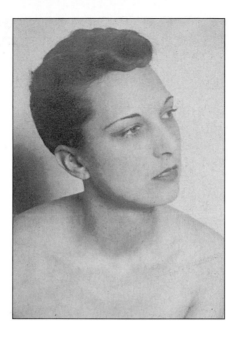

I first imagined her to be Spanish, and possibly with some gypsy blood…
but what was particularly noticeable was her air of discreet chic.

A surrealist to his fingernails.

ELT and Sybil in Venice in the sixties. Like many North Europeans he fell completely in love with Italy.

The Queen is dead. Long live the Queen' – corrected dedication of ELT's collected poems.

On the wall, the young Mesens by Magritte. In front of it, ELT in his sixties – old, tight and angry.

ELT dressing.

taking. While not best pleased I agreed to do so, but Roy quietly but definitively said it was impossible. Edouard asked why.

'I've arranged,' drawled Roy, 'to go into Brentwood with my mother.' 'What for?' asked Edouard, still calmly and politely, but with a growing edge to his voice. 'To buy a mackintosh,' explained Roy.

Edouard repeated the word 'mackintosh' several times, travelling through incredulity to rage. He forbade Roy to take the day off. He shouted that a gallery was not a factory, that Penrose or no Penrose he would give Roy the sack. 'The sack or your mac!' he told him. 'The sack in your mac!' This kind of word-play always amused him but he still meant what he said. Roy, as calmly as if there was no question of yielding, continued to give his reasons. His mother had made special arrangements. There was a sale on. He had already committed himself.

Gradually, in the face of Roy's polite intransigence, Edouard not only calmed down but began to laugh. 'Very well, Professor Mackintosh,' he said, 'we will manage without you. And so Roy became first Professor General T Mackintosh, then Mackintosh, and finally Mac. He turned up on Monday wearing the by now celebrated garment. Clothes rationing was still in force so it was nothing out of the ordinary. ELT praised it with suspect enthusiasm.

Roy spoke hardly at all of his childhood or current life in Essex. His father I supposed was dead, he had it seemed several unspecified siblings. His mother, while evidently formidable, remained a shadowy figure. Of his imaginative world however I became well-informed.

I don't know what kind of school he went to: I suspect it was probably a grammar school but I may well be wrong. Anyway, despite his competence in the traditional disciplines, it was not his formal education which interested me, but his astounding and presumably autodidactic grasp of so many diverse subjects, all of which nevertheless formed a cohesive world. His knowledge of Surrealism was encyclopaedic in both the historic and poetic fields. He had a keen interest in alchemy, necromancy and black magic. He had read and re-read the British gothic novelists of the early nineteenth century and the decadents of the nineties. He adored Dickens, Edwardian tales of boyish adventure, Firbank and Waugh. He introduced me to some of these fields. He was never pedantic as he always assumed, while discussing any subjects close to him, a somewhat camp approach. André Breton, in particular, a man he probably honoured above all other living men, he treated in conversation as a kind of solemn Pantaloon. Surrealism, the faith by which he lived, emerged as a kind of Gallic Punch and Judy show. I was, amongst other things, delighted to find that like me, he harboured considerable admiration for the films of Jean Cocteau, chief fiend in Breton's Parisian demonology. With all those hours of non-activity in the gallery, he kept me continuously amused, entertained and enlightened. He showed me his enviable poetry too.

Occasionally he would carry out a small practical exercise in humour. One month we had hired out one of the upstairs galleries to a Turkish mother and daughter ('In fact lesbians,' Edouard had categorically decided). Their paintings, indistinguishable one from the other, were better than some things we showed: heavy doe-eyed odalisques lying about in cushioned luxury a long way after Matisse.

Some days after the exhibition had opened Roy and I were astonished when the neatly dressed and extremely polite TS Eliot walked in and asked us where the mother and daughter were exhibiting; they had been very hospitable to him when he was lecturing recently in Istanbul for the British Council. We indicated the way and he went upstairs leaving his smart trilby hat on the desk.

Roy and I both worshipped Eliot and knew much of his work by heart. We would hardly have been more impressed if Picasso himself had come into the gallery. Roy picked up Eliot's hat and put it on. (I was slightly apprehensive about the Brylcreem marking the sweat band.) 'George,' said Roy at his most mock-solemn, 'you can tell your grandchildren that you saw me wearing TS Eliot's hat.' He replaced it on the desk when we heard the poet descending ('with a bald spot in the middle of my hair' we whispered to each other). It had been a very short visit, just long enough to sign the visitors book. He collected his hat, replaced it on his head and left, unaware that Roy and I were carrying on like groupies in his wake.

You will notice that Roy alluded to my grandchildren, not his, in relation to the donning of TS Eliot's hat. By saying his he was acknowledging his homosexuality. He would, he told me, never go to bed with a woman. He did however adore women, and not in the hypocritical way of some queens who favour only the grotesque or self-destructive. Women in turn loved Roy. Even Lee Miller, about whom Roy wrote one of his most beautiful poems, adored him until the end of her life and, uniquely, she never turned on him.

I can see him sitting at the desk when sad Peter Watson walked in one day. Passing Roy, he was unable to resist patting him on the head, modifying this temporary mild indiscretion by crying 'Pat Pat!'. This became Peter's nickname and we were flattered when Edouard, overhearing it and demanding an explanation, added it to his list. Roy usually went promptly home to his mysterious life in Brentwood but, very occasionally, he would come with me to a jazz club and get quite drunk on Guinness. Inevitably missing the last train, he would stay overnight in my versatile and expandable room in Chelsea. Once we made love. It was not a success, but it didn't affect our relationship in any way. When Roy finally left the gallery I was really upset and so was Edouard. Roy in his turn had become fond of him. He understood as I did how deeply Edouard felt the failure of the gallery, his need to caricature the businessman, his lack of any creative outlet, his fear that the surrealist adventure was drawing to its close, his fatal obsession with alcohol.

At seventeen, Roy's future was still undetermined and although I saw him fairly regularly until his death by cancer some thirty years later, I shall take leave of him here, at the point the army claimed him after one last mention.

Roy, completely innocently, was responsible for the worst row

Edouard and I ever had. It came about when Max Ernst made his first visit to London since the war, and quite naturally stayed with Lee and Roland on Downshire Hill. They gave a party for him, and it was this that gave Roland the perfect opportunity to get back at Edouard without appearing to do so. His pawns were Roy and myself.

Roland couldn't refuse to ask Sybil and Edouard to the party. After all, ELT and Max had been friends for twenty years, but he had no obligation to ask me and there was nothing to stop him asking Roy. Of course Roland was well aware of my passion for Ernst, of my collection of his work, but this made no difference. Roy was asked. I was not.

Edouard was upset. He sent me up to Downshire Hill with a parcel, thinking that perhaps Roland would relent. Roland did not relent. To make it worse I caught sight of Ernst's bird-like profile in the window. There was no doubt about it. Roland was determined to have his pound of ELT's flesh and I was that pound!

As one might expect, it was Sybil, the Portia of Brook Street, who really blew her top. To ask Roy and not me was pure malice on Roland's part and an insult to Edouard also. He must refuse to go. That, Edouard claimed, would be an insult to Max. So a compromise was reached. They'd go for a short while and leave in time for ELT to take me out for supper. I was, Sybil realised, genuinely upset although I in no way blamed Roy. I was left resentfully at the gallery hanging the next exhibition, when they set off at six thirty. They would be back, Edouard promised at eight thirty at the latest. It was ten before they returned, Edouard very drunk. Sybil, fuming with rage, went up to bed; Edouard, dangerously jovial, walked with me to the Barcelona, erstwhile centre of British Surrealism, which was open late. 'Max,' he told me several times, 'received me with tenderness.' He also stressed that Sybil had '*made* me to return'. All in all I could see we were in for a bumpy evening.

He started with a proposition. 'The Jazz' as he always called it was taking up more and more of my time. If I would relinquish it entirely he would double my salary. I pointed out (I was no longer afraid of Edouard. Roy and I had turned his rages into a shared joke) that 'The Jazz' was already earning me more than my salary. Another large gin and tonic arrived and was swallowed in one. It turned the corner. He began to shout. He was extremely eloquent and inventive, but equally venomous. I can remember clearly that he attacked first my mother and then myself on anti-semitic grounds (although I knew that ELT hadn't, when sober, even a grain of racism in his whole body). Through the paella and caramel custard he thundered on. My still largely gay sexual make-up was described and attacked to the prurient interest of the diners and staff. My possible impregnation of Sybil paraded. Why didn't I walk out? Partially greed – I was ravenous. Partially the rabbit in front of the serpent syndrome. How far would he go? What would he say next? How would he bring down the curtain?

I needn't have worried. He had an impeccable sense of drama. After his third brandy he rose to his feet (he never showed any signs of physical drunkenness). He called over the waiter. 'Mr Melly,' he told him, 'is to pay the bill. Because he is a young fool he has no money. If it is necessary, call the police. He is entirely without means!'

And Edouard stormed off into Beak Street and I couldn't help thinking rather sadly, how only a few years before the awed 'Petit Marin' had won his friendship in this very building. On the other hand I could completely understand why he was so angry. I could even sympathise. The waiter, an elderly man from Barcelona, was both kindly and fatherly. I was not to worry. They knew Mr Mesens. He was . . . (The waiter made drinking and staggering movements.) He would pay tomorrow.

I'd just enough money on me, about five shillings in the late forties, to take a taxi back to Chelsea. I had already decided what to do. I would not go in to work!

At about eleven next morning Sybil rang up to say that Edouard, full of remorse, begged me to come in so that he could apologise for his monstrous behaviour and, if he could, make amends. I said all right, bathed and dressed at a pace not much quicker than ELT himself and, at about one o'clock strolled in to the gallery. Mac was there looking mystified. I winked at him meaning later, and went upstairs. Sybil, probably because Edouard was too nervous to face me alone, hadn't gone in to work. The miscreant launched into a major *mea culpa*. Naturally I forgave him. We all embraced and Edouard burst into tears. He then announced that in recompense he was going to give me a Magritte. I felt that this was more than fair. We went down in to the cellar for a formal presentation.

Now although Edouard owned many early Magrittes he preferred to keep most of them in Brussels and bring them over only when organising a particular exhibition. His collection included a high proportion of masterpieces of both the twenties and to a lesser extent the thirties, but at the time of the apology there was only one picture in stock and in my view it was a real bummer. Entitled 'The latest customs' (1926), it depicted, in front of a black sky without mystery or luminosity, a large lump of ice stained, as far as I can recall, with what seemed to be raspberry juice, and with a flatly painted tree sprouting from its summit. Behind it was a tower or column with a classical statue bound in ribbon perched on the top of it. Considering the marvels painted in that year, it was a poor thing. I said so. If Edouard was going to give me a Magritte, I was not going to be fobbed off with such a weak one. Sybil backed me up.

Very well, said Edouard, but I must come over to Brussels to choose it. I accepted this condition unaware as to how long he would prevaricate. From then on whenever I suggested a visit it was inconvenient. When ELT, after the closing of the London Gallery, organised an exhibition for another gallery, I couldn't choose one because they all had to be reimported, unless sold, to Belgium. Sometimes I almost wished I'd accepted 'The latest customs'.

Seven

Jazzin', Jazzin, me oh my,
The world's Jazz crazy Lord
And so am I!
TRIXIE SMITH

With Mac gone for a soldier, Edouard was by no means as ogre-like as I'd anticipated. It was irritating that he refused to sit in the gallery for more than five minutes – I no longer took a lunch-break, but had to run to the rat café for liver paté or corned beef sandwiches and a bottle of Tizer which I ate at my desk – much condemned by Miss Fenton on professional grounds, but Edouard was much less critical. No doubt this was in part the after-effect of Sybil's pasting on the night of the Ernst party, but he also seemed to have accepted that the jazz world would eventually claim me and that the gallery would be forced to close down.

He even accompanied me once to a jazz club in Oxford Street where I was appearing, and although in general rather lukewarm about my performance, he was delighted by one of my numbers: a vaudeville song of the early twenties called 'I've got Ford-engine movements in my hips – ten thousand miles guaranteed' and this soon won its place in his late-night street medley. I don't know why he was quite so enthusiastic about this image (recorded originally by the mysterious Miss Cleo Gibson) but it may have been because it reminded him of the sexual-mechanical paintings of Duchamp, Picabia and Man Ray in the New York Dada period.

One weekend the Mulligan Band were invited to appear at a jazz festival in Holland. Having made enquiries and discovered it was possible, just possible, to be back in time to open the gallery on Monday morning, and having decided to exaggerate slightly my chances of this happening, I asked Edouard's permission.

Rather to my surprise, after a short dissertation on Holland centring around the fact that, while undoubtedly the cleanest country in Europe, it was there that he had contracted his only dose of crabs, he said yes. He also told me he would be away in Brussels. That was a bonus, and even if I was a bit adrift Sybil would already be in her office at Dickie and Johnny.

Of course I was late. It took longer than I'd anticipated to collect my luggage at Heathrow (still housed in Nissen huts) and there was a slight hold-up in the traffic (no M4 then of course), but it was still only twenty past ten when my taxi (about two pounds with tip) pulled into Brook Street. Surely I'd 'scaped whipping.

I was none too pleased therefore as we pulled up to find the gallery lights ablaze, the door unlocked and Sybil, with a brow like thunder, pacing the floor. While admittedly suffering from a mild attack of what my mother called 'dentist feeling', I was not too worried as I faced her. I could still hear the applause of the Dutch jazz fans ringing in my ears and was also stale-pissed on the vast amount of Hollands' gin I'd put away in the small hours – a literal case of Dutch courage.

Even so, it was a superb roasting from Miss Fenton. At great inconvenience to herself, she began, she had decided to go to work late because she didn't trust me and *she'd been proved right*! I was a liar, sly, disloyal etc., etc. It was especially bad as I'd known Edouard was away and thinking she'd be at work, I'd calculated I'd get away with it – Edouard would be deeply disappointed in me, so much so that she hadn't yet decided whether to tell him or not, for his sake not mine. With this final anxiety-primed threat and another reminder of how much nicer I'd been when I was 'Le Petit Marin', she swept off.

I was impressed but not cowed. Was it *that* important being twenty minutes late – no later than usual on many occasions – to open a gallery more often than not empty all morning. I sat at my desk remembering the enthusiasm which had greeted my version of 'Send me to the 'lectric chair'. She did tell Edouard of course, but he seemed to be, rather to her irritation, surprisingly unfazed. Indeed, he was becoming more and more relaxed, shrugging at my mistakes, indifferent to when I arrived, unprovoked by my telephone calls from Mick Mulligan. Was it simply depression at the gallery's escalating failure, or did he know something to his future advantage; something concealed from Sybil, certainly from me?

In the spring of 1950, ELT Mesens, Managing Director of the London Gallery since April 1938, printed a kind of apologia. By that time the monthly catalogue had shrunk to a folded sheet of coloured paper: pink, blue, green and so on. On the cover was 'ELT Mesens presents' and the name of the artist or artists. Inside was a list of the works on view and on the back the exhibition to follow. Although the production of these catalogues was as cheap as possible, the choice of typeface and the layout were, as always if ELT was involved, immaculate.

In the catalogue of spring 1950 however, there was a change. The list of works was moved to the back page, and the centrefold was given over to a list of artists exhibited at the London Gallery from October 1936 when it was directed by Lady Norton and Mrs Cunningham Strettel, through Edouard's reign both before and after the war, up to and including the previous month. It is not simply a list of names; there are references to Edouard's other activities including a note about the loss of a hundred pictures belonging to the directors during of the first heavy air-raids on London. ('The cellar where they are stored is completely flooded,' Edouard once told me. 'On the surface of the water is floating a fragment of an important canvas by Delvaux, a nude woman.' It was a pity Lee Miller wasn't there. This remarkable image would certainly have earned its place in those wonderful surreal photographs she took of displaced aspects of the blitz.)

Most of the catalogue though was a list which, despite (and correctly) including those who had paid to be shown, remains absolutely formidable. The document concludes with the following note. It is, for all its apparent factual content, extremely angry and with every justification:

> 'Up to the date of proofreading of the above
> text, the London Gallery Ltd has not sold a
> single painting or sculpture to a Public Art
> Gallery in Great Britain. All our internationally
> known artists are represented in museums and
> the most authoritative collections in Europe and
> the USA.'

This postscript is what Edouard would have called 'just', but equally it illustrates a curious element in his character – his provocation of the official establishment and at the same time his need to be accepted by it on his own terms. Trustees of public bodies, especially if they had once been revolutionary artists, were amongst those he most vigorously mocked and attacked. It would have been extraordinary if they had also helped support him, but to the end of his days he couldn't understand why the hand he'd already bitten, often with every justification from a surrealist viewpoint, didn't choose to feed him.

The visitors that month were as sparse as usual. Few bothered to pay the small amount to buy a catalogue and of these who, I wondered, bothered to read it? What was his object then in printing it? A cry of self-justification? To prove to the directors and himself that he had done his best? Who can say.

The exact moment when the directors decided to close down the London Gallery is difficult to establish as they are now all dead, but it was certainly not long after (or possibly just before) ELT's self-homage in the catalogue. My own memory is that we finally shut up shop about the close of 1950, but of course it took several months to wind things up. It was certainly closed between the beginning of July and half way through August although it was probably announced as a holiday. I know this

126

because ELT and I were both involved at that time in an entirely different project across the North Sea.

I wasn't the first to hear about the closure. Edouard came back from a directors' lunch, not completely sober but rather cheerful and at the same time mysterious. He winked at me and put a finger to his lips. Then he went upstairs where he discovered my sister Andrée and Sybil and told them, 'It is finished.'

Andrée told me this only recently. Sybil, she said, was very angry because Edouard had a pretty good idea it was going to happen and hadn't let on. Couldn't he at least have hinted? How would he support himself? They would have to move, to buy a lease and pay rent. Edouard listened to this tirade without reacting. It may well have been he was in the middle of negotiating a new venture and didn't want to tell anyone, not even Sybil, until it was in the bag. He eventually retired for a snooze. When I was told, surely the same day, I was far from unhappy about it. Although we weren't quite ready for it Mick Mulligan had already asked me what I felt about going pro, and of course, when it was all over, I would still have my pictures.

In his wonderful book on Magritte, David Sylvester maintains that, about this time, ELT came into a bequest which was much more than he expected. Was it from that father who had removed his hat to reveal to Sybil his identifying growth? Was it one of the mysterious 'aunts' who, to Edouard's indignation, always reduced Sybil to giggles? Perhaps Edouard knew of this windfall. It would not have been out of character for him to keep it from Sybil as she reproached him for his unworldly lack of concern over the future.

Knokke Le Zoute casino in Belgium is an impressive organisation and at that time its director, Gustav Nellens, was not content that it should be the tables alone which justified its existence. There was a season there, studded with cultural events: a film festival, fashion shows, concerts, a *concours d'élégance* and so on, and in 1950 he or his advisers decided to sponsor an important art exhibition.

Closely involved in the organisation of several of these events was Edouard's old boss and mentor, PG Van Hecke and his wife Nono, Belgium's leading couturier and Edouard's one-time mistress. It was probably PG who, perhaps aware that his old friend was soon to be unemployed, suggested that ELT be made responsible for the whole exhibition: choice of work, catalogue, transportation, hanging, the lot. Once accepted, and with Picasso as his brief, Edouard's self-worth which had dwindled seriously over the last few years was instantly restored as he wrote to collectors, consulted his documentation and made many 'paid' trips to Belgium.

To me alone he confided that one of the attractions of his task was its proximity to a casino. He had always had a weakness for the tables, not only for the excitement but because they gave him an opportunity to reinforce his belief in 'the certainty of chance' yet modified, as were so many areas in his life, by complicated mathematical systems of Duchamp-like impenetrability.

Some months before the grand *vernissage* Edouard asked me if I would accept to accompany him as his assistant. There wasn't much money in it, he explained, my fare would be paid of course, I would be given bed and breakfast in a reasonable hotel. I would also receive a daily allowance. I accepted immediately. Not only was it a glamorous prospect, but it was proof, after my nightmare years as his employee, that he was eager to repair the bridge of our friendship.

Knokke was indeed to prove as rewarding as I'd hoped, but both before and after it there was the dreary business of closing down the gallery. Most of the stock belonged to Edouard, a smaller but still substantial amount to Penrose and a few pictures each to Peter Watson and Anton Zwemmer. There was also my own collection. Even so there were still a lot of gallery-owned pictures to dispose of, and it was decided to hold an auction amongst the directors on an 'everything must go' basis. Edouard, perhaps because of my father's investment, had insisted that I too be allowed to bid which was kind of him except that, as usual, I had no money. Even so the prices were so modest that I was able to buy for a few shillings each, four large and beautiful ink-drawings by the distinguished Cuban surrealist, Wilfredo Lam.

My task was to remove the works one by one from the stacks and show them to the reluctant punters. Edouard (in part out of pride?) bought most, Roland very little (understandable in that his walls were already crammed with masterpieces), Zwemmer a few things to show goodwill, while Pat Pat bid for nothing, contributing only a few despairing groans when one of those inexplicably dreadful pictures which lurk in every gallery's stock was placed before him.

The amount realised was laughable and there was almost no bidding, certainly no competitive bidding. Someone would name a low price, no one would challenge it. This was perfectly understandable; the directors, well out of pocket after the whole catastrophe wanted whatever money could be raised. They certainly didn't need pictures. Edouard on the other hand, while having to accept a lot of rubbish but for practically nothing, was able to acquire some genuine bargains. For some reason this gloomy farce took place, not in one of the galleries but in an office on the second floor. It was a foggy day, you could hardly see across Brook Street, and that evening Edouard treated Sybil and me to an hysterical wake at the Ivy. We were all in high spirits including Sybil, now no doubt reassured that she wouldn't have to be the only breadwinner, and whenever the laughter died down I had only to imitate the groans of Pat Pat to re-ignite it.

During the last few days before we closed for ever, Edouard reverted to his role as Dada businessman to pull one more trick. The storeroom, most of the stock already gone, was half-full of an enormous quantity of paper he had refused to let me throw away and several boxes overflowing with bits of string, many still coated in whitewash, and of various lengths and thickness.

Edouard had read somewhere that the local authorities would pay for waste paper if tied into ten pound parcels and ('For the profit of the Directors') he ordered me to reduce this chaos to order. To this end he borrowed some commercial scales and left me to it. Despite having caught his passion for geometrical tidiness the task he had set me was both too arduous and monotonous to be enjoyable. As I might have expected he was always coming down to check the weight of the packages and to demand they be adjusted if more than an ounce or two out. The work took up several days before he was satisfied, and eventually even I took some satisfaction in the neat parcels stacked like hay bales along one wall of the cellar.

We rang up for the waste paper man to come. I can't remember how much paper there was but it looked a lot. 'Two pounds,' he said dismissively. We took it. I don't know if Roland, Pat Pat and Anton Zwemmer got their ten shillings each.

The next day I could get up as late as I pleased.

Interlude in Knokke

> ... a world of lovely women, butterflies, castles,
> jewels and glittering metamorphosis
> ANDRÉ BRETON

ELT Mesens assembled a wonderful Picasso exhibition for the Grand Casino of Knokke. Of the sixty pictures, the earliest was a watercolour of 1897, a study for a projected mural in El Quatre Gats, the legendary bohemian café in Barcelona where Picasso spent so much of his youth; the latest picture was an obligatory, rather weak still life of 1944, 'Now the man is finished'; but between those dates most of the exhibits were not only masterpieces, but a convincing if abbreviated survey of Picasso's whole career. They ranged from a beautiful Rose Period nude of 1905 to the greatest of the many pendants surrounding 'Guernica', the 'Weeping Woman' of 1937. Heralded by a seminal African dancer of 1907, they mapped out the evolution of Cubism to its decorative conclusion. Here Marie Louise Walters lounged sensually in her red armchair, there the minotaur watched his own death agonies in a glass held up by an impassive girl. It was a triumph.

At the same time I was mildly perplexed to note that almost a third of the show and nearly all the masterpieces were lent by Roland Penrose, despite the fact that he and Edouard were by now on worse terms than ever. Even today Roland's magnanimity still puzzles me. Was it his pride in owning such masterpieces and wanting the public to be aware of it? Was it to honour the genius of his friend Picasso? Was it because, in many ways, he was a genuinely nice man, and the ideological quarrel between them was entirely of Edouard's making? Nor did Roland seem to care that his generous loan ensured ELT's authority and prestige in Knokke Le Zoute.

Yet about ten days before the opening it looked as though the exhibition wouldn't happen at all. The British pictures were ready to be collected from the gallery (a modern curator would be appalled how casually pictures were handled in those days; a trellis of sticky tape if they were glazed, and a few blankets to separate one from the other when stacked in the van, were considered perfectly adequate), the catalogues printed, our tickets booked. And then, without warning, came a letter from a civil service department claiming that a form had been omitted and that without it the pictures couldn't leave the country, and that even when the form (enclosed in triplicate) had been correctly filled in it would take approximately a month before it could be rubbed stamped, we remain yours sincerely, etc. . . .

The morning this blow fell I found Edouard alternating between pessimistic paralysis and futile bursts of rage. Like all near-paranoids he was convinced of several alternative conspiracy theories. He believed the most elaborate the most likely. Roland Penrose, he decided, was behind this attempt to destroy him. He had never intended to lend his pictures. Why then, I asked, were they leaning against the wall? To convince and deceive us better. Meanwhile he had conspired with the art gang to throw a hammer in the works. After all he, Edouard, had insulted Sir Kenneth Clark in print. Perhaps, on the other hand, it was all the work of the Stalinist Paul Eluard . . .

My own theory, which I didn't even begin to explain to ELT, was that some minor civil servant, with a sharp eye on promotion, had spotted the form was missing and reported it to his boss who felt obliged to act on it. Our only defence was that when we had applied, perfectly properly, for a temporary export licence, the relevant form was omitted. I therefore proposed to ELT that I go forth to beard the bureaucrats on their own territory and, without enthusiasm, he agreed. Without telling Edouard, it would only have fuelled his suspicions further, it struck me that it might be sound strategy to head first for the offices of the British Council (later the Arts Council) and persuade them that our reputation as a nation of philistines would be confirmed by a refusal to allow the pictures to go to Belgium. Indeed I carried this idea through and was promised mildly supportive back-up should I need it.

Leaving the gallery that morning with a file of papers and a list of names I was, quite suddenly, flooded with adrenalin. Unique in my experience, it was as if I had just snorted a long line of pure coke. I have very little memory of my prolonged Kafka-esque struggles while, recognising that, inch by inch, I was beginning to break through. I wept here, shouted there, collapsed in fake despair like a deflating balloon if I spotted the least gleam of sympathy, dropped names like an ambitious society hostess, found an ally in a comparatively senior civil servant who liked, if not Picasso, at any rate John Piper, and another who was a closet jazz fan and finally persuaded the senior bureaucrat with the power to say yes or no to ring up the British Council, my hidden trump card. They didn't let me down. Outwardly calm, but fighting back the temptation to shout 'Fuck the lot of you!' and blow the whole thing, I watched the rubber stamp come down on the disputed form (it would have been in slow motion in a film) and tucking it into my file I returned triumphantly to Brook Street. Edouard was as relieved as he was surprised but, whereas Sybil was warmly congratulatory, he made no big deal of it.

About a month after the exhibition closed he gave me a catalogue inside which he had written

À George Melly
This 'souvenir' of the Picasso exhibition at
Knokke Le Zoute with thanks for his help.
and that was that.

Edouard and I set off early for Knokke travelling by train and boat, both of us in high spirits. From this point on we mended a friendship which had been fractured by our business association, if it may be described in such neutral terms. If our relationship was never to achieve the intensity of the days of 'Le Petit Marin' it was the more solid for it.

By setting up on my own as a jazz singer I had become, in his eyes, a grown-up rather than a blubbing office boy. He too was his own boss again and was able to discard his unpleasant business persona, at any rate most of the time. I dare say too that my saving of his bacon a week earlier, however unacknowledged, had helped restore me in his eyes. Meantime we were on our way to do what, as a team, we could do best; he to present a magnificent exhibition, me to hang it.

It was a wonderful morning, the light so strong as almost to bleach out the chalky landscape of southern England. On the boat Edouard was full of tales, amongst them a report of a conversation he had once had with Piet Mondrian. Although Mondrian, with his white backgrounds, grids of black lines and restricted use of primary colours, might appear to be the antithesis of Surrealism, all the surrealists, even Breton, awarded him some admiration for his uncompromising fanaticism. Nevertheless, Edouard's visits to his studio were probably kept secret from the café table. It was after all consorting with the abstract enemy.

Mondrian's studio was above the Gare Montparnasse. It was completely white with only the picture he was working on visible on its pristine easel. Mondrian's palette lay on a stool. I think Edouard said it was made of china but perhaps I've invented that. Arranged on it were black, red, blue and yellow. 'It resembled an operating theatre,' Edouard told me, 'and Piet with his big nose, spectacles and habitual white coat unstained with paint resembled a surgeon.'

There was another side to the austere Dutchman. Every Saturday night he locked his studio and went up the hill to Montmartre to dance 'with the whores to the jazz'. (Mondrian was a committed jazz fan. As an expatriate in Manhattan he was to paint his boogie woogie series.) It was a strange image, the serious stork-like painter jazzing all night long. I was reminded of Lautrec's cavorting skeleton with his top hat and pipe-cleaner limbs. 'I asked him if he ever fucked with the whores after the jazz,' resumed Edouard, and the idea of him not asking this question is inconceivable. 'He replied "No" with great emphasis, and repeating himself several times. I asked him why. Fear for disease? Refinement of taste? He answered me with an explanation I found completely strange in his case. "Every drop of sperm spilt is a masterpiece lost!" '

And strange it was, the idea of those austere structures relying on a vow of chastity, or perhaps not. Without it he might have wavered, allowed in other colours, curves and spirals.

Edouard was looking especially dapper that morning, understandably as he was returning to his native land, but puzzling in that he must have got up in the small hours to complete his prolonged toilet. This he confirmed – four thirty a.m. – and as he was in such an expansive mood I asked what I had never dared to do before. What took him so long? He explained at once. It wasn't his shit (completely without effort), nor his teeth, nor even a long soak in the bath. It was his shave, or rather *three* shaves, that took the time.

I had already observed when staying with him and Sybil that he used an expensive badger shaving brush, but I had missed the real clue: three neatly stacked piles of brand new, or apparently brand new, Gillette razor blades. I should perhaps explain for the benefit of those born into the age of the throw-away razor that the 'safety' razor, which had replaced the 'cut throat' of my grandfathers' day, unscrewed so that a blunt blade could be replaced. There were several models but Edouard's was rather solid and old-fashioned dating back, I should guess, to the twenties, perhaps the first he had ever possessed.

It was not so much the razor that obsessed him, he told me, as the packaging of the blades. Each was wrapped in blue, slightly shiny paper, framing an engraving or photograph (it was hard to tell) depicting the original manufacturer, a handsome moustached Edwardian, and below it his confident signature, 'King Gillette'. (King as in Duke Ellington or Earl Hines.)

I saw that three shaves might take some time, but not enough to account for those lost hours. I was right. What held Edouard up was never to throw a blade away. Using some elaborate Duchamp-like mathematical formula he would select the blade for the first shave and, when he had finished, dry it meticulously, rewrap it with extreme care and, with the aid of more obtuse calculations, replace it in one or another of the piles. In repeating this rigmarole three times ELT Mesens easily filled his mornings. I was, I admit, rather impressed by so rigorously observed an obsession.

Actually there was another clue under my nose, namely an image in one of his poems – a metamorphosis of bathroom objects needed to 'hunt the dragon'.

First he lists them without comment:

A shaving stick
A badger shaving brush
A safety razor
Ten blades
A face cloth
A cake of soap
A bottle of lotion
A comb
A toothbrush
A nail file

but later the same objects are transformed:

In the silence
The moon makes my weapons gleam:
A shaving stick for false beards
A badger shaving brush of pigs' bristles
A safety razor for drowned men
Ten under cutting blades
A face cloth in velvet
A cake of soft soap
A bottle of mandrake lotion
A cosmic comb
A toothbrush in fine gold
A nail file – phosphorescent.

Bathroom objects, the rituals of the bathroom were my friend's defence against the world!

I was later to speculate as to whether 'Personal Values', a post-war painting of Magritte's, one of his best later images in my view, was inspired by ELT's fetishism of the *salle de bain*. In a room whose walls are papered with a pattern of clouds, is a bed, a small Turkish carpet and a banal wardrobe. The room also contains a few enormous objects, amongst them a comb, a bar of soap and a shaving brush. To hunt the dragon?

We berthed at Ostend where James Ensor lived, although following Edouard's wartime 'obituary' on the BBC he could no longer visit him. We caught a small train straight to Knokke Le Zoute Albert Plage.

It has always been the fashion to mock Belgium as a provincial backwater. Baudelaire wrote of it with ferocious disgust, and the old joke, 'Can you name three famous Belgians?' has become a handy cliché whenever some aspect of the country is under surveyance. For me this distaste has no meaning. After all, ELT was a Belgian and so was Magritte. Brussels ('Our little capital' as Edouard called it, rather defensively) has much admirable architecture and, as a treasure house of Art Nouveau is almost on the level of Glasgow or Barcelona. The food, French cooking and German helpings, can be delicious. The artistic tradition is very rich. I've no doubt its rape by European bureaucracy has done much to ruin it but my memories of it (for now that both ELT and Magritte are long dead I can imagine no reason to visit it again) are very warm.

Travelling that short distance along the coast, recognising the architecture, landscape and seashore as typically 'Magrittian', I was in high, almost hysterical spirits. Edouard told me that, on our arrival, having registered at our respective hotels and 'freshened' we were to lunch in the principal restaurant of the casino complex with the Van Heckes, PG, his mentor, and Norine, his ex-mistress. 'Then,' he told me, 'we will begin our work.'

The casino complex was built around a huge expanse of lawn, punctuated by flowerbeds and so fanatically tended as to resemble the cover of a seed catalogue. I am relying on my inner eye here for, although I revisited Knokke with Jonathan Miller during the sixties when we were making a BBC film about Magritte, it was my arrival fifteen years earlier which remains so vivid, so hallucinary.

It was a perfect summer's day, the intense heat tempered by a gentle ozone-scented breeze off the North Sea. Edouard was put up at La Réserve, the top hotel, built to resemble a gargantuan Flemish farmhouse, or so I suppose for I can't think of what else could have inspired it. It was low, white, and with an enormous swoop of red tiled roof. While more than a touch vulgar, it emanated money and luxury, and as well as its no-expense-spared suites, contained a really grand restaurant.

I was in a more modest hotel on the other side of the green, but even so, Le Résidence Albert was grander than anywhere I'd stayed before. I was very impressed to find a bathroom *en suite*, something I had never previously encountered. Having unpacked and washed and feeling incredibly cosmopolitan, I strolled back to La Réserve, taking in *en route* the casino and the bronzed boys playing on the tennis courts, for I was still predominantly gay.

Was it this that touched me on the raw when I heard Edouard, shortly after introducing me to the Van Heckes, telling them, in French (but in a sentence so simple that even I could understand it) that 'like all English boys he is a pederast'. For some reason (and for the last time on account of ELT) I burst into tears; I must point out I had drunk quite a bit on the boat. Norine, while shrilly reproaching her ex-lover, led me from the room and comforted me. When we returned (even Edouard managed to mumble something mildly contrite) she sat me by her side and fed me morsels, *bonnes bouches* she called them, from her own plate. PG took to me also, and Edouard was pleased that his protégé was a success despite the lachrimose curtain-raiser.

Coming from post-war Britain, still rationed and austere, I couldn't believe the dining-room. I remember a blue and white tented ceiling, perhaps pink tablecloths, napiery, cutlery and glass well up to snuff, handsome young waiters serving very handsome or distinguished men and *soigné* women whose *haute couture* ensembles Nono (as she had asked me to call her) could identify at a glance and sometimes criticise severely. As for the food there was a still life of crustacians and bivalves draped in seaweed and dominated by giant lobsters. The hors d'oeuvres trolley (rare today, ubiquitous in the fifties) seemed the size of a house, main dishes were conjured up with theatrical panache from beneath silver-plated domes, the pudding trolley carried everything from tiny wild strawberries to elaborate architectural confections of impossible richness. I was thin then but almost obscenely greedy. The Van Heckes were astonished by the amount I put away.

Edouard pointed out to me a powerfully built man with that thick, perfectly cut hair and habitual tan which come with money and authority. He was Gustav Nellens, the director of the casino, and was sitting, Edouard told me with a certain roguish admiration, between his wife and mistress, who were both extremely elegant and almost interchangeable.

When even I had finished eating PG, who had chosen the most distinguished wines throughout the lunch, offered us the oldest brandy and the best cigars. It was not difficult to understand how, several times in his life, he had gone broke.

After lunch Edouard and I, flushed and optimistic and brandishing our Havana Havanas, made our way to the Grande Salle des Expositions. There the pictures were stacked against the wall, and there too was a Flemish handyman entirely at my disposal. This was a most welcome surprise as my first task would have been to remove the trellis of sticky paper protecting the glass. Today this is no problem as there is a transparent product available which tears off in one strip leaving the glass immaculate, but in the fifties it was another matter. You had to damp the paper with a sponge, taking great care of course that no excess water leaked through the edge of the glass onto the work, and then, after an exact interval, peel off the paper. Too soon and it wouldn't come away from the glass. Too long and it dried and readhered. Usually it tore, or left fragments of its glued surface. Even when it was done, the glass was horribly smeared and viscous. Getting that cleaned and polished took almost as long again. And here, in this palace of wonders, was a respectful Flemish workman, with the face of a Netherlandish disciple at the last supper, prepared and obliged to take on this boring task.

ELT and I decided on the best arrangement to show off the pictures, given that some of them were very small and the room was enormous. As Edouard had trained me to hang pictures there was very little disagreement. It must be chronological with a big gap between the periods. There should be plenty of space around the larger or stronger paintings, and the drawings and watercolours must be clustered together. It took quite a long time but finally Edouard was satisfied, and we left the impassive handyman to his monotonous task.

During the five days before the Picasso opening I had a really enjoyable time. If we'd been under real pressure we could have hung the work in a day but Edouard hinted, by tapping his forefinger against his nose, that we should take our time to justify what they were paying him. It really was easy-going and besides I had the dour Flemish handyman to do anything physical. Even if I hadn't it wouldn't have been difficult as the casino had provided brand new string, picture wire, chain, nails, eye-screws, hooks and rawl plugs, the antithesis of their miserable equivalent at the moribund London Gallery.

I'd stroll in about ten o'clock after a leisurely breakfast on my hotel balcony thinking, as I smeared apricot jam on my croissant and drank delicious *café au lait*, what a contrast it all was to the greasy fry-ups in the grimy bed and breakfasts I stayed at on the road with the Mick Mulligan Magnolia Jazz Band.

Once in situ I'd move some of the pictures about until about eleven thirty, when ELT would arrive, immaculate as ever but rather more 'sportif' in linen trousers and a dark-blue shirt. Together we would shuffle things around a bit more, or at least the Flemish *ouvrier* would, until it was time for Edouard to leave to have drinks followed by lunch with his ex-boss and ex-mistress and I'd hang on for about another half hour for appearance's sake. We had of course by this time decided exactly where everything was to hang but if we'd done it there'd be nothing left to do and, every now and then de Vlieger, the beady-eyed Secrétaire Général of the casino, or even Nellens himself would pay us a brief visit and we were in a position to consult them as to whether the cubist oils would be better divided by drawings of the same period or if the magnificent 'Weeping Woman' of 1936 didn't, despite being comparatively small, deserve a whole wall to herself. In consequence they would leave apparently convinced of our scrupulous perfectionism.

Every hour, on the hour, ELT had arranged for a liveried servant of the casino wearing white gloves to bring me a Campari-soda on a silver tray, a new drink for me but to which I soon became addicted. Meanwhile I would chain-smoke very black Belgian cigarettes from a yellow and white paper packet. When Edouard was there he was at his most charming, full of inventive jokes and prepared to feed my insatiable appetite for tales of Surrealism in its golden age. When he was absent I had the miraculous pictures to look at. I wished we could have gone on hanging the pictures for ever.

At one o'clock, for I could hardly expect to eat at La Réserve every day, I left the Grande Salle and, on gaining the main road, turned right and ambled, cigarette in mouth, for about three-quarters of a mile until I reached what Edouard called the popular end of Knokke Le Zoute Albert Plage. I was always confused by his use of the word popular until, much later I discovered that, in French, the word *populaire* means working class. He also advised me to eat 'popular' dishes, specifying Steak Americain (indistinguishable to me from Steak Tartare), eels in green (sauce), tomatoes stuffed with prawns and those delicious very thin, very crisp chips, and so I did and there was no doubt that it was a great improvement on the cuisine of the rat cafés in the alleys of Mayfair.

The weather throughout the week was as idyllic as a travel

poster. My daily walk along the sandy road was enhanced by the absurd villas of the prosperous bourgeoisie. The most grotesque was built to resemble a liner with portholes and funnels. It was made of concrete painted the colour of pistachio ice-cream. In the resort I was fascinated to see how the families, many of them grotesquely fat, ate continuously, in the main *pommes frites* and mussels. This did not in any way inhibit them when it came to consuming gargantuan meals at regular hours. I would sit among them, facing the sea, eating my lunch chosen from ELT's list, washing it down with dramatically strong beer, and finishing up with black coffee and a large cognac. My return to the casino was a little unsteady and sometimes I would even sing.

I paid for my lunch myself but would be reimbursed by Edouard on my presentation of the bill. To amuse him (and occupy myself) I would draw on a paper napkin what I'd eaten in the approximate manner of a modern master: a Guernica-like bull to represent a steak, convulsive eels escaping from their tureen *à la* Dali and so on. Edouard liked these drawings and kept them (but then he kept everything) and perhaps they may still be amongst his papers.

In the afternoon we took a long siesta and after a token reappearance in the Grande Salle called it a day. I soon became a familiar figure around the casino complex, and I played tennis a lot with Nellens's sixteen-year-old son, on whom I developed a passionate if unrequited crush. Sometimes I would visit the casino, but having very little money, could only afford few and low bets. If I did have a little run of luck, believing that I was about to become the man who broke the bank at Knokke Le Zoute Albert Plage, I soon lost it again. I have always been a very optimistic gambler. Edouard on the other hand played the tables with great flair and luck. He was of course superstitious and had contrived an elaborate false mathematical system for his betting, as indeed he had for almost every moment in his daily routine, including of course his selection of a Gillette razor blade. At the same time he was well aware of the odds and played to win.

Many years later I went to see him and he'd told me that he

had spent the previous night cruising the London casinos with Francis Bacon, and had been appalled by the way the great painter had scattered his chips at every table around the room, seldom returning to check if he was winning or losing. Edouard's system was probably no more logical but, if he hit a lucky streak, he'd nurse it along. The night before the opening of the exhibition he told me that he had trebled his salary at roulette, and I both believed and believe him. If he had lost he might well have said nothing but his nature compelled him to boast of his success. Equally predictably he then asked me not to tell Sybil. I don't think his embargo here was to keep his ill-gotten gains to himself; rather because Sybil would have been furious to find out that he had risked so much. It's true that, for the Mesenses, things were looking up financially, but it was still to be some years before they really hit it rich.

Such economic scruples played no part in the Van Heckes' calculations. Happily they had taken a shine to me so that, almost every evening, I was in a position to observe PG's legendary and profligate generosity. One evening I over-stepped the mark. At dinner he'd ordered bottle after bottle of vintage wine followed by several large brandies. When we had all trouped over to the casino nightclub for champagne, and he also offered Edouard and myself cigars. I was by this time ridiculously drunk, but perplexed as to how my huge cigar had suddenly disappeared. It had in fact slipped from my almost lifeless fingers and finished up in PG's champagne. He was, momentarily, furious with me, but then he began to chuckle, bought me another cigar and had his glass replaced. The evening surged forward.

The proprietress of the nightclub was a chic middle-aged woman dressed entirely in black and typical of her *métier*. After she had greeted us, Edouard explained to her that I was, in England, a famous exponent of 'Le jazz authentique de Nouvelle Orléans' and that I should sing a number with the rather dispirited trio grinding out the lacrimose French hits of the period. Unfortunately, although clearly reluctant, she eventually

145

agreed and, after a rather unsatisfactory conference with the pianist, I essayed a blues.

I know hundreds of blues verses but they all deserted me, as too did any sense of time, melody or pitching. Clinging onto a column and shouting incoherent rubbish, I eventually slid to the floor. Helped back to my seat by several waiters, I heard ELT telling the appalled manageress that she should book me 'in cabaret'. Her rejection of this notion was a masterpiece of diplomacy.

'Alas no,' she told him. 'He is too existentialist for my bourgeois clientele!'

The day of the opening: all the wonderful pictures finally hung and lit, the catalogues stacked on a table, the wine bottles at attention, the glasses glinting. Sybil and my sister Andrée arrived in time for lunch in La Réserve with the Van Heckes and naturally I was invited too. I was amused to note that Sybil, while on the surface all charm, was a little jealous of Nono, Edouard's mistress of thirty years before and hardly a threat now, while for her part Nono flirted with Edouard as if playing a role in *The Merry Widow*. Sybil's eyebrows shot up a little too when ELT signed what must have been an enormous bill. No doubt he explained to her later that he felt obliged to as his ex-boss had been generosity itself, but I knew that he was well able to afford it from his winnings in the casino.

As we were drinking our coffee Nellens came over and asked if he might accompany us round the exhibition which he had not yet seen hanging. It soon became clear, that although he was by no means a philistine, what really interested him was my ravishing eighteen-year-old sister. In Sybil's view (and not perhaps without a certain justification) Edouard acted like a pimp. Nellens was after all ELT's present and possibly future benefactor. Edouard complained to me later that when he and Sybil had returned to their hotel room she had given him a 'severe shouting'.

The opening, the men in 'Le Smoking' the women in

glamorous 'Robes du Soir', was both a formidable social and artistic success. ELT was congratulated non-stop and for once didn't drink too much. Andrée's hand was much kissed by gallant elderly Belgians, but, with Nellens on the prowl, she hardly left Sybil's side except to walk round the exhibition with me. I noticed too that Sybil, always well turned out, had taken particular trouble, and was indeed looking wonderful. This was no doubt because she was well aware that Madame Van Hecke had been Brussells's leading couturier during the twenties and thirties.

I had hoped my hero Magritte might have been invited, but I discovered to my disappointment that he and ELT were still on very bad terms, partly because of Magritte's temporary membership of the Communist party at the end of the war, but largely because, like Van Hecke and almost all his long-time admirers including André Breton, Mesens couldn't stomach Magritte's 'Renoir period'. In an attempt to frogmarch Surrealism into the open air, Magritte had broken up his smooth surface in favour of slap-dash splodges of very vulgar colour. It was in fact to be several years before Edouard wrote me an introductory letter and my finger pressed the neat chiropodist-like bell of that bourgeois villa in La Rue de Mimosas.

Edouard and Sybil stayed on as guests of the casino for another few days. It had all gone splendidly, Edouard told me later, Nellens had asked him to arrange a more ambitious show the following year, and had also agreed to ELT loaning him several enormous early Magrittes to hang on the vast walls of the casino. In fact the only moment of disappointment for Edouard was when he was asked to show his hero, Maurice Chevalier, round the exhibition he found himself unable to convince him that Picasso wasn't simply pulling everyone's leg.

Andrée and I returned to England on the ferry the morning after the opening. On the crossing – it was another cloudless and idyllic day – I fell asleep on one of those stout wooden grids through which warm air escapes from the engine-room. Stimulated by the heat, by alcohol taken the night before, and perhaps the memory of lithe young Nellens on the tennis court, I had apparently tried to roger the grid, but was woken by Andrée who told me that she'd overheard an appalled middle-aged English couple complaining about my involuntary behaviour to a steward, and had guessed it could only be me.

And so I returned to grim, rationed Britain and hit the road with Mick Mulligan's Magnolia Jazz Band, recently braving professional status. Unfortunately, whereas in our amateur days the work had poured in, now that we depended on gigs it had become surprisingly scarce. In fact it was ELT who came to my rescue.

One cold February evening, two weeks late with the rent and so broke that I'd nothing to spend in the pub, my landlord shouted up to me that Edouard, whom he'd met and liked, was on the phone. Running down the worn stair-carpet and wondering, despite the overdue rent, if I could ponce the bus fare if it was an invitation to dinner, I picked up the receiver.

What in fact Edouard wanted was to bring round – immediately – a Belgian diamond merchant who was becoming a 'serious collector' (ie buying through and on the advice of Edouard) as he might be interested in some things I had.

It seemed like a miracle and in no time at all I heard a taxi pull up. Edouard was there with a small but immaculately dressed man whom he introduced as Monsieur Urvater. 'As you can see,' he explained to his client as I showed them into my room, 'he lives like a student.' By this he meant surrounded by shabby furniture and walking on dusty and threadbare carpets under a cracked ceiling, and it was certainly true, but I could see Monsieur Urvater's bewilderment as he tried to equate this near squalor with pictures by Magritte and Ernst on the walls and graphic works by Klee, Arp, Schwitters and Picasso hung around the spluttering gas fire. He accepted to sit in a Victorian chair with very dodgy springs that had once belonged to a great-uncle. As there was only a limited wallspace in my single room, most of my collection had to be stored on part of the landing surrounded by banisters and jutting out over the stairwell.

At ELT's request I went out there and brought back two works, the wonderful orange and grey Max Ernst of the screaming figure of Lop-Lop swarming with phantasmagoria, and the 'ungrateful' Miro, that huge savage representation of two women from the later thirties. I rested them against one of the two beds and Monsieur Urvater was immediately convinced, and offered me £450 for the pair. I immediately accepted. Four hundred and fifty pounds was half what I'd spent on my whole collection. While it doesn't sound much now, it was a lot of money then, and Monsieur Urvater suggested he pay me in notes and that if I came along to the Savoy Hotel next morning with a suitcase . . . I let them out, and the following day found myself in a grand suite overlooking the river and counting out the bundles of money while attempting to give the impression it was a perfectly commonplace event. A week later they collected the works by van.

Having paid my debts, I should of course have spent some of the money on replacing the pictures. I could have bought a Francis Bacon then for very little and, worse still, I suspected him to be a genius. I didn't though. To quote a teetotal drummer of my acquaintance, I 'pissed it up against a wall'. And very typical of ELT was that the next time I saw him about three weeks later, he told me I shouldn't have sold the pictures. It was a great mistake. I would regret it.

Over the next few months bookings for the jazz band improved, but not so dramatically that I felt reluctant to accept Edouard's invitation to return to Knokke the following July to help him install his second exhibition.

This was called '75 Oeuvres du Demi-Siècle', and the catalogue was typical of ELT's painstaking scholarship. In this case he put aside his surrealist bias to describe, briefly but succinctly, the principal movements of the twentieth century from Fauves to what he called 'Les Tendances Actuelles'. With the exception of this last (for like most Europeans he had no knowledge of what had hatched in the lofts of Manhattan, and might well not have liked it if he had) it was a magnificent choice both aesthetically and didactically. In the first part of the catalogue each section was prefaced by a chart illustrating how the movement evolved. German Expressionism for example:

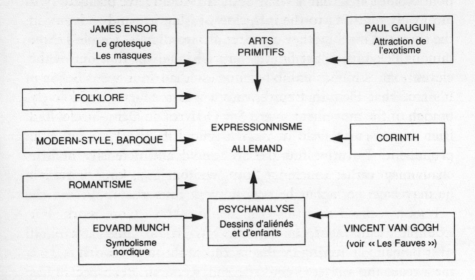

followed by a list of central participants and a quote or quotes from appropriate sources. Then came the plates, thirty-nine of them, and finally the catalogue proper with a short biography of each artist and the provenance of the work which represented them.

I have this little catalogue in front of me. The layout and typography are faultless, but the quality of the paper, the absence of any colour reproduction, would surprise those who nowadays expect a catalogue to be a luxurious and weighty indication of its purchaser's cultural pretensions.

As to the exhibition itself, Penrose yet again lent generously, and so of course did ELT himself but, as neither of them collected much outside the cubist-surrealist axis, Edouard had to look elsewhere for the rest. Luckily he didn't have to look far.

Belgium itself, that small nation of perspicacious and acquisitive art lovers, possessed most of what he needed, and with just a few loans from Paris it was all complete. There was certainly a slight bias in favour of Belgian artists. This was not entirely art-politics, although that is what Edouard would have pleaded. Nor am I only referring to the inclusion of Magritte and Delvaux in the surrealist section; they are after all two of most people's three famous Belgians. What faintly surprised me was that out of the eleven expressionists exhibited no less than four were Belgian. It's true that Flemish Expressionism was a coherent and lively branch of the movement, but if '75 Oeuvres du Demi-Siècle' had been organised in Oslo or Zurich would it have been quite so prominent? I always found ELT's mild and defensive artistic chauvinism rather touching. Born 'without god, king or rights' he may have been, but he was born in Brussels.

I soon realised that this trip would involve more work. For example I learnt that, the day after my arrival, I must travel all over Belgium collecting the loans. I liked this idea but felt it gave me a reason to suggest I could be paid a little more, especially as the year before I had saved the situation single-handed. Edouard, side-stepping the money question altogether, said that he acknowledged the value of my intervention and in consequence, as I would soon learn, he had shown gratitude in a way he knew I would appreciate.

He didn't lie exactly, but I wasn't overwhelmed by his largess. Here it is.

L'EXPOSITION
« 75 ŒUVRES DU DEMI - SIÈCLE »
A ETE ORGANISEE PAR
E. L. T. MESENS

L'INITIATIVE EN REVIENT A
J. - M. DE VLIEGER
SECRÉTAIRE GÉNÉRAL DU CASINO COMMUNAL
DE KNOKKE - LE ZOUTE - ALBERT PLAGE

ET A
P. G. VAN HECKE

GEORGE MELLY, ASSISTANT

Still, I suppose my name could have been printed in even smaller lettering.

'You see, Doctor,' he said, beaming, 'your role is recognised.'

Early on my first morning, when it was still a little misty and the grounds of the casino were empty but for a few gardeners, I climbed up into the seat of a large lorry and the impassive Flamand at the wheel switched on the noisy engine. He had no English of course, and even less French than I, but we communicated somehow. Most of the loans were predictably from Brussels, but we were also to make stops at Anvers, Gand, Liège and Ostend. The country in between was neat but very monotonous, like the duller bits of Norfolk or Holland without the tulips and windmills. I was impressed, however, by the number of very clean, very fat, very pink pigs in many of the fields. Years later, back in Belgium with Jonathan Miller for the Magritte film, and in a train *en route* to Knokke to record the artist's disappointing murals, the good doctor, as fascinated as I had been by the number of pigs and their immaculate appearance, suggested that in Belgium they didn't have to be slaughtered or butchered, but exploded spontaneously into hams, cured sides of bacon, pork chops and offal ready for the table. All one had to do was walk about the fields and pick them up.

For the moment though they were just pigs in fields, a mild diversion of limited duration, but the stops we made were interesting. In Brussels most of these were predictably luxurious (the Urvaters' for example) and at one stop I, but not the driver, was offered a cup of tea on a lawn where we sat on primitive African furniture, originating no doubt in the infamous Belgian Congo. Less expected, and mostly in the provincial towns, was the discovery of glowing masterpieces hanging in stuffy, fusty interiors full of hideous furniture and clutter.

We loaded the pictures into the back of the van, the driver following my gestural guidance as to the rules I had learnt at Edouard's knee: big pictures first facing the inner wall of the van, and then the next biggest and so on. Not too many pictures in any one pile, wood against wood, frame or stretcher never against the back of the canvas. Pictures with glass, criss-crossed with sticky-tapes. Each work cushioned by blankets and secured to the slats lining the van with thin rope, taut and secure. The van driver, while clearly uninterested in the pictures as images, knew they were valuable and quickly understood the logic of what we were doing. Indeed when we'd finished and had a beer to celebrate at a transport café, he actually smiled. I was rather touched, although I can't say that this friendly gesture was much of an advertisement for Belgian dentistry.

We got back to Knokke at about five and unloaded. Edouard inspected each picture as we leant it against the wall of the Grande Salle. There wasn't a scratch or a crack on any of them and he tipped the van driver generously, but not me.

Next day we were back in the old routine arranging the pictures. An easy task, because they represented different schools and had to be hung chronologically to make sense. It was mostly an exhilarating activity until we got to 'Les Tendances Actuelles'. Here Dubuffet was the only artist of any interest. The most fashionable painter of the day, Bernard Buffet was perhaps the lowest spot, although the vulgar false surrealist, Felix Labisse, ran him close. Edouard did what he could to conceal the aridity of post-war European painting by cunning placing of the movable screens he'd ordered to separate the movements. He almost achieved his aim to 'whisker them away out of sight'.

One of the most enjoyable and unlikely things that happened to me that year was when PG Van Hecke introduced me to a handsome middle-aged African-American who turned out to be the great Kansas City trumpet-player, Oran 'Hot Lips' Page, one of whose recordings, 'Just Another Woman', had long formed part of my collection. As American musicians were still banned in Britain on account of the Musicians' Union dispute with America, he was the first big jazz star I'd met and, as he spoke no French, he accepted without hesitation that we hit the town.

I can't remember why he was in Knokke. There was no jazz festival taking place. Perhaps he had already played a concert the week before I'd arrived, or was booked to do so the week after I'd gone. But there he was, and we had a magic evening cruising the bars and knocking back the cognac. The only thing was that I found myself paying for everything. Not that I blamed him; an increasingly noisy and incoherent twenty-five-year-old repeatedly singing the words of a tune he had recorded fifteen years ago was probably not his ideal evening, and it was only fair, as Edouard would have said, that I should 'cough out' for the privilege. On emptying my pockets in the small hours, I discovered that I had just enough left to pay for the cheapest chip at the casino. I could of course have borrowed from Edouard, but I didn't want to do that if I could avoid it so, win or lose, I got dressed again, went down in the lift, purchased my chip and put it on number seventeen. It came up. I then put five chips on thirty-two and that came up too. I don't know why this time I decided to cash in my winnings and leave, but happily I did so. I had more than enough to cover the rest of the week in comparative affluence.

As I left I'd seen Edouard at another table, but I deliberately didn't catch his eye. I saw that he was placing high chips with systematic application and that each time the croupier raked them in. Knowing his inability not to boast in triumph, this year he had probably lost or at best broken even. I realised it would be unpolitic to tell him of my own modest good fortune and took care not to spend more than I would have done without it. But on my last night (this year an engagement in Bradford prevented me from attending the opening) I treated the table to a bottle of champagne. I could see that Edouard was a little puzzled as to how I could afford this largess, but said nothing.

One evening during my stay, ELT asked me if I would care to accompany him to a fête in the country. It was to honour the eightieth birthday of the artist Leon de Smet, who had been a member of a school of Flemish impressionists who lived and worked in a village in the neighbourhood. I had been introduced to him the year before by PG and found him charming and modest with a quiff of snow-white hair and candid, slightly startled blue eyes, but I couldn't understand why Edouard of all people wished to pay him homage.

'Because,' said Edouard when I asked him, 'he is a good old boy, and besides he was the brother of my friend, Gustave de Smet.' This made more sense. Gustave was a leading Flemish expressionist and one of his pictures was in the exhibition. What's more, he had been influenced by the lyrical automatism of Max Ernst. 'Besides,' Edouard added, 'it will be a typical Flemish event, a Brueghelian evening.' And indeed it was, but what neither of us anticipated was that my friend would be provoked into surrealist confrontation, an act which finally exorcised the ghost of the penny-pinching bully of Brook Street.

We arrived by taxi – the fête was only about thirty kilometres from Knokke – and entered a wooden building resembling an enormous cricket pavilion. There were long tables laid out for what ELT called 'a serious feast' and a top table on a raised dais, the only one with a tablecloth and bowls of roses, and clearly reserved for the octogenarian and distinguished guests. It was a beautiful evening and as we walked in a shaft of sunlight caught one of the bowls of roses making it look, as Edouard pointed out, 'like one of Leon's completely banal still lifes'.

People were already streaming in, and Edouard gave me a ticket with a table and seat number on it. As the hall filled up I noticed that the middle-class Walloons, ELT among them, sat at the front, while I found myself far back amongst Flemish farmers, trades-people and the like. It was, I gathered, a subscription banquet, but those close to the high table were friends and collectors of the old artist. I was somewhat surprised that my neighbours were interested enough in art to pay to attend, and I asked the man next to me, a small fat man with a face 'like a coachman's fart'[1] who had tucked his napkin under his jowls even before the arrival of the cause of celebration, if he was interested in art. 'Art!' he snorted in worse French than

---

[1] Expression applied by the ur-Dadaist, Arthur Cravan, to the appearance of the painter, Robert Delaunay, a picture by whom hung in the Simultanéisme section of our exhibition.

mine, 'I don't care about art! I'm here for the grub and the booze!'

Shortly afterwards, the old painter and the VIPs arrived, and Leon beamed modestly as he acknowledged the applause. I sensed that those at the front applauded out of affection and admiration, whereas those who surrounded me (and certainly my neighbour) applauded because at any moment now the eating and drinking could begin. It was a gross yet innocent spectacle which followed. Most of the dishes were derived from 'the exploding pigs'. Not only roast pork sheathed in crackling, but such by-products as tripe, trotters, sausages, black puddings, cold ham and offal. There was also goose, capon, and calf's tongue. There were boats of sauces and gravy. Later there were rich cakes, solid puddings, and many kinds of cheese. Sturdy Flemish women moved constantly between the tables making sure that no plate was empty, no glass uncharged. There was a vast quantity of drink; jugs of red and white wine and strong beer for those who, like my companion, preferred it. If Brueghel were the host (and only the clogs were missing), Rabelais had done the catering. Meanwhile, those at the top end of the room chose with discrimination, ate with restraint, and sipped their wine, poured from bottles, with appreciative moderation.

At last, when even my friend had had enough, had mopped the sweat from his face, the grease from his lips and let loose a series of uninhibited farts and belches, there was a cry for order. The speeches were about to begin and I expected my replete companion to grumble about it. But he didn't seem to mind. It was a small price to pay in exchange for his recent visit to the Land of Cockaigne, and besides, he could always doze. I felt inclined to follow his example. I couldn't hear much from where I sat and wouldn't have understood most if I had. The first speaker, however, appeared so grotesque that I couldn't keep my eyes off him.

I gathered he was a cabinet minister or, more likely, an ex-cabinet minister for he looked almost as old, if by no means as amiable, as Leon himself. With his wings of white hair, pince-nez, a tail-coat, a sash and many ribbon medals, he resembled one of those establishment figures who attend the ambassador's party in Bunuel's film *L'Age d'Or*. He began (and from here on I had to rely on ELT's later account of what was said, but everything I saw confirmed it) by 'bombarding our friend with banal compliments' but then, starting quietly but with increasing vehemence, used Leon's work as a launching-pad for an attack on modern art. Edouard suffered this for some time, but then rose to his feet and marched through the gap between the tables shouting insults, until he was facing the minister who, shaking with impotent rage, was struggling to continue his peroration.

Edouard (and again I depend on his translation) attacked him thus:

> 'Monsieur le ministre, although, for our friend
> Leon's sake we were prepared to accept your empty
> and ill-informed praise of his amiable work, to
> listen, although sorely tried, to your rambling
> metaphors and inane rhetoric, YOU HAVE NOW
> GONE TOO FAR! Are you aware [there was by
> this time complete silence in the hall] that by using
> Leon's painting as a stick to beat modernism, YOU
> ARE ACTUALLY INSULTING THE OBJECT OF
> YOUR PRAISE! Didn't you know that Leon's
> brother, his much-loved brother, the late Gustave de
> Smet, was one of Belgium's finest modernists? That
> many of us who have come here tonight to honour
> Leon were admirers, collectors and friends of his
> brother also? You tedious old fool, by insulting
> Gustave de Smet, you insult us, and you insult Leon
> most of all . . .'

Everybody had listened with fascinated attention to all this. Even my neighbour had woken up and was listening. A number of people began to applaud and cheer, but others started to jeer and boo. Angry words were exchanged, fists shaken, and, as the rumpus increased, the minister, trembling with terror, was escorted to his official car rapidly followed by the other establishment guests. Leon de Smet however continued to sit there, appearing neither upset nor displeased. He and his brother were always, Edouard told me later, very close.

After a lot of shouting there was a very ineffective riot. Everybody was too drunk for their blows to connect, and would frequently stop as if by mutual consent, to throw back another glass of wine. One table was overturned, but only because a man passed out and fell across it. I shouted 'Vive l'art moderne' and so on. It was enormous fun. I next found myself sitting at the top table with Edouard, Leon de Smet and a few of his supporters.

I decided suddenly to fill my mouth with rose petals and no sooner had I done so than ELT, having explained to Leon that I was an exponent of 'le vrai Jazz de Nouvelle Orlèans,' asked me to perform. (Was it unconscious, or indeed conscious malice that led him to choose such inauspicious moments?) I did my best, but finding myself unable to swallow or eject the rose petals, I tried shouting through them, but was able to produce no more than a muffled high-pitched choking. Knokke Le Zoute, it seemed, was never to hear me at my best.

When I saw Edouard the next day he was looking both hang-dog and shifty. It would all be in the newspapers he told me. He had insulted a minister and the casino depended on the goodwill of the authorities. His action might well destroy all the credit he had accumulated. Above all, I was not to tell Sybil.

We turned a corner on our way to the Grande Salle and there, approaching us and impossible to evade, was JM de Vlieger, Secrétaire Général du Casino de Knokke Le Zoute Albert Plage. Had the news reached him yet? If so how had Nellens taken it? As he passed, JM de Vlieger wagged a roguish finger at ELT Mesens and then winked, and in retrospect this reaction was perfectly explicable. The casino, through direct purchases and the sponsorship of exhibitions, was investing a lot of money in modern art. The minister's speech, reported at length, would have given heart to those opposed to this tendency. ELT, without directly involving the institution, had acted like a guard dog. His insults would ensure attention, but his argument – brotherly love, a great Belgian modernist and in *Flemish* – would all be in his, and by association, the casino's favour.

As soon as we had passed de Vlieger and were out of earshot, Edouard began to indulge in mock-modest self-praise. After all, the minister deserved it. The forces of reaction needed to be reminded that others, more intelligent than they, had the courage to act – perhaps I should tell Sybil after all. This kind of nervous inconsistency never worried me, nor did the fact that it was usually in drink that the surrealist horse kicked open the door of the conformist stable. I loved Edouard for both his virtues and his faults.

However, one of his devices, the false and repetitive question, was a constant irritation throughout our long friendship. Sometimes he used it to wear one down, to wound or provoke. On this occasion it was innocent enough but none the less maddening. It derived from the fact he had insulted the minister in Flemish, something I hadn't realised until now. The question took various forms, for instance:

'Why did I speak in Flemish?'
'You know Géneral, I have not spoken with Flemish for thirty years. What made me return to it last night, and without faults or hesitations?'
'When I rose I had no intention of speaking with Flemish. Why did I find myself doing it?'

I knew what he wanted me to reply – that his use of Flemish was an unconscious return to his roots, an identification with the oppressed proletariat. This was pure bullshit. ELT Mesens had always been a Walloon. Paris was his spiritual home. His poetry was written entirely in French. As for the surrealist belief in the triumph of the proletariat, even that was fading as Breton was drawn more towards mysticism, the 'Great Invisibles' and the Utopian anarchist theories of Fauré. In answering a surrealist questionnaire, and in response to 'What do you hope for most?', Edouard had written: 'At one time I would have answered "Above all the triumph of the proletariat", but now that their leaders have proved themselves as stupid as any others . . .' Perhaps it was mean of me, but aware of all this, I refused to feed his sudden attack of Flemish sentimentality.

I would, on the other hand, have given him full credit for choosing to speak in Flemish (and it may well have been unconscious) as a politic device. The majority of those attending the banquet, albeit for the grub and the booze, were Flemish. The minister was boring them in ornate French. They may not have taken in why Edouard was so angry, but he was angry in *their* language and that was enough to put them on his side.

And so we entered the Grande Salle. There was almost nothing left to do – a picture to be raised an inch here, the smear on a piece of glass wiped clean – but the general effect was dazzling. From comparatively limited means and with what would now be considered a ridiculously small budget, Edouard had put together a miraculous refutation of the stupid old minister, far more effective than an anthology of insults. We embraced without further hesitation.

I returned to the jazz world the next morning. Edouard was later to arrange other exhibitions at Knokke Le Zoute Albert Plage (the following year it was Max Ernst) but he never asked me to help him again. In fact, as it transpired, this exhibition – 'a triumph?' said his postcard – was to be the last time he employed me professionally.

Part Two

Eight

Everything for him is good. However banal in origin,
he will know how to draw magic from it . . . He
makes collage like others do the garden.

BRUNIUS

During the rest of the fifties Edouard's financial position entered
a new and prosperous period. Not only did the Knokke
connection keep him solvent, not only had he acquired several
'serious' clients, not only had Sybil risen higher and higher in the
hierarchy at Dickie and Johnny with a commensurate salary, but
increasingly rapidly his collection became more valuable.

I was glad at their change of fortune but felt that it was a
shame that, although he kept in touch with the Parisian
surrealists and, when they weren't quarrelling, Magritte, he
seemed to have lost all faith or interest in writing. He had always
maintained, during the darkest days at the London Gallery, that
it was having to try and scratch a miserable living which had
blocked his creativity. It would seem not. I regretted this but
must admit that, while genuine, my regrets were somewhat
abstract. With my non-existent French, I was really in no
position to judge ELT as a poet; very little of his work had been
translated and most of that restricted to his burst of creativity
during the war. Even so, I am in a position to suggest what kind
of poet he seemed to be.

As in all his activities, his poetry alternates between a taste for
black humour of a somewhat dadaist persuasion (for despite the
years of faithful adherence to Breton's orthodox Surrealism, he
never lost his taste for Dada pranks) and a lyricism, at times

extraordinarily moving and most of it inspired by love. Like many of the surrealist painters and poets he was unable to suppress a resentful yet unavoidable nostalgia for his Edwardian childhood often in contrast to present disillusion. Here is an example, 'Sing Song', dedicated to his friend and mentor PG Van Hecke.

SING SONG

My weariness is equal to my misery
My misery handed over to the scaffold
My weariness is of lead
And my misery of gold
Calendar escaped from the past
I remember the time of crinolines
Orangeades, orangeades
Hair extinguished for ever.

Those who came to listen to me
Taught me to lie
Those who came to help me
Covered me with pitch
Calendar counting over the past
I remember a time of columbines
Orangeades orangeades
Hair extinguished for ever.

And here I am – lost in the desert
Immobile, but without a pedestal
Heavy as gold
And dull as lead
Calendar turned towards the past
I remember the time of mandolines
Orangeades orangeades
Hair extinguished for ever.

This poem makes it clear that, however surreal his imagery,

Edouard was a careful poetic craftsman. There is nothing of the automatist about him. His poetry is as considered as the visual images of his friend Magritte. Note for instance the careful inversion of 'gold' and 'lead' in verses one and three. How the 'calendar' having 'escaped from the past' is discovered 'counting over the past' and finally 'turned towards the past'.

His ability to write poetry was apparently directly linked to what he was up to elsewhere. He produced a quite substantial amount of work throughout most of his carefree twenties, but almost none between 1928 and 1939 when his work as a dealer and exhibition organiser was at its height. The war freed him again. The London Gallery and the bitter struggle to keep it open banished his muse. She never came back! As far as I can make out, the rest of his life yielded only nine poems, most of those written for specific occasions. My impression is that he was a good surrealist poet rather than a great one like Paul Eluard. There is however one masterpiece, a rare moment of inspiration that almost wrote itself.

In 1930, confined to hospital, he produced in two afternoons twenty-six short poems. The fact that there are also twenty-six letters in the alphabet is no coincidence for the book, when it was published later that year, was called *Alphabet Sourd Aveugle* (*Alphabet for the Deaf and Blind*) and has an admiring preface by Paul Eluard.

Lying there, ELT had this spontaneous image of a large capital letter, printed in alphabetical order, one to each page, and forming the first letter of each line, a form of alliteration, but it would be clearer to demonstrate than to describe:

ion
unaire jouant de
a
yre au bord d'un
ac sera tué par
egion
aique

The moon Lion playing the Lyre on the shore of the Lake will be killed by the Laique Legion. Child-like as a concept, not unlike those games, Exquisite Corpses for instance, the *Alphabet* manages to be both absurd and tragic. I am most reminded of Edward Lear, and would not be too surprised if the owl and the pussy-cat strolling on the shores of the lake after their wedding on the isle where the Bong tree grows should have recoiled in horror and pity to come across the slaughtered body of the moon lion, his lyre beside him kicked to pieces by the sandals of the legionnaires.

Alphabet Sourd Aveugle, if he had written nothing else, would ensure ELT Mesens a place in the pantheon of surrealist poets.

In regretting Edouard's inability to turn again to poetry after the war, I was correct in thinking that the fire was out. Later, when I interviewed him for *Art and Artists* in 1966 he admitted it: 'I wrote a few poems but discovered words were inadequate to express myself as I wished.' Where I was wrong was to be pessimistic. It was verbal poetry which had turned her back on him. A new mistress had him in view and waited her chance.

In 1954, at the Venice Biennial, among the old and modern Belgian masters including Magritte and Delvaux, hung three of ELT's pre-war collages and, rather to his surprise, 'they held their own'.

On his return to London he began to work. From then on, and for the rest of his life, collage became his chosen means of expression, much of his material drawn from those drawers full of accumulated rubbish which had so irritated Sybil.

I have already mentioned Edouard's collages, but only in relation to Magritte's hurtful dismissal and David Sylvester's low valuation of the later work in comparison to his pre-war, Ernst-like images. Magritte, in that he admired almost no contemporary art, may be dismissed as bitchy. Sylvester's opinion is his own. As for myself, while making no claims beyond my belief that ELT Mesens was certainly a *petit maître* in this field, I would maintain that he was a true artist and, on one occasion touched by greatness.

ELT's post-Biennial collages fall into two main categories: on the one hand visual punning and absurdist humour, and on the other the pleasure principle, sometimes lyrical but more often constructivist. Both tendencies are established in his first two works after his return from Venice.

The first, 'The Evidence I Love' shows the white silhouette of a hand which simultaneously represents the upright body of a cat with a realistic head floating above a night landscape in a void between two cliffs. The cat-headed hand is both funny and disquieting. As to how five fingers can form the four legs of a cat, the answer is that the middle finger represents its tail.

In one sense 'The Evidence I Love' is a transitional work. The cat's head would seem to be cut out from a nineteenth-century steel engraving; the weapon which Ernst, Mesens and almost everyone else during the thirties used to suspend our disbelief when faced with dream or nightmare-like events.

His second collage, 'Valori Plastici' is a long, narrow composition using tickets and labels, the first fruit of Edouard's accumulation mania, and a marriage of Schwitters's respect for the discarded, and Mondrian's strict geometry. Its potential severity is betrayed by the harmony of pinks, greys and blues, the colours of those faded proofs of distant or recent journeys. A later but rather similar work is entitled 'Comings and Goings'.

Sometimes, in the works that followed, geometry and humour combine, most notably in 'The World of Plenty'. Hundreds of letter Ts of all sizes and type faces are crowded together in near-claustrophobic conditions, and yet the rigidity of the letter T imposes an order on the composition, which Edouard has quite consciously exploited.

After 'The Evidence I Love', Mesens never again resorted to steel engravings, he would sometimes use photographic images: perhaps a set of thirties cigarette cards depicting footballers, their faces concealed behind black rectangles like criminals, or a reference to his shaving rituals incorporating many immaculately flattened blue wrappers repeating the moustached likeness of King Gillette himself. Less often he would incorporate real elements. In 'Cult Object' (his titles are carefully chosen) the picture surface is divided into three strips containing, respectively, a rubber glove, a satin bow and a lipstick. Glove, bow and lipstick are all an identical dark red. It's a glamorous object, but also a clear reference to Chirico's 'Love Song', the picture which had alerted Magritte to the existence of an alternative path.

It is Mesens's diversity of means and intention which distinguishes his work. His friend, the cineaste and essayist Jacques Brunius, wrote:

> 'So we arrive, precisely, at the manner in which
> the techniques of collage, the elements of
> collage, are utilised. But of manner there is
> none, properly speaking, or rather all manners
> are there. Only the spirit remains a recognisable
> constant.'

This is broadly true, although I believe that Klee and Schwitters are often present; the latter at times a little too much in evidence, and that the violin, the leaf, and the hand can also become overused. But not always. One of his finest works is called 'Starry Violin Giving Birth to a Pointillist Child', and its title, leaving aside its ravishing colour and minutely adjusted composition, is completely accurate. I can still hear ELT laughing at its dead-pan absurdity.

With the exception of two years when he did not work, ELT Mesens produced up to a maximum of forty collages a year almost up until his death. Why forty and no more? I never asked him, but I suspect it to be related to the same absurdist Duchamp-like mathematics as the selection of the razor blades. At all events, forty a year between 1954 and 1971, even allowing for gaps and shortfalls, is a great many collages and the majority are at the very least interesting and frequently admirable. I saw almost all of them as they were completed, because whenever I visited him he would first give me 'a good helping' of whisky, and then show me the latest work or works and ask my opinion. He was never stupid so there was no point in praising everything even if I had wanted to, but one morning in 1955, he placed a larger piece than usual on the mantel-shelf in front of me, and there was nothing I could say but 'It's a masterpiece' and nothing he could do but agree with me. He had seventeen years left and would never produce its equal. He gave it to Sybil and so in effect it stayed with him. It is now in the Tate Gallery. It's called 'The Sleepwalker'.

In a black night floats a large varnished fragment of torn newspaper somehow resembling an imaginary continent. Through a hole in this newspaper a moon, trapped in a sack or jug, throws a little light despite its short black rays.

To the right of the picture is a wall, the colour of the newspaper and, skirting it, a pavement along which (the same colour, always the same colour) stomps the Sleepwalker. Crude and expressive as a child's drawing, wearing a hat yet featureless, his club-foot crashes down ahead of him. His navel, the centre of his being, is a tiny wheel. He is both pathetic and malevolent; a true surrealist phantom.

In this picture, born of the night (for he worked mostly at night), ELT Mesens touched greatness.

There were occasional failures among Edouard's collages. The odd injection of Belgian Expressionism was seldom helpful, and equally intrusive were his rare resorts to hand-drawn elements. Edouard couldn't draw, he never denied it for an instant, but every now and then he would introduce a tracing of his hand, that after all required no draftsmanship, and a simplified face or a star or an isolated eye. The effect was inevitably clumsy and unconvincing. Happily such elements are rare.

What he did have, however, was a faultless colour-sense. This he never applied for aesthetic reasons only, but to intensify the impact of the image.

He always titled his work – most of them light-heartedly, some were deliberately absurd, many involved puns, none were merely descriptive. He named them, he once told me 'to protect them from a certain banal interpretation'.

Almost as soon as he started to make collages again Edouard began to exhibit his work, finding dealers not only in London and Brussels, but with particular success in Italy. Cynics, not exactly thin on the ground in the art world, might and did say that, at a time when Magritte's prices were beginning to climb, not to mention those of Dada and Surrealism in general, it would be advantageous to dealers to offer a show to a man with an enormous holding of the former and important pictures by many other artists associated with the two movements. In some cases there may have been something in it, but even if ELT suspected it, he would have enjoyed manipulating and outmanoeuvring those who imagined they were stringing him along. There was a strong element of Volpone in ELT Mesens. For whatever reason, at the front of the catalogue of a large exhibition at the Grosvenor Gallery in 1961, there is a list of over sixty museums and private collectors who had bought his work.

ELT was a true and fastidious artist. The last decade of his life, for all its escalating despair, was in part made bearable by the acceptance of his work by others. Of course it was never enough. He used to send me from abroad not only catalogues, not only major reviews, but any mention of his name, even in the provincial Flemish press. To the very end he thought of the world as his father who, whatever he achieved, treated him as a disreputable lunatic, and refused to pay his fare 'even on the platform of a tram'.

Nine

Temptation of ordering a new drink; for instance a
wrecking with a drop of plane tree.

BRETON AND SOUPAULT

After the gallery closed and the Mesenses moved into their new
flat, Edouard asked me to help him hang his collection. Knowing
that this meant doing all the donkey-work – he had a convenient
hernia when it came to lifting anything heavier than a leaf – I
agreed, but on condition I was given money to buy new tools. I
suspected, and rightly, that he had transported every twisted eye-
screw, bent nail and all the white-washed string from the gallery.
He was very reluctant but eventually, realising I meant it, he gave
in.

The flat was in Montague Mansions, a rather dark, fairly
narrow street of tall Pont Street Dutch apartments just off Baker
Street. The hanging took a long time, partially because I was
often on tour with Mick Mulligan, partially because it was the
period when Edouard was most insistent on sexual experimenta-
tion, but mostly (and I was by no means averse to this particular
ploy), because as soon as it was opening time, he proposed we
visit one of the two public houses on the other side of Baker
Street which had replaced the Democ and the Aristoc. One was
called the Beehive the other the Barley Mow. (Despite my
sustained efforts to correct him he always pronounced Mow to
rhyme with cow.) When the hanging was finally done I saw him
less often.

In 1956 Edouard and Sybil moved a mile or so north, to a
larger and lighter flat in St John's Wood. It was on the first floor

of a three-sided neo-Georgian mansion block, built during the thirties, faced Lord's Cricket Ground and, more to the point as far as Edouard was concerned, Lord's Tavern.

It was much more convenient. There was room in a recess in one of the corridors to build a wooden rack for those pictures he didn't choose to hang, and much more wall space for those he did. A room at the back was transformed into a studio for his collage-making while another, shelved from floor to ceiling, housed his immaculate library. In the living-room, over the grand piano, hung Sybil's once despised, now cherished Léger and elsewhere most of his best pictures were interspersed, in the manner of Breton's apartment in the rue Fontaine, with tribal objects.

The front door had enough locks, bolts and chains to satisfy a nervous fence or crack-dealer, but then ELT was always paranoid about security, especially because he never insured anything, to avoid having the escalating value of his collection on record. As it is impossible to secure bolts and chains from outside, the flat was actually more secure when he was in, but this flaw in logic never seemed to occur to him. Even if he had seen me arrive by appointment through the window and acknowledged it by waving, he would wait until I was outside the door and then take over a minute pulling back bolts, releasing chains, and finally un-double-locking the Chubb before letting me in ('Good morning, Doctor') in his expensive silk dressing-gown. In the living-room his latest collage would be already at hand for my appraisal.

Edouard, rather to my relief, hadn't asked me to hang the pictures this time round but had hired a handyman. I suspect this was because our physical liaison was over and he thought I might be hurt at his failure to renew it during the long periods which would have been available. Bearing this delusion in mind, I have always exercised scepticism in my ability to seduce or to believe my younger lovers.

During most of the fifties I saw less of the Mesenses than at any other time. This had nothing to do with a waning of interest and affection on my part, although I admit I did become a little weary of Sybil's sustained disapproval, whether justifiable or not, at my scruffiness, drunkenness and boastful promiscuity. I was not, after all, any longer an employee of the London Gallery, still less under Miss Fenton's supervision at Dickie and Johnny. Still, Sybil was at work all day, and Edouard was far less inclined to carp. There were other reasons for the temporary gap in our relationship.

I was more often than not on tour with Mick Mulligan while Edouard was often on business in Europe. Quite early in the fifties I married for the first time, and, although my wife very soon left me to live in Rome, her lack of empathy with the Mesenses and their mutual antipathy to her meant that our rare meetings were distinctly chilly. (In the very late fifties she returned to try again. It was no more successful and neither had her opinion of Edouard and Sybil changed nor theirs of her.) My bursts of libertinism alternating with short but absorbing affairs and more or less constant 'derangement of the senses' left me little time for quiet domesticity in St John's Wood.

Another move I made wasn't too popular either, at any rate with Sybil. After the collapse of my marriage (Round One) I had moved in with Simon Watson Taylor, ex-secretary of the by now almost completely atrophied Surrealist Group in England, and they had never really got on. An actor when I first met him, he had become an air steward by this time, flying mostly to New York. We suited each other very well, both being fanatically tidy (a surrealist characteristic) and both of us lovers of drink (Simon bought several crates of Merrydown Cider every month for which I paid half). Blond, almost white hair *en brosse*, eye sardonic, tongue witty but merciless, he was a formidable figure. Although he owned some nice things himself, he was delighted with the surrealist 'Old Masters' I brought with me, as indeed I was with his enormous collection of rare jazz 78s, which he kept in strict alphabetical order in a walk-in cupboard.

Finally, he was not only sexually tolerant, but encouraging

and even at times participatory. He always claimed his motto was 'Man, woman or dog – we throw it on a bed'! The few years I spent in that rather dark basement flat were, for the most part, extraordinarily happy.

One evening, I have forgotten why, we visited St John's Wood together and I was surprised that Edouard, usually generosity itself when it comes to pouring out drinks, seemed reluctant to offer us any. I realised he must have his reasons, but Simon, whose middle name was never tact, felt no compunction at all in asking for and eventually demanding a scotch.

ELT at first pretended not to hear him but finally, under Sybil's increasingly suspicious eye, poured him out a very small one, and asked (hopefully) if Simon took water. Simon made it quite clear he didn't, accepted the glass, took a mouthful, and spat it out in disgust. 'But this *is* watered!' he protested. 'In fact it's almost all water!' Sybil picked up the bottle and sniffed it. She said nothing, but her look spoke volumes. It was obvious what had happened. In an attempt to limit his drinking, she kept an eye on the bottle. ELT, perhaps during a night working on a collage, had sought increasing liquid inspiration, but on his final visit took in how little remained had topped it up from the tap, intending to replace it later. He had either no opportunity or had forgotten to do so when Simon and I turned up.

Edouard could match Sybil as a martinet, particularly when it came to etiquette in restaurants. This in no way applied to his table manners; he would always use his fingers rather than relinquish a tasty but knife and fork resistant morsel, and was especially rigorous when it came to the sparse segments of fish entrapped along the very bony fringes of a Dover sole. I resisted following his example but I was always reproached for it: 'No, Doctor,' he would chide me as he rather messily put precept into practice. 'You should always suck the beard. It is the most distinguished meat!'

His rancour then was aroused not by any petit bourgeois gentility when it came to transferring food from plate to mouth (here Gargantua would have passed muster) but in the correct behaviour of a guest in relation to the host and, as the latter was almost inevitably ELT, it was as well to watch ones Ps and Qs.

The most memorable demonstration of this hazard yet again involved Simon Watson Taylor, although it was only indirectly responsible for the subsequent explosion. Shortly after the incident of the watered whisky, ELT invited Simon and myself to dine at the Ivy. Sybil was not amongst the company (perhaps she was away on business or had made an excuse, for she had no love of Simon and his refusal to compromise for the sake of social ease). The other guest was Simon's mistress, a warm-hearted, doe-eyed, olive-skinned Italian girl called Lorenza whom he treated rather badly although, it has to be said, the more cavalier his behaviour, the more she seemed to adore him.

Perhaps because of Sybil's absence, Edouard plied us with bottle after bottle of excellent wine and, as so often when drinking, but not yet drunk, was at his most charming and inventive. Finally there was the best brandy ('Give me a good helping,' he told the perplexed *sommelier*) and cigars. Edouard chose one, with much rustling close to his ear, and so did Simon and I. It was then that Lorenza, emboldened perhaps by drink, asked if she too could have one. Edouard, while surprised, said of course she could, but while the waiter was reverently applying the cigar-cutter, noticed her slipping her Romeo y Juliet into her bag.

In a deceptively soft voice (which I recognised as a harbinger of trouble from my days at the gallery) Edouard asked Lorenza if it were for Simon to smoke later. Eyes proud with love she admitted this to be the case. After brooding for a few moments, Edouard shouted so loudly as to silence the entire restaurant: 'A REAL WHORE'S TRICK!'

Lorenza, hurling the cigar on the table, burst into tears. Simon did nothing to comfort or defend her, but smiled slightly with what I suspect to have been a certain pride. Eventually Edouard calmed down. Lorenza stopped crying and we parted outside Zwemmer's without further incident, but leaving behind us the ruins of what, up until then had been an enchanting evening.

ELT as hen-pecked husband, ELT as social arbiter, but his next encounter with Simon showed him up as still capable of that financial deviousness which I found the least attractive of his various personae. One Sunday at about midday he arrived in a taxi at Tregunter Road with a picture-shaped parcel under his arm. Leaving this for the moment in the hall he entered our living-room and demanded 'a good helping of whisky'.

As it happened, my father was staying with me on one of his rare visits to London and preferring, as was his nature, to sleep on a sofa however uncomfortable to being put to the expense of an hotel. Meanwhile my current girlfriend, a Bahamian night-club dancer given to unpredictable outbursts of violence ('Decorative but not restful,' was my father's fair if understated description) was cooking us brunch wearing a baby-doll nighty, a spectacle which predictably enchanted ELT.

'Is it not marvellous,' he said while apparently addressing an invisible spectator, a constant trick of his, 'to discover George's mistress cooking toasts for his father!' Yet despite his geniality I was perfectly aware that this was no social visit and, with the wrapped picture in the hall, I'd a good idea as to what he was up to.

Shortly after, Simon emerged from his bedroom, wearing a dressing-gown, and none too amiable as he had only flown in from New York late the previous night. Almost immediately ELT turned into the nose-tapping businessman I hadn't seen since I'd left the gallery six years before and had hoped never to re-encounter. The reason for his visit was actually my doing. I had mentioned at our last meeting that someone had left Simon two Max Ernsts. They were not major works, I'd told him. One was a tiny although cherishable picture of a frog, the other a not especially distinguished example from a series of 'flower' pictures – the flowers were produced by some automatic process and, I imagine, were very saleable, hence their proliferation.

After examining them with modified rapture, Edouard went into the hall. I realised what he was up to, but daren't try to alert Simon because most likely he would have asked me why I was shaking my head and pointing at the Ernsts. ELT returned with his parcel and unwrapped it to reveal a medium-sized picture by Edith Rimmington; the British surrealist whom I had first met at the Barcelona almost a decade before. Edith, an immaculate crafts-person, was an uneven surrealist, but the picture we were looking at was, in my view, her very best.

It was called 'The Oneiroscopist' and was painted in strong yet sombre colours. On a wooden pier-like structure sits a strange anthropomorphic figure wearing an old-fashioned diving suit. Although it has large, dark-red hands resting on its knees, the creature has the skeletal head and feet of a man-sized bird. By its side, resting on the platform, is its helmet but it is immediately evident that its long beak would render it impractical. The platform on which the creature sits is clearly very high up as it is surrounded by clouds and, through a gap, there is a glimpse of the wrinkled sea far below and the top of what must be an extremely tall ladder just peeping above the edge of the diver's perch to show how it gained this lonely eminence.

Edouard rested it deliberately close to the Ernst flowers (which in consequence looked rather drab) and launched into a panegyric on Edith's virtues. I suspect his intention was to offer a small amount of money and 'The Oneiroscopist' in exchange for if not two, one of the Ernsts. He had no chance to formulate such an offer. Simon interrupted him and in that world-weary way he had of exorcising a possibly boring conversation, declared himself willing, with no money mentioned, to swap both Ernsts for the Rimmington.

I glanced at Edouard and, as I'd suspected, he looked rather put out, deprived of opposition and the consequent slow wearing-down of objection, which would have made his inevitable victory the sweeter. After a few more 'good helpings' he left 'with' a taxi and both Ernsts (his objective after all) but with an air of defeat.

As soon as he'd gone I reproached Simon. They may not have been very good Ernsts, but they would always be worth much more than a Rimmington, however superior in quality. Simon said he knew that perfectly well, but he liked the Rimmington better. He had recently deserted Breton to join the pataphysicians, a group of malcontent, largely ex-surrealists, who had founded a mock-academic 'college' devoted to the works of Alfred Jarry. Nevertheless that day, in ignoring any financial considerations, he proved himself more truly surreal than me with my realism or ELT in his manifestation as a petit bourgeois Belgian tradesman.

My father was rather relieved at my realistic analysis of the situation. He had after all lent me money to invest in modern art, and it remains a regret of mine that he died just before the upswing in the value of the surrealist masters. Not that he ever reproached me, that wasn't in his nature.

Simon's benign, indifferent or possibly sardonic acceptance of Edouard's con-trick puzzled me considerably. Yet it turned out to be a mere exercise, a limbering up in comparison to what he was to do some years later, long after we had parted company.

Resigning from his airline not far short of a substantial pension, he sold everything he had: his library of rare books, his amazing collection of early jazz records (many on their original labels), his pictures, and what's more, sold them far short of their real value, accepting the first offer without argument. With this money he became a lotus-eating beach-bum on the shores of the Far East, returning to this country only intermittently (and typically) to visit his dentist.

Although he turned his back on Surrealism over forty years ago, no one I've ever known has followed with such literal dedication, one of its earliest precepts – 'Change Your Life!'

Although I was seeing less of Edouard during the fifties he spontaneously did me several real favours. There was the letter of introduction to Magritte, but also the telephone number of André Breton who seduced me utterly; the most charismatic figure I've ever met.

Towards the end of the decade, my life was about to change. My Bahamian girlfriend left for Europe, my wife had returned from Rome and after renting a posh flat in a smart postal district, we bought a rather twee terraced cottage on the Golders Green edge of Hampstead Heath.

At the same time my satirical script for Wally 'Trog' Fawkes's strip-cartoon 'Flook' had gradually attracted a lot of favourable attention and, as a result, I'd begun to be asked to write for the glossies and quite often to compère on the BBC light programme. Disillusioned with touring, I began to think that I might leave the jazz world and see if I could earn a living through my pen. Victoria was not best pleased to realise that I'd be at home most of the time, but as I had as yet several months of contracts to fulfil it turned out she had no reason to fret.

One Saturday morning in the early sixties I called, by appointment as always, on Edouard and Sybil, and found them both in a very friendly mood. I'd already told ELT that I was to leave the jazz world, and no doubt this accounted in part for Sybil's change of tack (my mother was equally pleased). Sybil had also read my piece in *Vogue* and heard me several times on the radio. 'We thoroughly approve of what you're doing,' she said.

It did occur to me of course that what I was actually doing was becoming a journalist (weren't they meant to be 'hyenas, scorpions, vultures, swine first-class?') and that furthermore I was in direct breach of ELT's edict that surrealists must only contribute to surrealist publications, but I didn't push it. Anyway, my *Vogue* piece was entitled 'Where are the Surrealists Now?' and stressed that the movement was intended to be a revolutionary concept rather than an aesthetic school, and on top of that the article was illustrated in the main by the early work of René Magritte.

No doubt all that had pleased Edouard too, but what had restored me entirely to his good books was that I had recently written an insulting letter to Roland Penrose. I didn't write it for Edouard's sake, but for my own, and even today I feel I was right to do so. In 1960 Roland organised a wonderful Picasso retrospective at the Tate Gallery. So far so good. It was, however, to be opened by the Duke of Edinburgh, and whether or not this had been Roland's idea was in my view immaterial. He had accepted it.

I imagine I'd have written whichever member of the royal family had been chosen, but Prince Philip, an open philistine, was by far the least appropriate. Here was a man who frequently delighted the saloon bars by openly mocking modern art, now called upon to introduce a great artist, arguably the greatest of the twentieth century. Worse! Picasso was meant to be 'honoured'. (It seemed to me 'insulted' would be a more appropriate word.) What was Roland thinking of in asking this tetchy ram-rod to read out a speech written no doubt by some establishment creep like Sir Kenneth Clark? 'Are you after a title?' I concluded rhetorically. Only it wasn't rhetorical after all. Some years later Roland was knighted.

Roland always struck me as a weak rather than a wicked man. His wife, Lee Miller, was, on the contrary, immensely powerful ('A tough wench,' was Sybil's description) and he never really stood much of a chance. If she fancied being 'Lady Penrose', then it was inevitable that Roland must kneel before his sovereign.

Years later, when Roland and I became friends, he never mentioned this letter. Perhaps he never got it. Perhaps some secretary at the Tate or ICA opened it, read it, concluded it was from a lunatic, scrumpled it up and threw it in the wastepaper basket.

In 1961 Victoria fell in love with a rich film director, told everyone our child wasn't mine, and left Sandy Road for Grosvenor Square.

She let me in on her intentions the very morning I'd gone into her bedroom to tell her I'd fallen desperately in love with a girl called Diana Moynihan and so I was leaving her. Although naturally it took some of the wind out of her sails, Victoria took this quite well, and, within a very short time she'd gone and Diana had moved in.

Naturally enough we began to meet each other's friends, and eventually I took her down to St John's Wood to introduce her to

Edouard. I asked her the other day what she remembered of this first encounter.

'Not much,' she said, 'a picture with biscuits [de Chirico] and a man carrying on like Maurice Chevalier.'

While never denying his intelligence, Diana didn't take to Edouard. She was completely unmoved, repelled even, by the exaggerated continental gallantry, still more by the poetic appraisal of her breasts. Knowing that he meant a great deal to me, she remained perfectly correct, although quite soon after we were together, she encouraged me to visit him alone. Sybil she found 'all right', but even so they were both definitely 'my friends'.

They, on the other hand, were enchanted with her. No doubt, given half a chance, Sybil would like to have 'smartened her up', for at that time Diana wore rather extreme, slightly tarty clothes which in only a few years were to become the norm, but in 1961 were still the antithesis of the 'garments' displayed in the windows of Dickie and Johnny. Sybil recognised, behind the rather Sally Bowles façade, an idealistic realism in direct contrast to Victoria's acquisitive whimsicality. It was obvious that she looked to Diana to restore me to my pre-jazz persona – less of a hooligan; cleaner and more presentable – and here she was in part gratified, but more as a result of my obsessive and exclusive love than any Fenton-like resort to snaffle and bit.

Edouard had no criticism at all to offer. For him she personified one of the two surrealist feminine ideals: not the 'vampire-seductress' but the 'child-woman'. She did somewhat resemble the identical tumble-haired girls of that chic and decadent figure Leonore Fini, the painter of hats, swamps and sexually convenient railway carriages, and in one of Leonore's paintings especially, there are a number of sphinxes so like Diana that she could have modelled for all of them.

In 1959, when I was still with Victoria, Edouard's collected poems had been published in Paris, and he'd presented us with an exuberantly inscribed copy illuminated in coloured inks. 'Celebration of victoriennes fêtes' he wrote at the top and then

'To Vicky and George Melly'. On the opposite page he ammended it to 'Succession as queen by DIANE the huntress'.

Ten

Then the snake
Got entangled with the rake,
And the cock
Got a very nasty knock,
And the hen said: 'We'll never come again to
Johnny Crows's garden.'
                    LEONARD LESLIE BROOKE

The first half of the sixties (excluding his early days with
Magritte) were perhaps the happiest years of Edouard's life. Like
many north Europeans he fell completely in love with Italy and,
once Sybil had retired, they spent a lot of time there.

Milan was the centre of his activities. Not only did he exhibit
at the Galleria del Naviglio, but he became much loved and
cherished by a group of lively young artists whose leader was
called Enrico Baj. Baj was a talented man who made collages
utilising wallpaper and cloth to construct satirical portraits of
figures of authority wearing medals, orders and epaulettes, and
related to the more sombre personages of Dubuffet. But if Milan
remained, partially for professional reasons, the centre of his life
in Italy, he and Sybil often travelled elsewhere for pure pleasure,
and he would send me postcards pressing us to join them.

I believe he only visited Rome on one or two occasions, and it
was certainly as far south as he ever went, but he came back
from it full of enthusiasm despite the proximity of the pope. It
wasn't so much the famous sights he told me. What they liked to
do was turn off the main thoroughfares at random and to find
themselves in a small square with a café and a fountain or an

ancient statue. He described these discoveries with great enthusiasm. He loved the life of the streets, the exaggerated gestures, the shouts and embraces.

Yet there is no doubt in my mind that Venice was his especial favourite, not just because it resembled Bruges. During one visit he sent me a menu in a large format of a small trattoria they had discovered. 'You and Diana should come here,' he wrote, 'look at the prices!' The prices were in no way his reason for sending us the menu. It was its cover, a collage by him, to which he wished, and why not, to draw my attention. I found this naïve device rather touching. 'Look at the prices!' indeed.

Many years later, long after he was dead, I was in Venice making two films for the BBC about pictures in the Guggenheim museum. By chance, in that rather bleak district behind the Accademia, I entered a trat and recognised not only the menu cover, but several of Edouard's framed collages on the walls. I almost burst into tears. 'The Certainty of Hazard' can be very disturbing on occasion.

The only bone of contention between Sybil and Edouard, or so he told me, was that she insisted on sunbathing on the Lido instead of exploring the city and discovering its hidden treasures. It quite upset him, he said, that with all the wonders to explore she preferred to lie on the beach, to read a 'tecy'. Then he said something which seemed to me very odd, a truism today but certainly not in the sixties: 'Besides Doctor, the sun. It's not good for her by the way.'

Throughout the sixties ELT Mesens was establishing himself more widely as a collagist. As well as Milan there was an exhibition at the Grosvenor Gallery in London in 1961. In Brussels he showed at the Palais des Beaux-Arts, scene of his earlier employment. He exhibited at the Galerie de la Madeleine in 1966 and several times at the Galerie Isy Brachot, both in Brussels. In 1963 Knokke Le Zoute, home of his earlier triumphs as an exhibition organiser, mounted a full-scale show. He was invited to participate in many important mixed shows in Belgium and elsewhere, he was represented in innumerable private collections and began to enter museums, including the Tate. Every day the sun shone brighter on ELT Mesens, but never enough to warm away his paranoid suspicions and, as is so often the case with paranoics, every now and then something happened to reinforce his beliefs.

In 1964, at a time when Mark Boxer's *Sunday Times Colour Supplement* had overcome its teething problems and established a new form of journalism, I was approached by David Sylvester, the great art critic and employed by Mark at that time, to ask me to contribute to a series they were intending to run on modern British artists. I proposed Edouard and this was accepted. Then I did something which was, in retrospect, very foolish. I told ELT and naturally he was delighted.

A week or two later Mark himself rang me up and said he was withdrawing the offer. He had decided that all the artists had to be British-born. I didn't believe him and I was proved right, when a month or so later, the series started and an article was devoted to the American-born Ron Kitaj. Admittedly he was domiciled here, but so was Mesens.

My own conclusion as to why my piece had been rejected was that it broke one of Mark's editorial rules. It would have been about someone he had never heard of. He believed, and *vis-à-vis* the *Colour Supplement* was probably right, that he was absolutely 'in touch' and that anyone he hadn't taken aboard wasn't worth bothering about. I based my supposition on experience. Whenever I wrote for him there was usually something, given my dada/surrealist background, that he cut. A reference to Jarry's *Ubu Roi* was one such example, well enough known I'd have thought, but not it seemed to Mark, so out it went.

The other day I asked David Sylvester if he remembered the Mesens case. He didn't, but recalled the series and that there was something suspect about it. It was meant to be long-running but after only four pieces had been published Mark had dropped the whole thing. His explanation was that following the appraisement of Patrick Heron his entire contemporaneous exhibition had sold out, and Mark felt that people might suspect that the *Colour Supplement* was acting in the interests of Cork Street. It sounds plausible enough, but David is convinced, and he was after all there, that it was probably a lie, and the real explanation was concealed. Yet, whatever the truth of it, the cancellation of my piece was only a small side issue, but not of course to ELT.

I had to tell him and was very nervous about it. I simply repeated what Mark had said, and I was especially apprehensive in that it was based, or appeared to be based, on British artistic chauvinism, the central argument (and not without foundation) in Edouard's paranoid system. However, greatly to my surprise and certainly to my relief, he did no more than shrug. What I didn't know, but should have suspected, was that the name Mark Boxer was being filed under 'E' for 'Enemies'.

In the winter of sixty-four Diana and I moved from the twee Heath to one of the imposing stuccoed mid-Victorian houses in Gloucester Crescent, NW1 where, on quiet nights, you could hear the lions roaring in nearby Regent's Park zoo.

Once posh (Dickens had lived there for a time), most of the houses had become cheap B and Bs for Irish labourers or squalid bedsits. Then, with that cunning ability to spot potential in a run-down area which is the gift of those connected with the media, the colonisers landed, and within a remarkably short time they'd taken over the whole street.

With their knocked-through kitchens and sanded floors, their Morris papers and their children with names like Emma and Tristram, the families of Gloucester Crescent became a rather 'in' joke, chronicled at first by Alan Bennett, and later by Mark Boxer in his other role as elegantly waspish cartoonist.

We were amongst the second wave of middle-class, Labour-voting, CND-supporting settlers (the Nicholas Tomalins and Jonathan Millers were true pioneers), but the houses were still absurdly cheap. Admittedly they were also in terrible repair so they didn't turn out to be as cheap as all that, but they were pretty impressive all the same.

When we were more or less straight the Mesenses came to inspect it. As they were leaving, ELT assumed his persona as a paid-up member of the Belgian bourgeoisie. 'This is a real house,' he said, a statement almost as disconcerting as Magritte's 'This is not a pipe'.

In 1965 my first book was published. It was called *Owning Up* and described my life in the jazz world during the previous decade. It had been commissioned by George Weidenfeld whom I had met through Diana. It was George's custom to throw rather grand book launches in his luxurious house or flat. For me however there was no such party. Perhaps he was apprehensive of the number of swear words and mildly explicit sex on offer. Perhaps he didn't think I was established enough to warrant the expense. I'd have got over it anyway (and especially as the reviews, with the exception of Philip Larkin, were exceptionally positive) but then George went too far. He sent me a message, through an employee, that he'd give me thirty pounds 'to entertain some journalists in a pub'!

Diana and I were furious, and in revenge decided to hold our own book launch at Gloucester Crescent and invite, not only George, but every glamorous person we knew. Although, predictably, George didn't show up, we made sure he heard all about it. Naturally we asked the Mesenses, and I was pleased that amongst those who did accept were David Webster, an old Liverpool friend of my mother's, by now managing director of Covent Garden and, more particularly in this instance, his partner Jimmy Bell. Jimmy was a top executive at Aquascutum, the smart Regent Street shop famous for its raincoats. Sybil had met him before through business and I thought it would be nice for her to recognise someone, as she tended, unlike Edouard, to be rather shy in social situations. As it was she never got to exchange a word with Jimmy Bell.

Apart from distinguished neighbours like Jonathan and Alan and many friends unknown to the general public, I am able to write down a list of some of the people there because the children answered the door, and having shown the arrivals a piece of kid's writing paper on which they'd scribbled: 'Come to the Di and Goge party if you are inVitid', they then collected some of their autographs, albeit on a haphazard basis. Amongst those 'inVitid' were: James Joll, distinguished historian; John Russell, art critic of the *Sunday Times*; Rory McEwan, artist and folk singer; Alun Owen, TV playwright; Dee Wells, journalist and televiser; Penelope and John Mortimer, 'Pumpkin Eater' and 'Rumpole', Joan Bakewell, broadcaster; Suzi Gablik, writer and collagist; John Golding, painter, art historian and exhibition curator; David Sylvester, art critic and exhibition curator; Polly Devlin, novelist; Mark and Arabella Boxer, editor and cartoonist and cookery writer; Francis Wyndham, writer. These were just the names the children collected and they soon got bored. David and Jimmy weren't on it, for instance, because they arrived rather late.

'Your wife must be a genius,' screamed Jimmy as I showed them down into the vast kitchen where the food was, 'getting all these people to come to a party on a Friday night!' David, who was very greedy, headed for the buffet.

Edouard and Sybil also rang the bell after the children had given up. Sybil looked petrified at the size of the crowd, but Edouard was perfectly at ease. Jonathan Miller, whom I'd asked to pay him some attention, was doing just that, and I knew also that David Sylvester and John Russell wished him well. I felt able to circulate with a clear conscience, having made sure that Edouard was standing close to a bottle of whisky and could decide himself what he considered to be 'a good helping'.

It was really going well (the only fly in the ointment that George Weidenfeld wasn't there to see it) when someone, I entirely forget who, rushed up to me and said: 'There's a bit of trouble upstairs. This little short man with a foreign accent is shouting that he "wants to box Mr Boxer".'

So up I ran and there was Edouard, in a pugilistic stance, repeating at the top of his voice his not undiverting pun; a threat he would now be unable to fulfil as someone had tipped off Mark and Arabella and they had prudently made themselves scarce. Finally, although still threatening Mark spasmodically, Edouard calmed down sufficiently for Sybil to get him into a taxi. While we were waiting I grumbled about his behaviour, but she said she was entirely on his side. She thoroughly disapproved of 'socialite ostentation'. As the taxi drove off I could hear Edouard shouting with renewed single-minded emphasis that he was still determined to 'box Mr Boxer'.

The party continued into the small hours. The 'box Mr Boxer' incident, far from spoiling it, provided a talking point and added lustre to those who'd witnessed it. I, on the other hand, was a bit upset although naturally I didn't let on. It wasn't so much Edouard – he was, after all, reacting as he quite often did in his cups (as on the night of the Max Ernst party). Sybil I found altogether harder to excuse. I understood of course that when it came to handling ELT when out of control, it was easier to justify his behaviour, but she wasn't pretending. I found her accusation of 'social ostentation' ridiculous. My motives for giving the party may have been suspect, but those I invited were, in the main, serious creative people.

Sybil never mentioned the party again and nor, at any rate directly, did Edouard. Things returned to normal.

Eleven

The door someone opened
The door someone closed
The chair on which someone sat
The cat someone stroked
The fruit into which someone bit
The letter someone read
The chair someone upset
The door someone opened
The road where someone ran
The wood someone crossed
The river where someone threw himself
The hospital where someone died.

JACQUES PREVERT

One fine Saturday morning a few months after the party Sybil rang up to tell me, quite cheerfully, that she had leukaemia. I hadn't heard of it but as she sounded so matter of fact about it I thought it couldn't be too serious.

'Oh dear,' I said.

'Apparently you can live with it for quite a long time,' she said in that bright, neutral voice, 'even for several years.'

I began to realise that it was not only more serious than I'd at first imagined, but a death sentence. I told her I hadn't taken in what she'd said and I was desperately sorry. She didn't react to this, but described how they'd changed all her blood and she felt fine again. Would I like to have a word with Edouard?

Edouard didn't sound cheerful at all. He was coherent but only just, and had to keep stopping so as not to break down. I asked him how they'd found out she'd got it. He told me that she had been 'tired since several months', and that the other day she had come in from shopping and 'fallen into a chair with exhaustion and tears'. So he'd insisted she see her doctor and . . . but he couldn't go on, so I told him I'd come and see them that afternoon.

It didn't surprise me that Sybil should behave so well. It was equally predictable that Edouard should take it so hard. He loved Sybil obsessively, knew only too well that it was she who held his life together, and that when she died, now sooner rather than later, he would not be far behind.

After I'd put the phone down I walked up the crescent to ask Dr Miller about leukaemia. There is nothing Jonathan likes better than to expound, and within the hour I had learnt great deal about Sybil's condition, including the fact that although changing the blood instantly restored the patient to apparent health and well-being, it could only be effective a limited number of times. The disease, Jonathan explained, didn't kill you but, by destroying the white corpuscles, it left the body with no defence against infection and you died of any opportunist infection.

When I got home I spoke to my sister Andrée who loved Sybil dearly and was desperately upset.

Over the next few months Edouard, in Sybil's company at least, struggled and largely succeeded in controlling his despair, an effort which given his temperament verged on the heroic. In private he made no secret of his misery. His love, he explained, was no longer carnal. For several years now he slept in his studio, where in any case he often worked very late, 'sometimes it is dawn', on a collage. 'But if we met in the night [she presumably to pee, he to replenish his glass] we embraced with tenderness.'

For the rest of that summer and the subsequent autumn and winter Sybil, despite the occasional remission, began to decline. We asked them for Christmas lunch (no religious significance we assured them). Sybil brought us a poinsettia, that curious plant whose flowers are really terminal leaves. Unlike Edouard, I am not very superstitious, but I became convinced it wouldn't long outlive her.

Sybil made an effort to eat but could only manage a few mouthfuls. She was soon exhausted and went home. Very soon after she was moved into a nursing home in Circus Road, only a mile from their flat. It was staffed, ironically enough, by the White Sisters, an order of nuns, but Edouard made no protest. Perhaps as a continental he accepted it as the norm.

While controlling himself when visiting her, Edouard was drinking a terrifying amount, which always led to bursts of very inventive black humour and floods of tears.

I went to see Sybil almost at the end. She had great liver-coloured bruises under her eyes and was painfully thin, but her spirit was unbowed. When I bent down to kiss her she asked me to 'Look after the old man'. I promised to do my best, but I thought 'easier said than done'!

Sybil died on 7th January 1966, aged fifty-seven.

Edouard told me that the same night 'Le Noctambule', the beautiful collage he had given her, fell from the wall with a great crash. He also told me that when, alone, he had gone in to view her corpse, he had lifted her breasts: 'They were once so fine,' he said. 'So beautiful and proud, but now they were like two dried leaves.' Through racking sobs he repeated this simile, 'Two dried leaves! Two dried leaves!'

The year before ELT had not only completed his quota of forty collages but, uniquely, executed two extra. I don't know the subject of forty-one, but forty-two was called 'Ma Pauvre Chèrie'.

In 1966 he only made one. It was called 'Goodbye my beautiful darling'.

In 1967 he did none at all. In 1968 he began to work again.

A few days after her death, on a crisp and beautiful winter's morning, Sybil was cremated at Golders Green.

There were not many mourners. There was Andrée and her husband the actor Oscar Quitak. There was Diana and me. There was a quiet Belgian couple I believe Edouard and Sybil saw something of, and about sixteen or so employees of Dickins and Jones, for although Sybil had retired it was comparatively recently. I was surprised not to see Jacques Brunius or Conroy Maddox or indeed any of the surrealists, but especially Edith Rimmington and Eileen Agar who were Sybil's particular friends. Perhaps Edouard hadn't let them know. Perhaps there had been nothing in the newspapers. Perhaps he wanted to keep it discreet and, as it transpired, he was quite right to do so.

ELT arrived with André and Oscar wearing a good overcoat and a rather jaunty black persian lamb Russian hat. It was soon clear that, while physically in control, he was blind drunk. The first thing that happened was when one of those Magritte-like men whose job it is to add a note of solemnity to the battery-system of modern death handed Edouard an ornate card on which was a list, in gothic calligraphy, of those who had sent floral tributes, the majority of them from Dickie and Johnny (who let *them* know by the way?). Edouard looked at it with bemused incomprehension. Then he gave us a sample of what was to come. 'What's this?' he shouted. 'The menu?'

I don't remember the hearse arriving. My next clear recollection is of sitting next to Edouard with Andrée on his other side. We were flanked by Oscar and Diana while the Dickie and Johnny contingent sat together at the back of the Romanesque chapel. Even so, they would have heard every word Edouard said. It's a small building with excellent accoustics, and he was shouting.

Sybil lay in her coffin on the slip-way. As usual I found it hard to imagine someone I'd known and loved inside that neat box.

ELT kicked off fairly mildly. 'I asked for Satie,' he said, 'but it was not on offer, so it is Bach – the non-religious Bach, naturally. It is played not too badly by the way.'

We listened for a bit in grateful silence to the not-too-badly-played non-religious Bach, but it was not alas for long. Without warning Edouard suddenly shouted first at Andrée and then at me, 'Why do you not weep?'

This line of accusatory questioning continued for some time but then, after another brief pause, he veered on to another tack.

'Our little Italian cleaner,' he began, comparatively quietly, 'asked of me where "Madam is to be buried". I explained to her that Madam was to be cremated. Naturally she is a Catholic and was completely shocked. "Poor Madam is to be burnt, burnt!" ' and by now he was really shouting, 'POOR MADAM IS TO BE BURNT LIKE A CHICKEN!'

It was during this account that, unseen by Edouard, 'Poor Madam' was indeed *en route* to the oven. The horrid little blue velvet curtains had swished open, the coffin, wobbling only very slightly, had glided out of sight and the curtains fallen back into place. It was at this point Edouard turned back towards the production belt and did a double-take worthy of a great silent film comedian. 'Where is she?' he yelled in fury. 'What have they done with my darling! It's a disgrace!' Andrée and I eventually persuaded him as to what had happened, but this didn't satisfy him at all. 'But the flames,' he demanded, 'where were the flames! In my country you see the flames!' Behind me I could hear the representatives of Dickie and Johnny making their escape. They'd remember Miss Fenton's funeral all right.

No flames of course, but at least a thin plume of pale smoke rose from the tall chimney as we came out of the crematorium desperate for cigarettes. I pointed it out to Edouard, and it seemed to reassure him although of course there was no proof that the smoke was Sybil. I'd always heard they burn people in batches when they are busy (the next cortège was already waiting at the other entrance as we came out) but perhaps, like Edouard's Belgian flames, that is a myth.

We went back to Andrée and Oscar's for wine and sandwiches. They were conveniently living close in a house they'd been lent in the Vale of Health, just up the hill.

Edouard, who predictably demanded whisky, was by this time passing through the dictatorial stage of drink. He forced us all to swear, not once but many times, that we would each contribute a memoir to a book in Sybil's homage. I was reminded of that scene were Hamlet forces Horatio and Marcellus to swear over and over again that they will never reveal what they've seen and heard on the battlements of Elsinore. Then Edouard changed tack. We, her friends, must honour Sybil with an orgy. When it becomes dark we must take all our clothes off, rush out onto the heath and LICK EACH OTHER UNDER THE MOON!

Long before it was dark we'd got Edouard into a taxi and sent him home.

He had behaved outrageously, without dignity, and extremely embarrassingly too. Yet there was something I found rather marvellous about his carry on. It was fuelled by drink certainly, but it was fired by grief and love.

Twelve

... Gin in small quantities, Hollands' Gin (in a small glass), Scotch whisky and IRISH in large quantities and without water.
PART OF ELT'S ANSWER AS TO WHAT HE LOVED MOST IN A SURREALIST QUESTIONNAIRE OF 1946.

Alcoholism, Edouard's long-time mistress, moved in to take her late rival's place. Unable to destroy his obsessive devotion to order, she was nevertheless free to seal everything in dust and grime. She was delighted also that he began to spend more and more time unshaven and in his pyjamas and dressing-gown, but made sure that, when he did go out, dapper as ever, it was in her company, and that if he did eat, despite a long, irritating perusal of the menu, it was in tiny quantities and only as an excuse to drink even more.

Abroad I gather she was less sure of herself. There he was surrounded by old friends and young admirers. She was at his shoulder certainly, but he chose to pay her less attention. On his return to London however, where there was no need to keep up appearances, she would resume her dominant role, sneering at Andrée's spasmodic dusting, laughing sardonically at my hopeless suggestion of a longer pause or smaller 'helping'.

From 1966 on, ELT Mesens tried conscientiously to drink himself to death. It took him a surprisingly long time to achieve his purpose.

When embarked on one of his stormy pub-crawls across north-west London, Edouard established a few harbours in which to cast anchor. One was the flat of the veteran surrealist painter Conroy Maddox, who lived in Belsize Park. Conroy (whose renaissance in spry old age is genuinely remarkable) still had a day job, but he gave Edouard a key so that he could get in and rest, and some materials so that he could try his hand at a collage if he so chose. The flat was also convenient for a small Italian restaurant of which Edouard had 'become fond'. As Conroy never fails to mention this even now, I presume he had introduced him to it in the first place. With the ungrateful and resentful sarcasm of the confirmed drunk Edouard's reaction to Conroy's generosity was to refer to him behind his back as 'the office boy'.

To begin with we too were a port of call, but we didn't offer the same unconditional freedom as Conroy and certainly no key. With us he felt obliged, as he himself would have insisted, to telephone first. In our favour, we were much nearer St John's Wood, and there was always drink. What's more, providing I wasn't writing to a deadline, I was pleased for any excuse to stop and listen to him for as long as he chose.

While we remained alone in the living-room it was all right. He banged on obsessively about Sybil of course, but I could sometimes persuade him to return to the past. He could still be witty at times.

So far so good, but when Edouard decided to go down to 'embrace Diana' in the kitchen things became more difficult. Despite making allowances for Sybil's death, Diana, who had never cared for Edouard much in the first place, began to find him more and more irritating. For his part, Edouard showered Diana with flirtatious compliments, but chose to needle her to provoke her hostility, and capped it finally with a physical gesture guaranteed to lead to an open break.

The climax took place at the kitchen table one fine Saturday morning. His opening salvo was to resort, as I explained earlier, to the fake question; a question to which both he and his audience understood what he conceived to be the answer perfectly well: 'When Sybil was dying,' he began, 'she said to me

"Don't let them get George." Now what can she have meant by that?' It was perfectly possible that Sybil had said this, but what Edouard wanted to get across to us was that it seemed to them both that Diana, like some latter-day Olga Picasso, was determined to transform me into a society figure, a member of the art-establishment, the host of fashionable parties and that somehow he must try to prevent it.

There was certainly some truth in it, but it was more of my making than Diana's. After years of rattling round the provinces in a moribund van, sleeping in damp digs and eating in greasy transport cafés, I was both delighted and flattered to breathe the scented air of great drawing-rooms, to be greeted warmly by head-waiters, and acknowledged by my peers in El Vino's. Without Diana I doubt I would have achieved these short-lived aims (Jimmy Bell was right to recognise her genius as an oganiser) but it was I who wished to wallow for a time in these warm seductive waters.

After asking us over and over again what Sybil 'meant', Edouard introduced an alternative weapon. With no evidence whatsoever, he began to air his belief that Sybil's aborted child was mine. He then developed his theme as follows: 'Is it not strange,' he'd begin, 'to think that if she had decided to keep it, your little son, Tom, might now be sitting at this table with his older half-brother?' Both Edouard and I could see that Diana strongly resented this somehow repellent fantasy, but it didn't stop him – he was now completely drunk – from alternating it relentlessly with Sybil's alleged deathbed command.

How long ELT would have been allowed to continue with this verbal torture it is impossible to guess, but what he did next was to resolve the whole issue. Diana had got up to fetch a bowl of fruit. As she was returning to the table Edouard rose also and extending his arms over the bowl, cupped her breasts while declaiming, with typically false objectivity, 'What charming little breasts.'

This was too much! Diana pushed him away with the edge of the fruit bowl with such force that he was propelled across the room and crashed against the opposite wall. 'I know George is your friend,' she told him with icy calm, 'I will do nothing to prevent him seeing you where and when he likes, *but never in this house*!'

Nor did she relent, but for me the mystery is why he, so enchanted by her to begin with, should have deliberately set out to alienate her. Sybil's death and drink are not enough in themselves to explain it. Did he resent our love for each other? Was he jealous of her? Did he simply prefer to see me by myself 'as in the days of yore'? ELT was too subtle to criticise Diana in front of me. From the very next time I saw him he asked politely after her health and well-being and continued to do so. But he never asked me to try and lift the ban, not even to effect a reconciliation in a public place.

Edouard continued to drink and I continued to visit him for an hour or two, usually at around midday on Fridays.

The time of day was deliberate; I have had several alcoholic friends and still have some, and the odds of enjoying their company are much better in the mornings. Friday was for my convenience. I used to get up at six to write my television column for the *Observer* and deliver it to Fleet Street on my moped at around eleven. This allowed me to make a detour via St John's Wood on my way home for lunch. Another bonus was that Edouard, still in his dressing-gown, had often emptied the flat of drink the night before and being, by temperament, unable to drag on a pair of slacks and a sweater to go out for more, was forced to wait for my arrival before hitting the bottle again. I hadn't far to go. Like many pubs in the days before you could buy alcohol in every corner-shop, Lord's Tavern had an off-licence. One of the two pretty cockney barmaids was usually serving there.

'Is it for that Edooard?' she'd ask, for they'd seen us together. 'Thought so,' she'd say when I confirmed it. ''E can drink that one – I should say so!' Edouard was, of course, when dressed a regular in the bar, and would frequently propose marriage to one or the other of the two young women. They told me they used to lead him on but of course they didn't take him seriously. 'That Edooard,' they'd giggle. ''E's got a bleedin' nerve – at 'is age!'

That was true. Sybil's death had left him incredibly lonely, and he proposed to everybody, especially in his cups. It also left him feeling incredibly randy. Left alone with any woman he would automatically make a heavy if clumsy pass. Edith Rimmington told me when I visited her in her old age in Bexhill, that she had called on him shortly after the funeral to offer her condolences, and he had pounced immediately. 'But Edouard, I'm an old lady!' she protested as she struggled clear. 'The little Italian cleaner' was another victim. Edouard claimed to have dismissed her, but I discovered recently that she'd rung Andrée to hand in her notice. She said that she was very sorry to leave but she hoped Andrée understood. She'd been very fond of Mrs Mesens.

Some of his 'fiancées' took him seriously, but none lasted very long. Andrée tells me that he brought back from Brussels a short, young, low-bottomed, rather hairy Belgian girl he called 'Little Block'; I vaguely remember another Belgian woman, middle-aged and tall like a stork. I think her name was Renée.

There was one serious contender who actually pursued him, and from whom he was fortunate to escape. Her name was Vera Russell. She'd been married to the art critic John Russell who had somehow found the courage to leave her. She was of Russian origin, of iron will, dramatically beautiful and she set her cap at ELT. Significantly she was also an art dealer and famously ruthless. I trembled for Edouard when he began to extol her virtues, but then one day he dismissed her totally. 'Why?' I asked. 'Because she is a liar,' he explained. 'She asked me to dinner promising fresh salmon flown specially down from Scotland, but it was not with oil and juice. It was completely dry. From McFish!'[1]

So Vera was defeated by her failure to realise that ELT Mesens, a life-long gourmet, would be able to recognise the

---

[1] McFisheries, a fishmonger chain of the period.

difference between fresh and long-frozen salmon. Edouard was lucky, at the end, to have met Ruth.

Strangely enough though, according to my sister, when alone in the flat Edouard would eat what she described as 'appalling food'. For a few months after Sybil died, and mostly for her sake, Andrée '. . . cleaned and tried to take him food', but cooled off as it got more and more squalid and he more and more drunk. 'The sheets got more and more shitty,' she wrote to me recently, 'the kitchen filthier.' She told me something else I hadn't realised. Apart from drink Edouard was heavily hooked on Doctor Collis Brown.

I was unaware of the worst. I had no reason to visit either shitty bedroom or filthy kitchen and, while dismayed by the dust in the living-room, could live with it while he, relatively sober at that hour, banged on about how the British chose to ignore him. I could help him there. Having by now achieved some clout in journalism and radio, I would do my best to spread his reputation. In July of '66, I managed to place quite a long article in *Art and Artists*, a serious publication most of which in this instance was devoted to Duchamp – a far from displeasing coincidence as far as Edouard was concerned.

Through my radio work I had become acquainted with a charming Third programme producer at the BBC. Leoni Cahn looked like one of the mice the Tailor of Gloucester discovered under his upturned tea-cups but she showed no timidity when it came to getting her way. Under her deceptively mild direction I recorded two talks with ELT, one on his early friendship with Magritte (this to coincide with Sylvester's magnificent exhibition at the Tate) the other on Edouard's youth and his initial contact with André Breton and the surrealists. I have both these broadcasts on cassette. It's very strange for me, so long after his death, to hear his unique diction. Moving, too. He is in sparkling form and I can only wish that he had recorded far more.

Then, not long before he died, I arranged a television interview for ITV's *Aquarius*. I have the typescript of that, including the arrival of the director and crew prior to the talk. Edouard is at his most bossy – it's almost as if I was still working for him at the London Gallery. You haven't shaved. It's a disgrace, and fetch this lady a chair etc., etc. Needless to say, although I had especially warned them to be careful, one of the crew knocked over and broke a tray of glasses. To my surprise Edouard remained completely unmoved. ITV replaced the glasses the next day. Edouard didn't like them. He called them 'too plump'. I can't remember seeing the *Aquarius* programme. Edouard certainly didn't. By the time it would have been shown he was dead.

In 1968, Edouard began to make collages again, and while no more sober, began to feel more at peace with himself. Sometimes I even persuaded him to lunch at a good restaurant in the West End (I owed him enough meals) and we went once to a retrospective at the Academy (Futurism? The Bauhaus? I can't remember) and he was like his old self. It was hard to imagine this immaculate and perceptive gentleman returning to the squalor of his flat. Surely I thought, if he could curb his drinking all might yet be well. I knew very little about alcoholism then. I know a lot more now. I too have had an on-off affair with drink and at times it seemed serious, but she let me go.

Sometimes, when he was feeling mellow, Edouard would tell me his plans for his old age. He would buy a property in a Provençal village. There, attached to the simple but substantial house, he would build an open-air dance hall with tables and a bar where local couples could dance to an accordian band under stars and Japanese lanterns. In the house, open by day to the public, he would hang his collection. He would call the whole thing 'Musée-Musette'.

Occasionally he would elaborate further. He imagined himself seated at the café in the village square arguing amicably with the local *curé* over a pernod. Was this a common old surrealist's dream? According to his biography it was exactly how the film-maker and anti-cleric, Louis Bunuel passed his last days in Mexico. Not Edouard though, and there would be no Musée-Musette either.

Thirteen

I want a clean white shirt to walk in the mire.

MESENS

In 1967 those of us who had been connected to the surrealist movement gathered in Exeter to participate in a manifestation called 'The Enchanted Domain'.

At the centre of this was an impressive exhibition staged at the city art gallery/museum, and including not only the official surrealists, but those contemporaries admired by the movement (Picasso, Klee, etc.) and certain young British artists (Earnshaw, Patrick Hughes) whose work and thought fell within the surrealist canon. As well as the exhibition, there were lectures, symposiums and a great dinner in a Chinese restaurant.

Why Exeter? Not because in the museum there is a stuffed giraffe so tall that it can only be exhibited in the stairwell, so that as you ascend you may examine segments of its neck until finally, at the top, you confront its long-lashed glass eyes. Nor did the institution's magnificent collection of tribal art come into it except as a bonus. The answer is that the whole concept and its realisation was the work of John Lyle who lived in Harpford, a nearby village.

Lyle was by profession a bookseller, specialising in surrealist publications, some of which were extremely rare, and dealing mostly by post. He came originally from Blackpool, ran a shop in London for a time, and then moved to Devon. He is retired now and lives in France. Bearded, wiry and intense as a biblical prophet, he was in violent disagreement with those who wished to relegate Surrealism to the past and dwell only on its 'Golden

Age'. It was his aim to resurrect its revolutionary offensive and to recruit the young and ardent. To this end he edited an admirable magazine for several years called *Transformaction*. Given his disapproval of Breton's recent beatification, I am forced to admit that John tended to assume his mantle when it came to excommunications and laying down the correct line of surrealist conduct. All of us sympathisers were given a smack from time to time, but he had taken on a formidable task.

Formidable and finally impossible. In his cynical cups ELT referred to John as 'a General without an army' and it turned out to be true.

Given Lyle's anti-historic approach, the Exeter event may seem inconsistent. The old veterans would inevitably turn over the past; the exhibits, with only a handful of exceptions, were drawn from the past. Nostalgia was inevitable amongst the invitees. I've never asked him for an explanation, I never even thought of it at the time, but perhaps in 1967 John Lyle had not fully recognised the dangers of this Lot's wife-like turning back, or perhaps he thought that a recognition of earlier achievements might fire the young revolutionaries. At all events it was a brilliant exhibition and, as it turned out, the last public manifestation of Surrealism in Britain as a living force. The surrealist spirit however lives on. Within a year of Exeter, it reared up in the streets of Paris. Defeated there, it bides its time.

I had fully expected Edouard to refuse to participate at Exeter because I'd noticed on my invitation that Roland Penrose had also been asked. I'm sure if Sybil had been still alive he would have felt obliged to refuse, but Sybil was a year dead, and ELT had no intention of relinquishing his position as the legitimate surrealist leader in Britain. If this meant patching it up with Penrose he was prepared to do it. I was delighted. I'd been asked to lend several pictures and write a preface. I've just re-read this and it's not too bad. 'Surrealism is dead' it concludes, and then 'Long Live Surrealism'. I'm not ashamed of it anyway.

And so one fine summer day Diana drove me down to Exeter, a beautiful cathedral city with twisted lanes and closes, and haunted by the rebellious victims strung up by Judge Jeffreys. Also *en route* that morning were Conroy Maddox (who had designed the cover to the catalogue), Roland Penrose, ELT and Jacques Brunius. I have named Jacques last for a reason that will become apparent.

Every exhibitor listed in the catalogue is backed up by a biographical note, part factual, part poetic. Here is Jacques's:

> BRUNIUS, Jacques
> 'The Uprooted Giraffe.' Born a heretic-Cathar in the year 1244, the year of the massacre of Montsequi – known as Doctor Faust, Count of San Germain, St Leon, Melmouth and the White Knight. Educated in Paris. Trained as a designer of motor cars and aircraft. Has since declared war on the internal combustion engine. Film director, actor, writer and poet. Lives in London and Paris.'

This leaves out his quiet but devastating charm. I appeared with him several times on the BBC's *The Critics* and everyone, especially Dylis Powell, the doyenne of film critics, fell completely under his spell. His charm certainly complicated his love-life. He was usually in some kind of passionate muddle which was perfectly in accordance with the surrealist belief in '*l'amour fou*' but caused him, and his mistresses, considerable anguish. He arrived in Exeter in what appeared to be a moment of calm with a rather beautiful young woman.

Edouard was, if I remember right, accompanied by Renée, the tall stork-like woman who gave an impression of the colour grey, she was so silent and unobtrusive.

Jacques and ELT were old allies, but Edouard was very scornful, in his unpleasant Belgian businessman persona, of Jacques's inability to make money. Quite often Jacques would be forced to borrow money from ELT who no doubt lectured him on his improvidence, yet for all that both would have described the other as a friend.

For the rest not much happened that first evening. I think there was a private view and the exhibition itself was much admired. John Lyle was present but modestly discreet. (His name only appears once in the catalogue and that as one of the four contributors to the notes.) Patrick Hughes and the Earnshaws turned up. Penrose and Mesens seemed friendly enough. Diana and I had dinner alone, but on our way there we pulled up at some lights, and ELT spotted us and came and leant through the open window. Diana stared straight ahead. Nothing was said. The lights turned green. Edouard drew back. Diana drove on.

We were in bed early. During the night, with no prior warning Jacques Brunius, 'The Uprooted Giraffe' died of a heart attack.

Although we were scattered in hotels and boarding-houses all over the city, by breakfast everybody knew and a meeting was called at ten a.m. in the gallery to decide whether to continue or call it a day. It was a foregone conclusion, exactly the same as if Jacques had been a comedian who had died in the wings. The show must go on. Jacques would have wished it. He probably would have, and especially as the whole manifestation was re-dedicated to his memory. Not a bad death anyway. Instant, and in a city temporarily celebrating a movement which had directed his life, and surrounded by friends.

So the lectures and forums and meetings went on, many people visited the wonderful pictures and, in the evening, we all assembled among the writhing dragons of the large Chinese restaurant.

At the top table, on a low dais, sat Mesens, Penrose, Maddox, Robert Melville, the surrealistically inclined art critic, and their wives and mistresses. Was there also an empty chair? Surely not. Although given my years connected with the movement I was probably entitled to sit up there with the nobs, for Diana's benefit I chose the young people's table: the Earnshaws, Patrick Hughes and others mostly from the north. I'm glad we did. It looked pretty sticky up there, whereas we had quite a jolly time with plenty of jokes spiced with black humour.

It was impossible, if predictable, not to notice that Edouard, his chop-sticks more or less unemployed, was knocking it back at an amazing rate. His speech in honour and memory of Jacques Brunius, while clearly passionate and heartfelt, was largely incomprehensible. His conclusion, however, was delivered with great clarity and force. Whether based unconsciously on the cry of dismay from the 'little Italian cleaner' over a year before I cannot say, but what he shouted was, 'We must burn poor Jacques!'

Next day the surrealists left Exeter, all of us more or less perpendicular except for poor Jacques who was horizontal.

Back in London that small part of an increasingly diverse and busy life that I reserved for Mesens – the weekly visit, the occasional telephone call, the exchange of postcards when he was abroad – continued as before.

No doubt he looked terrible, but if you see someone regularly you don't notice a steady decline. Certainly others noticed. On a visit to Paris I called on André Breton's widow. She told me that she'd seen Mesens (he had not seen her) in a street in north-west London. He looked, she said, at death's door. I had a letter from Marcel Jean, painter, object-maker, and latterly the biographer of the surrealist movement. He had visited Edouard recently and found him (Marcel loved to show off his excellent command of idiomatic English) 'in poor shape'. I tended to reassure them. He drank too much of course, and Sybil's death had been a bad blow, and he was getting on, he was in his sixties after all.

They were right and I was wrong. When and how I have never discovered, nor can I remember who told me, but in the autumn of 1968 he collapsed from alcohol poisoning and was rushed into a nursing-home for the prosperously addicted near Primrose Hill. They told me later that it had been touch and go on arrival, but by the time I'd heard (perhaps after all it was Edouard himself who asked them to let me know) he was on the mend and allowed visitors.

I found him in one of those aggressively clean white rooms very like that in which he was to die some four years later. He seemed rested, had been well shaved (presumably by another – the only time) and was wearing silk pyjamas. He seemed cheerful and pleased to see me. The nurse who showed me in ('She has distinguished legs') took away the flowers I'd bought him and returned with them almost immediately in a cut-glass vase. Both the speed with which she accomplished this task and the quality of the vase implied a formidable bill, but then by this time, although ELT would inevitably check it several times, he could certainly afford it.

Left alone we talked and I soon realised, that rational as he seemed, Edouard had a long way to go and was suffering from happily benevolent DTs. It wasn't so much his belief that the 'pansy' male nurse was 'obsessed with my bottom'. Sexual vanity and ELT Mesens were far from strangers although here, while his blanket baths offered the male nurse an excellent opportunity to 'fondle' his buttocks, I couldn't help but feel he was exaggerating wildly.

It was after we'd dropped the male nurse that Edouard said something that really startled me.

'Are they not beautiful?' he asked me.

'Are not what beautiful?' I responded.

'The little blue-birds with red tails who fly everywhere. The little blue-birds with long red tails who fly all over the room.'

Half a mile away, in a kind of shed-cum-conservatory, prevented by a double door at each end from escaping into Regent's Park Zoo proper were the humming birds, free-flying within their artificial habitat, and hovering in the air to drink the sugar solution suspended in glass tubes from the branches of the Rousseau-like vegetation. It was my favourite house, but there were of course no humming birds in Edouard's sterilised private room.

'Are they not charming?' he asked me again. 'The little birds.'

After several weeks the little birds winged it back to their quarters, the male nurse lost his obsession with Edouard's bottom and finally, free from any trace of alcohol, ELT Mesens was discharged. For some time he remained clean. Somehow I got the impression that there was some improvement in the squalor of the flat, and for the first time since he had made 'Goodbye my beautiful darling' in 1966, he began to consider the possibility of working again. In 1968 he went back into production. The collage-making continued almost until the end of his life. So did the drinking . . .

Why do detoxed alcoholics, although warned by their doctors that if they go back on it they will die, return to the bottle? This is not quite as naïve a question as it may seem. Beyond the addictive factor there is another aspect, shown to me in a conversation I had with the late Peter Langan, celebrated piss-artist and restaurateur. As a result of a substantial bet with Michael Parkinson, Peter was dry for a month. He sat down at my table, usually a two-edged compliment, in a clean suit and articulate. 'Peter,' I said to him after a time, 'you know when you are sober . . .'

Here he cut me short to finish the sentence: 'I'm intelligent, witty, well-informed and good company . . .' These were almost exactly the words I'd been about to say, but Peter wasn't finished yet. 'AND BORED SHITLESS!' he shouted.

I think this was the case for Edouard too. On my only visits after his discharge when he was still not drinking he seemed curiously vacant, almost as though lobotomised. If I tried to interest him in something his only response when I'd finished was 'and then?'

One Friday as soon as he'd opened the door Edouard asked me if I'd go across to the off-licence. 'Of course,' I said. I might regret for his sake his decision to jump off the wagon, but in my view, then and now, it was *his* decision. 'What do you want?' I asked him as he gave me some money (and woe betide me if the change wasn't correct). 'Dry Vermouth,' he told me, 'Noilly Prat.'

I was surprised, but have since learnt to recognise this self-deluding syndrome amongst drunks. Somehow by rejecting gin, whisky, brandy and so on with an air of virtuous martyrdom, they convince themselves that products like Martini, Campari, and sherry are not *real* drinks and don't count. I found the Noilly Prat was both refreshing and delicious, but I soon discovered that he only drank it in London. Abroad he changed to pernod, absinthe's legal brother. I tried to persuade him to give it up. It was certainly as bad for him as anything else. He replied on a penultimate postcard from Brussels: 'Pernod is a very efficient anti-spasmodic with the qualities and faults of being also paregoric.'

For the second time I walked a few doors up Gloucester Crescent to consult Dr Jonathan Miller on a medical matter. He was wryly amused. He told me ELT's explanation was drawn from a totally discredited theory of medicine of the seventeenth century based on the 'humours' of the body, but what puzzled him (and me) also was how ELT came across it and why, beyond the useful concept that 'bullshit baffles brains', he should have decided to put his trust in it.

Meanwhile there was proof that paranoia and alcoholic rage had moved back in residence. Not that I, either then or later, was ever a victim.

In his last years ELT Mesens was never anything but sweet and generous to me. Of course there were reasons: I had consistently supported him and had been in the position to put his name in front of the indifferent British public (he didn't need this service in Brussels where he was already becoming a national treasure) but I don't think they were uppermost. The main point was I loved him warts and all. And I believe that he loved me.

Not that this prevented him from making a sly little joke in the catalogue of an exhibition held in Milan as early as 1965. Printed in a box on almost the last page is the following announcement in English.

> There are Acting and Technical Vacancies in all
> Companies affiliated to ELT. If you would like
> more information, please contact Mr G Melly,
> Public Relations Officer.

But this, which probably refers to my attempts to publicise his work (and which incidentally I hadn't noticed until researching this book) is friendly enough. Signs that he was on the turn came from elsewhere and one such signal was a letter I received from Marcel Jean dated April 1969.

Dear George

I had written to Mesens to ask him if we could
meet next time in London so he could show me
documents and tell me which poems he'd wish to
have reproduced in my Anthology. [*The
Autobiography of Surrealism*, edited by Marcel Jean,
1980, Viking Press] In all innocence I think I told
him that I'd also asked information and documents
from Penrose!!!! I received in answer the following
postcard: 'Either you deal with Penrose or with me
but not with both! I am more and more severe and
I don't need you or Penrose. You've already been
lousy "moche" enough with me and opportunistic
in your first book [*The History of Surrealist
Painting*, Marcel Jean, Weidenfeld & Nicolson,
1959. It contains seventeen references to ELT!]. I
am a *true* surrealist *poet*. That's that; and he, I
don't deny him some talent, but is he even an
English poet?'

Marcel went on to write that initial stupefaction soon gave
way to intense amusement. He thought of writing back to say
that as far as procuring documents was concerned he'd rather
deal with an obliging and courteous English knight of the British
Empire than an uneducated and unscrupulous Belgian art dealer,
even if the latter is a better poet than the former. He didn't
though. He'd heard Mesens wasn't well, 'He's got now a terrible
sloping handwriting and what is this "near death" he speaks of?'

The 'near death' was of course the visitation of the little birds.
The handwriting was only temporary, when sober his writing
was as neat as ever, but the postcard is a prime example of ELT
Mesens at his most paranoid and absurd, a state of incoherent
rage which always put me in mind of Shakespeare's Ancient
Pistol.

By the late sixties my own exposure to such an outburst was
long past. There'd been nothing serious since his attack on me in
the Barcelona restaurant almost twenty years before, and its still
unrequited promise of a free Magritte in recompense.

Yet Edouard's angry and grotesque letter to Marcel Jean, while certainly dictated by the Demon Drink (and proving that the rapprochement with Penrose in Exeter was purely opportunistic) was as nothing compared with a later full-length incident in which the DD, accompanied by her attendant imps: Malice, Prevarication, Manipulation and Bullying, set out to prove his ability to possess his victim, at whim and for as long as he liked, before claiming him for ever. I was responsible for placing this opportunity in the Demon's path and feel in part guilty, but take some comfort from the fact that there was a satisfactory outcome. As to whether this was sufficient acceptance for what he had suffered, you'd have to ask Professor John Golding.

John is a very fine painter, art historian, essayist, lecturer and exhibition organiser. In appearance he is small, bald and gives the impression of considerable inner tension. Perhaps it is this which has attracted the attention of bullies. Douglas Cooper, his first mentor, behaved disgracefully to John, and so on this occasion did Cooper's enemy Mesens. In both cases, however, in the end, despite considerable anguish, John Golding won through.

At a dinner party, towards the end of the sixties, John told me that he was in the process of organising an exhibition at the Tate to be called 'Léger and Purist Paris', and couldn't find a major example of an abstract Léger townscape of the twenties. Like a conjuror producing a Parisian purist rabbit out of a London hat, I told him that there was a wonderful Léger exactly fitting this description only a few miles from where we sat. Would the owner lend it? I was sure he would, but must warn John that, since the death of his wife and the escalation of a severe drinking problem, he could be very tricky. John said he was willing to take the risk if the painting was as good as I claimed; I assured him it was.

A week or two later, by appointment, we stood outside the front door where the withdrawing of bolts, the rattling of chains and turning of keys signalled the proximity of ELT Mesens. As I'd anticipated John was instantly dazzled by his first view of this Aladdin's cave of modern art, but the Léger surpassed even his most optimistic dreams.

When he asked to borrow it, ELT mimed serious thought on the subject but as I'd expected, finally agreed. However, he used a word that only too often had to be taken quite literally. That word was 'eventually'.

John, obviously delighted, produced a standard form for the loan of a picture and suggested they fill it in there and then. This was a grave tactical error. ELT said it was not possible. He must check the provenance, where and when previously exhibited, any references, catalogues . . . My heart sank. Mischief was afoot. John naturally suspected nothing. 'Perhaps by the end of the week?' he asked. 'Eventually,' said Edouard as he prepared to relock, bolt and chain us out. 'Eventually, Doctor!'

We left, John in high spirits. I saw no reason to worry him. Mesens *might* complete the form that week, *might* get around to posting it. He'd made no mention of course of it having belonged to Sybil or that, as a surrealist, he had ever disapproved of it. This gave me some hope. He was now so proud of it. He would surely avoid the risk of not having it in the exhibition. I underestimated him. Several weeks later John rang me up in despair. Despite telephone calls and written reminders that the catalogue would have to go to print at any moment, there had been no response from St John's Wood Road.

I'd been half expecting it. I told John our best and only hope was to revisit ELT as soon as possible. So we did, and Edouard, after some provocation, showed us the completed form, that is to say complete except for one essential detail – his signature. John pleaded with him. Edouard unscrewed his expensive fountain pen and lifted it above the paper. Then he paused, screwed it up again and said, 'I will just check the details one more time and then post it. Good morning, Doctor.'

John, white with anxiety, controlled himself until we were outside the ogre's castle. He was on the edge of breaking down but, with a confidence I didn't feel, I told him that as ELT realised that this time the deadline loomed, he would post it as soon as we were out of sight. (I had seen him, without making it obvious, watching us furtively through the window.) Happily, this time I was right. John rang me next morning to say the form had arrived. So later did the picture, but ELT wasn't quite finished. Despite all that checking and double-checking, he insisted on a correction in the errata: 'add The Late Sybil Mesens.' This may have come from guilt, or the knowledge that Sybil would have been furious at being excluded, but for all that it was a final little irritant, a flourish of the scorpion's tail.

John phoned again a week or so later. There was to be a dinner and a viewing of the exhibition for those who had loaned pictures, helped in some way, or were on the Tate's VIP list. Did I think (and I could well understand his hesitation) that he had to invite Edouard? I said I was afraid he did. If he didn't ELT's paranoid feelers would ensure he picked up a newspaper recording the dinner and listing the guests and, if he did, he might well, and with some justification, withdraw the picture altogether. However, I told him, Edouard was very unlikely to accept. There I was wrong. He accepted (by return of post). He came. He behaved very badly. This is what John told me later.

At dinner Edouard had found himself sitting next to Lady Norman Reid, wife of the Tate's director. In between trying to empty the gallery's famous wine-cellars, he delivered an enthusiastic but repetitive eulogy on the beauty of Lady Reid's breasts. It wasn't appreciated. Then, as the guests were beginning to circulate around the galleries, Edouard discovered a pretty employee whose role that evening was to sit behind a desk and hand out catalogues. As ELT was flirting with this girl, John happened to pass and Edouard attracted his attention. Having first complained that there was no reproduction of his loan in the catalogue (John reminded him there was almost no picture, let alone a reproduction) Edouard asked him to take the young lady's place for a few moments while he showed her 'his' Léger.

Hypnotised by this cool affrontery, feeling as though trapped in one of those nightmares where all action is denied us, Professor John Golding at the very hour when he should have been justifiably basking in the admiration of his peers for curating an exhibition clarifying a decade in art history hitherto left unexplored, at that very hour he found himself handing out catalogues from behind a desk. Why didn't he refuse or protest? For a very good reason – he was not prepared to take the risk that ELT might make a public scene compared with which the 'Box Mr Boxer' incident (and John had actually been present on that memorable occasion) could have faded into insignificance. ELT spent forty-five minutes showing the no doubt flattered young woman around the whole exhibition.

Finally the nightmare appeared to be over. John stayed on for a few minutes after everyone had left deciding on a few small adjustments to the hanging before the press view next day.

It was pouring with rain outside but John had his car. Unexpectedly the by-now only too familiar voice spoke out from the shadows. 'There are no taxis, Doctor,' said ELT Mesens. John, who lived south of the river, finally offered at least a token revolt. 'I'll drive you,' he said, 'to Victoria Station where there are plenty of taxis under cover, but *no further*!' On the way there, upset and exhausted, John drove over rather than round a roundabout.

'Why are you nervous, Doctor?' enquired Edouard mildly.

This tale, certainly from John's point of view, is horrific. For me it's simply embarrassing in that I acted as the catalyst. It is also a textbook example of drunken and angry behaviour. What is interesting though is what he was up to. My explanation is that he believed, and with some justification, he had not been given his due. John's appearance, cap as it were in hand, gave ELT the perfect opportunity to get his own back, to strike at the very heart of the art world establishment as he understood it. John, alas, was cast as the symbolic fall-guy.

Without drink I doubt he could have carried it through, but even so I cannot, in retrospect, deny ELT Mesens, in his handling of the Léger case a certain dadaist *éclat*.

Fourteen

That's what it is to go on a Sunday to Rue de
l'Echaudé to see the Unbraining. To see the Pig-
Pinching or Comanche-Disjointing. You start out
alive and you come back killed off. . . .
ALFRED JARRY − *TRANSLATED FROM THE FRENCH BY*
SYBIL & ELT MESENS.

But for the miraculous appearance of Ruth, the young German
gallery-owner from Switzerland, ELT Mesens's last few months
would have been much more tragic than they turned out.

His Belgian friends and relations might think of her as an
adventuress, and perhaps she was, albeit an unsuccessful one, but
in exchange she gave him devotion, nursing and, whether
genuine or not (it is my belief it was), at the very least the
simulacrum of love. Nor was she blind to his absurdities, nor
was she prepared to put up with bad behaviour or bullying. She
insisted on spending a reasonable amount of time at her gallery,
and I don't think she ever came to London, but she was on his
side and under her influence and despite the misery of the drink
the human being showed itself still there and the Demon seemed
less in control.

Just after Christmas 1970 I received an invitation to the
vernissage of an exhibition of Edouard's collages at the Isy
Brachot Gallery in Brussels. He was very keen for me to go; he
may have realised this was perhaps his last show, and I decided
to accept but only on condition that he delivered the Magritte he
had promised me after our quarrel on the night of the Max Ernst

party twenty-three years before. At first he pretended to have forgotten about it, but after I had begun to remind him of the circumstances at deliberately tedious length, he 'remembered' and finally, after I demanded a definitive promise with no 'eventually', he agreed.

Diana drove me to the airport and took me on a bet that I wouldn't get it. I thought she was on a winner, but of course I wouldn't say so.

The private view was a great success and Edouard was at his most charming and in excellent form. The collages looked very convincing in their diversity. ELT's old chums Scutenaire, Nono Van Hecke (PG was already dead) and the rest, were very warm and congratulatory, but I couldn't help but notice that they had all ganged up on Ruth and more or less ignored her. I'd met her earlier, when I had gone to register at Edouard's habitual hotel, the Canterbury, and taken to her immediately. At the private view I did my best to make her feel included, but of course she knew the score perfectly well. We must have gone on to a restaurant, but by this time I was terribly drunk and don't remember going back to the hotel. I didn't forget, however, that I was to collect ELT and Ruth at eleven a.m. from their room to go and collect the picture.

I knocked on the dot. Ruth answered the door and behind her I could see Edouard in socks and vest staggering about. He looked absolutely ghastly. He told me he was too ill to go and get the picture, and I thought Oh well, Diana has won. My plane's at four, but then, as I was leaving he shouted after me, 'Come back in an hour. I may feel better!'

So I walked about the streets and looked at the shops full of expensive handmade chocolates and, after exactly an hour, returned and Edouard, while looking no better, was at least dressed and so we set off 'with a taxi'.

ELT's hoard of pictures in Brussels (infinite riches in a little room) were stored in an air-conditioned *camion*, the body of a van, one of many, stacked in neat rows around a central courtyard on several floors and mostly used by diplomats to hold their furniture between appointments abroad. When they were needed, which of course Edouard's never were *en bloc*, they were lowered by crane into the well and secured to wheels and a driver's cab prior to being driven to the embassy in Madrid or Athens. But disasters still faced us. At first they couldn't find the key to Edouard's 'cabin' but eventually it turned up.

First, Edouard told me with proprietorial pride, he was going to show me a few of Magritte's masterpieces. Then he would offer me a choice from several pictures he had selected.

'Why not let him choose a masterpiece?' asked Ruth, but he pretended not to hear her.

So we looked at the masterpieces which were brought out by some very careful if indifferent employees of the storage company and displayed against the iron balcony. As far as I can recall there was 'The Musings of a Solitary Walker' (1926), that wonderfully pessimistic image of a bowler-hatted man retreating from the spectator along the banks of a gloomy canal while, between him and us, floats a bald nude male corpse parallel to the ground. There was 'The Use of Speech' (1928) in which, against a blue background, two abstract bits of white fluff or wool attached to thin stalks were identified as The Wind and The Normandie in copperplate writing. And finally there was a more famous picture, 'The Collective Invention' (1935), the reversed mermaid with the torso of a fish and the belly and legs of a woman, cast up upon a shore.

We looked at these wonderful pictures for some time – all indeed masterpieces but all very different – as David Sylvester wrote, 'If anyone knew a good Magritte from a bad one it was Mesens.' Then they were put away, and for a long time Edouard couldn't find the picture he thought I'd choose. He found the alternative at once; one of those near abstracts of 1927 and actually very beautiful, but not his first choice. Finally it turned up; the third version of 'The Lovers' of 1928 where a woman, very much of the twenties, framed by an architrave and in front of a featureless plain, is aware of her lover's disembodied head resting his cheek against her temple. It is a beautiful minor work, and I was delighted with it. He had one more trick up his sleeve. He directed the men to pull out one more picture, much larger than the others. Its title was *The Terrestrial Shadow* (1928). It depicts a prehistoric monster, a carniverous one, standing on a flat terrain against a greenish sky. Although difficult to read and decidedly 'ungrateful', its interesting feature is that it seems to have a massive woman's legs and arms.

'You know,' said Edouard as I was looking at it and aware the children with their taste for dinosaurs would love it, 'in that it is bigger, it is worth more.'

That decided me instantly. I chose 'The Lovers III'. Not only because I liked it best anyway, but I realised that if I'd chosen the monster, he might well have cancelled the whole deal claiming that I was being greedy.

While I was signing for the picture in the office, Ruth asked Edouard how long he had owed me a Magritte. When she heard it was since 1948 she became hysterical with laughter. Edouard looked rather put out. 'It shows I'm serious,' he said.

I'd promised the pair of them a 'serious' lunch and booked at the restaurant of Edouard's choice for one thirty with a taxi to pick me up and drive me to the airport at three. It was a tight schedule.

Leaving my picture wrapped in brown paper in the cloakroom I followed them in. It was indeed a 'serious' restaurant but Edouard could do it little justice. Returning from one of his many and rapid visits to the loo, he told us he had 'renounced the fish', but also that he had ignored the Prince of the Belgiums who had tried to catch his eye. Was this true or hallucinary? He was in a bad way and when I left to take my taxi and embraced them both his forehead was beaded with cold sweat. I didn't really expect to see him again.

On the aeroplane I'd taken on the Magritte as hand-luggage (I'd have had more difficulty doing that if I had chosen 'The Terrestrial Shadow'). As there was an empty seat next to me I leant the canvas against the cabin wall. It was then I noticed with considerable emotion that the wallpaper was covered with small birds formed from a bright cloudy sky; a Magritte image that was then the Sabina Airways logo.

Diana met me at the airport. I showed her the picture in her headlights. She was delighted she'd lost her bet.

Edouard, despite my presentiment, had four more months to go. Most of the time he was in London and I renewed my visits.

The television interview took place during this remission and, despite knocking back the Noilly Prat, Edouard worked hard towards another show in Brussels in April. While he looked pretty ropey, he seemed calm and happier than he'd been for ages. He told me he rang Ruth every evening.

From abroad, as usual, he sent cuttings and catalogues. For his exhibition opening on 23rd April, 1971, he'd printed various homages from Breton, Eluard and so on but also 'two birthday poems which the London Gallery employees, Roy Edwards and George Melly, had given him on the morning of 27th November, 1948'. Roy's was by far the better, but he didn't write back by return of post to thank ELT for including it, and I was told to reproach him firmly.

The last letter Andrée got from Edouard was shortly after his final return to Brussels for yet another exhibition and is dated 14th April, 1971. She had become quite fed up with him. Far fonder of Sybil anyway she saw no reason to be constantly at his beck and call. Here however he demands a final service and, she told me, with rage in her heart, she fulfilled it. It is however a wonderfully typical outpouring. Here it is:

14th April, 1971

My dear little Andréas,
I left *finally* London yesterday evening to land at the CANTERBURY after 11 p.m., and write to you at once, having been unable to get you on the phone. *You would be very kind to go to 34 St John's Wood's Court* on the very first occasion you go to town and to de-frieze the frigidaire: I do not dare to undertake a job you know very well.

222

Meanwhile you will see how clean my flat looks: from that point of view. Maria Dubucq is a 'star', but her *cuisine* is too rich and in 10 days she made me very ill, instead of feeling better. I have humorous things to tell you about the Dubucq's stay! Still, such people can not help to be very narrow minded. And Marcel repeats twenty times the same stories which I know already from before. I told to Maria *not to use* butter in *my* food . . . But she could not *help* doing so! I discovered that, one night I could not sleep, in looking at 'beautiful soup' she had stored in the frige! Marcel had meals like a . . . ! Scores of lamb cuttlets, and Maria took even a whole rib with her 'for the home'.

How is our lovely little Natacha? The Dubucq's were a bit shocked not to have *seen you at all*; they love George, of course, as you can guess.

Lots of kisses to Tacha and you, and love to my 'indian philosopher' Oscar.

I trust you do not neglect the frigidaire, please.

And now, the doctors!

Yours ever, Edouard

N.B. I sleep very very badly, but I expect Ruth this week-end.

The last letter I got from Edouard came from the Hôtel Canterbury and is dated 30th April, 1971. Most of it is given over to a high evaluation of an exhibition called 'Metamorphosis of the Object'. He suggests I bring it to the attention of Sylvester, Ronald Alley and (with a rather touching faith in time's ability to heal) John Golding.

He claimed to be in good health (a lie) and to love Ruth (true).

At that year's Edinburgh Festival there was to be a show of Belgian Surrealism comprised of Magritte, Delvaux and Mesens, and by chance at its most ironical (Mark Boxer having long departed), David Sylvester asked me to write a substantial piece on Mesens for the *Sunday Times Colour Supplement* to complement this event. Not wanting to repeat the earlier fiasco I asked David to let me know when it was absolutely certain, so that I could tell Edouard.

David rang to give me the go-ahead on the day ELT collapsed in Brussels in a terminal coma.

You learn some things long after the event. Either I never knew or had completely forgotten that my sister went over to say goodbye to our unconscious friend in his hospital bed. It must have been a day or two earlier than I. Ruth had not yet arrived from Geneva, and the 'nice cousin' was in a state in case she turned up with a later will or a signed claim to some important picture while at the same time worrying about Edouard's tenacious hold on life in relation to the price of the room.

Otherwise Andrée's impression when we discussed it recently was much the same as mine, although she did witness a grotesque tableau worthy of Bunuel at his most inventive. When a person is dying of an addiction, it is necessary for them to be fed small quantities of what is killing them in order to stay alive a little longer. When Andrée entered the room where Edouard lay unconscious, she discovered a nun in full fig feeding him gin from a teaspoon. He'd have loved that.

ELT Mesens was unconscious for six days and died, appropriately enough for one as superstitious as he, on Friday, 13th May, 1971.

Edouard's last words to me were: 'I remain a surrealist to my fingernails!' He shouted them on the eve of his final return to Brussels.

Coda

The good lady of milk has returned to the good country of milk.

Enoch and Ramsbottom, senile and miserable, can't remember each other, 'me', nor even their former employment by the British Broadcasting Corporation.

The daughter of the *concierge*, despite a visit to Lourdes, still limps.

Having passed ten thousand miles the Ford Engine movements in the owner's hips are no longer under guarantee.

This, we're afraid, is the end.

Monsieur et Madame M. DUBUCQ-FRANCAUX, ✝
Monsieur et Madame A. DUBUCQ-SAINT-VITEUX,
Madame P.-G. VAN HECKE,

très sensibles aux marques de sympathie que vous leur avez témoignées lors du décès de
Monsieur E. L. T. MESENS
vous expriment leurs sincères remerciements.

Bibliography

Alphabet Sourd Aveugle: ELT Mesens (Brussels: Editions Nicolas Flammel 1933)

Troisième Front: Poems de Guerre suives par pieces detaché: ELT Messens (London: Gallery Editions 1944)

Magritte: David Sylvester (London: Thames and Hudson in association with the Menil Foundation 1992)

Magritte Catalogue Raisonne: David Sylvester and Sarah Whitfield; ed. David Sylvester (London: Menil Foundation/Philip Wilson 1992 and 1993)

A Mon Ami Mesens: Louis Scutenaire (Brussels 1972)

The Autobiography of Surrealism: ed. Marcel Jean (New York: Viking 1980)

Surrealist Painting: Marcel Jean (London: Weidenfeld and Nicholson 1960)

ELT Mesens, Surrealist Jusque au Bout des Ongles: Diana Naylor (thesis: Essex University 1973)

ELT Mesens, L'Alchemist Meconnu du Surrealism: Christiane Guerts-Krauss (thesis: Université Libre de Bruxelles 1993)